4|11

Of Mice . . . and Murder

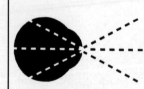

This Large Print Book carries the
Seal of Approval of N.A.V.H.

NOSY IN NEBRASKA, BOOK 1

OF MICE . . . AND MURDER

A MAXIE MOUSE MYSTERY

MARY CONNEALY

THORNDIKE PRESS
A part of Gale, Cengage Learning

GALE
CENGAGE Learning

Detroit • New York • San Francisco • New Haven, Conn • Waterville, Maine • London

GALE
CENGAGE Learning™

© 2008 by Mary Connealy.
Scripture taken from the HOLY BIBLE, NEW INTERNATIONAL VERSION®, NIV®. Copyright © 1973, 1978, 1984 by International Bible Society. Used by permission of Zondervan. All rights reserved.
Thorndike Press, a part of Gale, Cengage Learning.

Thorndike Press® Large Print Christian Mystery.
The text of this Large Print edition is unabridged.
Other aspects of the book may vary from the original edition.
Set in 16 pt. Plantin.

LIBRARY OF CONGRESS CATALOGING-IN-PUBLICATION DATA

Connealy, Mary.
  Of mice— and murder : a Maxie the mouse mystery / by Mary Connealy.
    p. cm. — (Nosy in Nebraska : bk. 1) (Thorndike Press large print christian mystery)
  ISBN-13: 978-1-4104-3650-4 (hardcover)
  ISBN-10: 1-4104-3650-0 (hardcover)
  1. Large type books. I. Title.
PS3603.O544O37 2011
813'.6—dc22   2011000627

Published in 2011 by arrangement with Barbour Publishing, Inc.

Printed in Mexico
1 2 3 4 5 6 7 15 14 13 12 11

Dedicated to:

Lois Crinklaw and Clark and Anna — Lois's terror of mice exceeds my own. Which makes me feel far closer to normal.

Linda Swenson and Jim, Amanda, Chris, Samantha, Alex, and Nick. Linda helped me chase a mouse once. It was a one-time act of courage. Lois sat on the couch with her feet up.

And Mardelle Connealy, who could teach classes on how to be properly afraid of mice. I'd be an A+ student.

1

MELNIK, NEBRASKA — POPULATION 972
HOME OF MAXIE —
THE WORLD'S LARGEST FIELD MOUSE

Being named in Great-Grandma's will was
like hitting Bankrupt on *Wheel of Fortune.*
The whole family held their breath while
the wheel ticked around and around — or
rather, while the lawyer opened the enve-
lope. Then they all heaved a sigh of relief
when the wheel stopped on Carrie's name.

Carrie the heiress. *Great.*

Clean up the house.

Clean up the yard.

Clean up Great-Grandma's rap sheet.

"I don't know why it has to be me," Carrie grumbled.

The empty kitchen — empty except for
the garbage that Great-Grandma Bea had
been amassing all her one hundred and
three years — mocked her with its silence.

Silence except for the hammering on the

porch, which stopped when Carrie started talking to herself.

Carrie froze, hoping the carpenter hadn't heard her. Spooky old house, spooky new resident.

The banging resumed. Now that her great-grandma wasn't around to drive off the hired help, the work would finally get done — except, of course, Carrie had no money. She'd have to break that to the carpenter pretty soon.

And while he pounded away, Carrie could break her back by cleaning up this old wreck. What a waste of a beautiful, brisk, fall afternoon. She had to figure out how to get out of Melnik before she went nuts. But first she would —

A mouse dashed out of the kitchen pantry twenty feet away.

"EEEEE!" Carrie shrieked.

The mouse skittered toward her. Carrie ran the opposite direction and collided with the carpenter, who was dashing through the door, clutching his hammer.

"What happened?"

The mouse skidded to a halt under the table and squeaked.

Carrie squeaked even louder and jumped toward the carpenter. He caught her against his chest, hooking one arm under her legs and the other behind her back.

It was nice of a stranger to come to the rescue. He was the kind of man who could do the whole "white knight" thing, with his lovely height and broad shoulders. The hammer he held — in the hand now under her knees — would make a fair lance, too.

"Forgive me." Carrie barely moved her lips.

"For what?" The carpenter's whisper pulled her attention away from the mouse.

Carrie noted the tidy logo of his company on the pocket of his shirt where a little polo player ought to be. *OC* with the word O'CONNOR arced above and CONSTRUCTION in a half circle below. Both of the placket buttons were neatly closed, and his hair was combed and gelled as if he were afraid it would break out and go its own way. His eyes glowed with humor and kindness, though.

"Oh, you weren't supposed to hear that. I was praying for forgiveness."

Their eyes locked. His were dark blue, a rich color that begged for a closer look. Hers were blue, too, but washed out like her white-blond hair, the wimpy coloring of a pure Swede, not strong and clear like his.

After way too long, he smiled and whispered again, "For what?"

"Huh?" Her brain functioned slowly, somewhat like Jell-O.

"What do you want God to forgive you for? Jumping into my arms?" His smile faded as if that hurt his feelings.

"Oh, no."

The smile returned. "Good."

"It's something I do when a mouse scares me."

"Why?"

"Because it's a sin to be afraid of a mouse."

A dimple appeared in each cheek as he smiled wider. "Is not. Where in the Bible does it say, 'Thou shalt not run and scream when you see a rodent'?"

Carrie switched from studying his eyes to studying his dimples. Really, a woman could keep busy forever watching him. "It should be. It's a sin to be this stupid about a tiny little creature obviously put on the earth by God to feed cats. Cats need to eat."

"Oh, well then, because cats need to eat, you've sinned for sure. And what does that have to do with you jumping into my arms?"

"There's a mouse." She glanced back at the floor.

The knight eased her back on her feet. "Mouse, huh?" He gave her an I'm-not-rolling-my-eyeballs-through-sheer-willpower look that tarnished his shining armor. "It's more afraid of you than . . ."

"Than I am of it. I know." And hadn't Carrie heard that a hundred thousand times before in her life? Hadn't helped then, didn't help now. Carrie saw the mouse turn and streak back under the closed pantry door. She grabbed a handful of the carpenter's shirtfront. He steadied her with a strong arm.

"Yeah, right, it's more afraid of me. Not even. Does that mouse lay awake nights fretting, 'What if a woman runs up my leg?' I don't think so."

"Uh, have you got a trap?"

Carrie turned back to the knight. "My hero." The words sounded reverent. "In that sack on the table. Thanks." She was just inches from him, and since she was there anyway, she let herself get lost in his eyes again. This close, she could smell his warm, clean scent.

"I'll see what I can do." He seemed even closer. "By the way, I'm Nick O'Connor. My hired man and I are repairing your porch."

"Hired man?"

"Wilkie Melnik."

Carrie gasped and backed off. *"You hired Wilkie Melnik?"*

11

The corners of Nick's mouth turned down, and the smile wrinkles on the corners of his eyes disappeared along with his dimples. Carrie regretted seeing them go, but it helped her mind work.

Nick smoothed the fist wrinkles she'd made in his shirt. "Yeah, he's not working out too well. He didn't show up yesterday or the day before, and he hasn't come today, either."

"That sounds like Wilkie. I'm Carrie Evans, and my great-grandma Bea died and left me this house. Thanks for the help. I heard that Grandpa tried to get you in earlier to fix things up for Great-Grandma Bea."

Nick rubbed his forehead absently. "Bea wasn't interested. So I'm doing it now."

A soft rustle of paper in the pantry made Carrie step closer to Nick.

"You know, clutter like this is mouse heaven. This house is probably infested."

Carrie shuddered.

"What you really need is a cat."

A loud "Meow" turned Carrie's head toward the porch. The ugliest animal Carrie had ever seen crouched outside the back door.

"That isn't a cat." Carrie kept Nick between her and the grisly beast.

Nick turned and tilted his head. "Um . . . I think it is."

Carrie saw his hand tighten on the hammer.

With a couple of ruthless slashes, the cat shredded the already tattered screen and slipped onto the porch.

Nick and Carrie stepped back, their motions in such perfect harmony that they could have been a pair of synchronized swimmers. The cat slunk across the porch on its belly, emitting a deep, humming yowl that sent a chill up Carrie's spine. It slithered into the kitchen, slipping under the table. He was mottled yellow, his fur matted to his body as if he'd been sleeping on it the wrong way for seventy-five years. He had one eye. The other was closed by a nasty scar. One ear stood up straight; its mate was slit and hung in tatters. Clumps of fur hung from under his belly. His tail had a nice upright S shape until the tip, where it took an alarming ninety-degree turn.

He was alley-cat thin and, from the look and sound of him, cougar-mean. It went against every instinct in Carrie's body to let him in the house. If she had a brain in her head, she'd be a thousand times more afraid of this cat than of a tiny mouse. And yet there was no eeeking and jumping.

A loud rustling noise came from the pantry. Carrie jumped sideways and shouldered Nick forward a step. Since she was hiding behind him, that shoved him closer to the cat. The cat jerked its head up and focused its eye on the pantry, the intact ear pointed forward. A low growl vibrated out of its throat. A real hero had arrived.

"I could, uh . . . catch the cat . . . and put him out." Nick glanced at Carrie as if he was terrified she'd say yes.

"Give him a minute. Maybe he'll eat the mouse."

"He looks like he'd eat you."

"If I close my bedroom door at night, the cat couldn't get me."

Nick shuddered. "You're thinking of keeping it?"

Carrie was seriously sure that, unless the cat cooperated, she couldn't get rid of it. "Sure. If it *is* a cat. It looks more like one of those moth-eaten animals in the Dead Zone."

Nick jerked his head up. "The Dead Zone?"

Carrie nodded. "Great-Grandpa came from a long line of big-game hunters. He personally assisted in placing over a dozen species on the endangered list. There are

14

dozens of moldering murdered mammals upstairs."

Nick's eyes widened. "Cool."

"You can look as soon as you've taken care of the mouse." Bribery. Carrie wasn't above it.

Nick grinned and Carrie filled the silence by studying his dimples until he said, "Got it. Priorities."

"Speaking of priorities, where's your hired man again?"

Nick's smile faded. "Uh . . . I may have made a bad hire."

"Everybody knows Wilkie Melnik is a bum, Nick."

"He didn't seem like a real go-getter, but his name is the same as the town. I figured he was special."

"*Special* — fair description. In fact, I think that was stamped in red ink all over his permanent record at school." Carrie shook her head. "He's got a nasty temper and a complete lack of respect for the law." She suspected she'd just described her cat. "How long has he been working for you?"

"A week. And I need the help. There's a lot of work to do here. Your grandpa already paid me for it."

"Why'd he pay you before you did the work?" Carrie asked.

"Well, that's a funny story." Nick rubbed his forehead again and flinched. "I've been in Melnik six months. The first week I was in town, your grandpa called me and . . ."

Someone knocked at the back porch door. "Anybody home?"

Dora Clemson. Carrie would recognize that voice anywhere. Dora was a living, breathing crowbar come to pry loose all her secrets. And Carrie had a big one.

The screen porch door squeaked mouse-like on its hinges. Nick obviously knew Dora because his smile shrank like generic plastic wrap in an overheated microwave. "Hi, Dora." Nick greeted Dora, slipped past her rotund figure, returned to the porch, and resumed hammering.

Some hero. Sure, he might fight a mouse, but where was he when there was *real* trouble?

"Come in," Carrie called — like saying "Stay out" would even slow the old bat down.

Dora said hi to Nick but didn't pause to talk. Carrie was sorely afraid she was Dora's prime goal. Dora and all her extra chins came through the kitchen door. "You're here, Cindy Lo–o–o–u." Dora dragged the name out, just in case Carrie didn't get the joke. Play a Who from Whoville in the

16

elementary school Christmas play fifteen years ago and live with it forever. That was the nightmare of a small town.

Dora laughed until her chins, ample breasts, and more than ample stomach bounced off each other. Wearing an age-old beige coat, the woman bore an unfortunate resemblance to a really grimy three-tiered wedding cake with a gray dust mop in place of the bride and groom.

Through the porch screens, Carrie saw a police car pull up. Tires scrunched the leaves, newly fallen in the early November weather and blown onto the cracked driveway.

Great — another casserole. Funeral food had been pouring in since Great-Grandma was found dead on Wednesday morning. They figured she must have fallen Tuesday night.

Dora heard the car, turned, and peered out the porch door, afraid she'd miss something good. "Wonder what Junior wants?"

Junior and Cindy Lou. He probably wants a new name. "He probably has another casserole," Carrie said.

Junior Hammerstad. Age fifty-five, a one-eyebrowed, blowhard redneck, born to hassle kids, give out-of-towners speeding tickets, and hold loose dogs for ransom.

He'd been employed as chief for thirty years at the exciting Melnik, Nebraska, police department — part time. Still, that was better than Carrie was doing.

The Crown Vic's door opened. Junior emerged, clutching a cream-colored file folder five inches thick. He defied the chilly fall wind and only wore his gray police uniform. But he had a substantial insulating layer of fat to get him through the tough times. A puff of white came through his lips, and the breeze blew his comb-over off his head. The thin hairs kept their curved shape and hung like an open lid over Junior's left ear, revealing to all the world that Junior was bald. What a shock.

"I heard Junior was coming over with all Bea's police paperwork," Dora said.

Carrie didn't ask how Dora found that out. It only would have been worth mentioning if something went on in Melnik that Dora *didn't* know about. "Grandpa said the police had a *talk* with him every few months about Great-Grandma Bea and all the crimes she reported."

"I can't believe she's dead. And from a fall." Dora patted Carrie on the back.

"Grandpa said she hadn't gone upstairs in years." A shot of electricity jagged through Carrie, reminding her of the *World-Herald* reporting job she'd started in August right after she graduated from college. She'd felt like this every time she'd latched onto a big story. Her instincts told her that there was something more here than a tragic accident. Of course, her instincts were garbage.

But in spite of that one tiny misstep in Omaha, at Nebraska's biggest newspaper — a mistake that ruined her whole life forever — she decided to ignore her garbage instincts and trust herself. Why had Great-Grandma Bea gone upstairs after refusing to do so for years? If she hadn't been one hundred and three, someone might ask questions — even investigate.

The screen door screeched and Junior came in. "Hey, Nick."

The hammering paused. "Hi, Junior."

Carrie circled Dora — no small journey — and met Junior at the kitchen door. "Hi, come on in. Grandpa Leonard said that someone needed to deal with all of Great-Grandma's complaints."

Carrie leaned forward to see Nick on his hands and knees, next to a pile of lumber perfectly stacked near his right side. He lifted a board and deftly slipped it over the gaping hole in the porch, running his hands over the smooth wood as if he enjoyed touching it. Nick snapped a nail into place,

19

hammered it home with three quick blows of his hammer (i.e. lance) and reached for another board. Carrie could have set it to music.

She wondered what neat, orderly Nick thought of this messy old mansion.

Junior, his cheeks as close to maroon as the human body could muster and belt cinched low to give his belly plenty of room to overlap it, looked back past his bulky shoulder. "You might as well come in, Nick. Beatrice accused you of stealing her lawn mower."

Nick sat back on his knees, a furrow in his brow. "Uh, when was that?"

"Just last week. I hadn't gotten around to arresting you yet. Sorry to be so slow."

"No problem. For the record, I mowed her lawn all summer with my own mower."

"Yeah, everybody knows that." Junior's no-nonsense voice raised Carrie's regard for Melnik's hiring practices.

Dora, eyes gleaming, headed for the kitchen table, the only clear surface in the kitchen — possibly in the whole house.

"I also know she doesn't have a lawn mower. Still, she insisted on filing a complaint." Junior hefted the file.

"Set it right there." Carrie waved him toward Great-Grandma's cherrywood table as Dora pulled up a chair and sat down.

The chair creaked alarmingly. Bless Great-Grandma's heart, she'd always had a knack for buying furniture that, as the years passed, dwindled into junk instead of becoming valuable antiques.

Nick appeared in the doorway, his hammer hanging dejectedly at his side as his gaze slid between the file and Dora.

Carrie lifted stacks of magazines off chairs and dragged them from various corners of the kitchen up to the table. Then she stationed her seat as far from the mouse's pantry as possible, hooking her Nikes on the rungs so the mouse couldn't reach her.

Junior sank into a creaky wooden chair and flipped open the file. Nick rounded the table, dragging his heels (practically a perp walk), and sat beside Dora, straight across from Carrie.

"I've got some old clippers of Nils's that I'll give you to take care of that nose hair, Nick." Dora scooted her chair closer to Nick, the legs screeching in pain over her weight. She folded her arms on the table and turned to, apparently, stare straight up Nick's nose.

Nick flinched but stayed put. He did lay the hammer on the table, as if he thought

Dora might back off, knowing he was armed.

In his dreams.

Carrie checked but saw no nose hair. Nick glanced up and caught her staring and narrowed his eyes. She looked away.

"I need a signature on these forms to officially close these cases. For example, when Nick here stole Bea's lawn mower . . ."

Nick clenched his hands on the table and leaned forward. "I did *not* steal —"

Dora snickered.

"Okay, fine." Nick rolled his eyes. "Is there a paper for me to sign to officially deny it?"

"Nope. Not necessary if Carrie drops the charges." Junior waved a sheet under Nick's nose then slid it in front of Carrie. "Your grandpa told me you're Bea's sole heir and executor of her estate."

That sounded like a big deal. If only Great-Grandma Bea had owned anything but this wreck.

"You've also got power of attorney, so you can clear up all these cases."

This was the first Carrie had heard of any power of attorney. She wasn't even sure what that was, but she was pretty sure she had to agree to it and sign some legal document. But this was Melnik. They'd probably just ignore the finer and more inconvenient points of law. "Show me where to sign. I'm dropping all the complaints."

Junior shook his head at Nick. "Got away with it again, you scofflaw."

Nick grinned. Carrie took a second to enjoy his dimples, and he caught her staring again. He probably thought she was checking for nose hair. She decided to let him think that since the truth wasn't something she could admit — that he was so gorgeous she could hardly take her eyes off him.

"I'm just going to need your signature on each one of these one hundred and sixty-two complaints, Carrie." Junior shoved the stack in front of her with a twinkle in his eye.

"I've got to sign my name one hundred and sixty-two times?" Carrie flexed her fingers, feeling writer's cramp already.

Dora's lips thinned. Honestly, when she made this face, her lips looked so much like another of her many chins, the woman needed a bookmark to find her mouth. "It won't be the first time."

Carrie cringed. *No, not the story about ninth grade, not in front of . . .*

"When Carrie was in ninth grade she had to write 'I will not disrupt class' on the blackboard five hundred times." Dora crossed her arms on the table again and settled into the tale. "The girl in front of her . . ."

2

Nick wondered if Dora was right and he really had disgusting nose hair. He'd never noticed before, but he was such a loser that it'd be about right.

Carrie looked across the table at him and distracted him even further from Dora's story by whispering, "It's the only bad thing I ever did. I promise." She held up one hand, flat, like she was being sworn in to testify in court, then turned back to her legal work.

She pulled a paper off the stack on her left, signed it, and slid it sideways to the right. As she worked, Nick picked up her growing stack of signed papers and tapped them on the tabletop, keeping the pile neat. He should whisper back. Try and convince her he was cool. *Think of something to say, idiot.*

He'd given up sitting in an office, pushing a pencil through complicated blueprints and math formulas for a reason — to try to make a human connection. Now if he could just speak to the prettiest woman he'd ever seen. A woman who needed a hero. And here he was, completely unafraid of mice. *Look out, Lancelot!*

"It's true," Dora said. "She was so well-behaved we worried about her."

"The whole town blew a gasket over the *shocking* event." Carrie clenched her fingers on the pen.

Junior snickered. Dora kept chattering. Carrie sighed.

Nick glanced from Junior to Dora and then at Carrie. "Event?" He'd tuned out Dora's story. He might be new in town, but even he had heard about Carrie, the small-town girl with big-city ambitions. She'd been hired at the *Omaha World-Herald,* with her eye on being an investigative reporter. She'd dreamed of bringing down presidents — but only if they were bad. And, more shocking yet, exposing the seamy underbelly of Cornhusker football — in the event she found a seamy underbelly, which was unlikely, the Huskers being above reproach and far too nearly worshipped.

Nick was going through his first Husker football season right now. He'd never seen so many red and white flags flying. He'd better get one.

"I pulled the chair out from under Amy Clark in English class," Carrie confessed.

Nick arched a brow.

"And then I said to Bea, my best friend even then," Dora reclaimed possession of the story. " 'Carrie'll pull out of it.' And Bea said, 'Don't say the word *pull* around me, Dora.' And I repeated that at the Community Club Spaghetti Dinner, and before you know it everyone in town was talking about Carrie 'pulling' a stunt. It even made the *Bugle*."

"Famous sayings in Melnik history. Not exactly 'Give me liberty or give me death,' " Carrie muttered into the police reports. She looked up at Junior. "You know, Junior, I can't find Grandma's skillet."

Junior intertwined his fingers like a man preparing to beg. "Please tell me you're not going to accuse Nick of stealing that."

Being accused of something by Bea Evans was practically a badge of honor. But Nick didn't want Carrie accusing him of anything, not when he was trying to work up the nerve to ask her to be the mother of his children.

Carrie tapped the current complaint with the clicking end of her pen.

Nick read it upside down. "Hey, she accused Leonard of that." Leonard, Carrie's grandfather and Bea's son, a retired carpenter whom Nick suspected didn't have a single black mark on his record, not even for ninth-grade hijinks.

Carrie pulled a paper from the pile. "She accused you," she jabbed her pen at Junior, "of stealing her cat."

"Not that mangy, bad-tempered, one-eyed, one-eared, broken-tailed yellow cat that just slashed Carrie's porch screen?" Nick glanced at the doorway to the living room, wondering where the cat had disappeared, as he tidied the pile Carrie had knocked askew.

Junior rolled his eyes. "Yep, caught me. My dream pet. I had him in my clutches."

"Great." Carrie looked at Junior. "I can make your dreams come true. Grizzly's yours."

"Grizzly? You're naming the cat?" Nick was pretty sure that meant that Carrie was stuck with the shaggy beast for life.

"You'll have to catch me first." Junior smirked.

Carrie looked back at the complaint she needed to sign. "Grandma always kept her skillet on that nail." She pointed at the heavy-duty nail head sticking out of the cracked plaster just behind the cookstove.

"So where is it? In all my twenty-two years, it's never been anywhere else."

"Maybe your grandpa really did steal it," Junior suggested.

Carrie rolled her eyes.

"I remember that skillet." Nick rubbed his forehead. "She nailed me with it the first time I came to the house to work. She'd let me mow the lawn, but she'd come after me if I so much as set foot on the porch. My head still hurts."

"That's motive." Carrie wrinkled her nose at him.

Nick's heart beat erratically. All that white-blond hair and those amazing, pastel blue eyes. She weighed just the right amount, too. Catching her in his arms was no hardship.

Junior grunted. "Yeah, you owe Leonard a thousand dollars' worth of work."

"Grandpa paid you a thousand dollars, and you've never done any work except mow the lawn?" Carrie glared those baby blues right at Nick.

He wondered if *she'd* start filing complaints on him now. "He actually paid me separately for mowing the lawn. The thousand dollars was to repair the house. We had a deal. I'd come over, your great-grandma would chase me off in some semiviolent

29

way, and he'd still pay me twenty bucks for trying."

"Which means" — Carrie did the math — "she ran you off fifty times."

Nick shrugged, feeling like the dopey math geek he'd been in junior high, beaten up by a one-hundred-year-old lady. "But who's counting."

"Leonard is. It's costing him a fortune," Junior grumbled.

"I came here twice a week for six months."

"Since there was never any chance she'd let you in," Carrie pointed out, "that was easy money."

"Easy? Before I learned to duck, she gave me a concussion. I spent three hours in the emergency room."

Junior snorted. "You drove yourself. You weren't hurt too bad."

"And Nick wouldn't even really try after that one time she nailed him with her skillet." Dora shook her head. "I was in the kitchen when she did it. I can still hear the metallic clang against his skull. After that, he just walked up, kind of slowly, until she came out and started hollering at him, and then he'd leave."

"Quitter." Carrie grinned at him. "Why didn't you go swear out a complaint of your own? Assault is a felony."

Nick scowled. "Because she was a century old, and I would have been laughed out of town."

"That still doesn't tell me where the skillet is. I loved that skillet." Carrie studied the paper and tapped the pen on the table.

"I hate that skillet." Nick rubbed his forehead again. After six months, he still had a lump. Bea Evans had reshaped the contour of his head.

"I want to know who stole it."

"I didn't do it." Junior raised his right hand as if it was now *his* turn to testify. "I was too busy taking care of that nasty cat I stole."

Grizzly yowled from another room.

"Someone did. I'm not signing this one." Carrie shoved it back at Junior.

Nick eyed the lone sheet of paper, wondering if he'd have to keep another pile in order.

Junior groaned and took it. By the time Carrie was finished, her signature had deteriorated to a scrawl Nick couldn't even recognize as being human. Grizzly could've done better.

Apparently deciding that nothing interesting was going to happen, Dora hoisted her significant weight out of the chair, its squeaking joints groaning in relief. "I'm going to the smorgasbord at Jansson's Diner. I'll be back to help tomorrow, Carrie."

"No need," Carrie said to Dora's receding back. "I'm not sure . . ."

The door slapped shut.

"So you inherited this . . . uh . . . house." Junior looked around the jam-packed kitchen.

"Dump, you mean?" Carrie's shoulders slumped. "Every countertop, every drawer, every end table, every flat surface in this house, including the floor, except this kitchen table and Great-Grandma's bed, are piled high with junk." Carrie glanced around the room.

Nick could tell she couldn't see the potential. "You've really got your work cut out for you. But it's a majestic old house. The lines and layout are fantastic."

"You might find some valuable antiques." Junior studied the room, flicking the corner of his manila file folder.

Carrie snorted inelegantly, which, when Nick thought about it, was really the only way a person *could* snort.

"My great-grandmother had a knack for only holding onto junk."

Nick's eyes skimmed the papers stacked to the ceiling on top of the refrigerator behind Carrie's back. There was a cardboard box full of magazines overflowing on the stove next to the refrigerator.

"But still," Nick said, "old magazines, dishes, furniture that doesn't seem valuable — some might have worth as collector's items."

"It'll take me a year to get it sorted out, listed on eBay, and shipped." Carrie's voice sounded so grim that Nick couldn't help smiling. "And when it's said and done, it's still Don't-Give-Up-Your-Day-Job money."

"Oh, speaking of day jobs, you want a job?" Junior jammed Nick's neat stack of complaints back in the overworked folder with complete disregard for keeping them tidy. He held up the remaining unsigned paper and scowled at it before he set it on top of his folder.

Carrie sat up straight. "At the police station?"

Nick couldn't tell if she was intrigued or horrified.

"No, the job's at the *Bugle*."

Carrie wrinkled her nose. "What position is open there?"

"Editor."

"They've turned over another editor?"

"Yeah, Edith Eskilson had been doing it, but she quit because Marlys Piperson complained about . . ."

Nick tried not to daydream as the two townies chattered away.

"So, did you arrest Jeffie?" Carrie snickered.

Nick's mind wandered to the wreck of a porch. He itched to get back to repairing it. A couple more hours replacing rotten floorboards and then he could . . .

"And then when Marlys called Edith an old . . ."

Carrie leaned in. Nick began a mental inventory of repairs. If he had his way, this would be a showplace.

"And of course Muriel saved her marigolds."

"Well, sure. Muriel isn't going to let anything hurt her flower bed."

Junior nodded. "Got a green thumb, that woman. But still, they . . ."

The screens were in shreds, but Nick loved the graceful way the porch wrapped around all four sides of the house.

"So Edith misspelled Stu Piperson's name?" Carrie asked. "Big deal."

And the complicated, gabled roof — what a nightmare to shingle, but so elegant . . .

"She spelled Stu Piperson, 'Stupid Person,' " Junior said.

Carrie gasped and started choking. "She didn't!"

Nick sat up, glad he'd caught that.

Junior nodded. "Mrs. Stupid Person and her son Jeffie were Friday afternoon coffee guests at Luella Hasting's home on . . ."

Nick dropped his head back and laughed.

"She's lucky she just got fired and not hanged." Carrie giggled.

"She didn't get fired," Junior scoffed. "Jeffie's mom threw such a fit that Edith quit in a huff, so now the job's open. Interested?"

Carrie sighed. "Sure, why not. I need a job. Do I go see Gunderson?"

Nick wondered why she'd given up her job in Omaha. He'd heard it was her dream. Of course he'd given up his job and moved, but engineering hadn't been his dream.

"Nope, I told Viola I'd ask. She knew I was bringing the reports over. Besides, Old Man Gunderson died about a month back. Rumor is his son Sven is coming back to town, but I haven't seen him."

Carrie's brow furrowed. "Maybe Sven will want to be editor."

"I doubt it. His dad got rich collecting rent on all his property. He owns most of Main Street. Why would Sven jump in and take over the *Bugle*?"

"What does it pay?"

Nick wished he'd kept daydreaming. "You know, this is one of the more bizarre job interviews I've ever heard."

"Yeah." Carried turned to glare at Junior. "Is that what this is, a job interview? Why would you interview me for a job at the *Bugle*?"

"I'm not interviewing you. I'm the grapevine."

Nick remembered the infestation and turned toward the pantry. "I forgot about setting your mousetraps."

Carrie shuddered. "This town grows really big mice."

Nick thought of Maxie, stuffed, his black, beady eyes fierce, posed by a local taxidermist and preserved forever in a glass case at city hall. With a shake of his head to dislodge the memory of that gigantic mouse — "The World's Largest Field Mouse" and Melnik's greatest claim to fame — Nick strode toward the pantry, a little spooked by what might jump out at him. Carrie's phobia was rubbing off on him. Prepared to stay and fight no matter how big the mouse, he grasped the handle and yanked open the door.

Wilkie Melnik came tipping out of the closet straight at him wearing Bea Evans's skillet like a cast-iron baseball cap.

3

Nick staggered backward into the table, banged his hip, and rammed into Carrie, who was striding toward the toppling body.

Wilkie tilted in slow motion until the skillet tumbled off his head and clanked to the floor.

"What happened?" Carrie pushed past Nick. Junior came up on the other side.

Wilkie — eyes fixed and dilated — was dead beyond a doubt. Scaredy-cat Carrie approached the body as Nick backed away. She crouched beside Wilkie, reminding Nick she'd worked the police beat at the *World-Herald.*

She pressed two fingers to Wilkie's neck.

"Stay back, Carrie. Call 911. I want both deputies down here, ASAP. Tell Sandra to contact the Dodge County coroner, too." Junior knelt by the body. "Whoever's on duty there will need to cover this."

Carrie stood, rounded the body, grabbed

the wall phone, and dialed. She rapped out her name, the address, and Junior's orders.

A siren blasted at the police station two blocks away. Carrie laid the phone on one of Bea's countless stacks of papers and knelt by the body again.

"Back off, Carrie." Junior reached across Wilkie's body and grabbed her shoulder. "I'm serious."

Carrie's hand froze inches from a bruise on Wilkie's forehead. "I know. What's that on his mouth?" Carrie inched closer.

Nick squinted. Junior dropped to one knee and leaned down. "It's hair. It looks like gray fur. Funny we were just talking about big mice, because it could almost be . . ."

A mouse scrambled out of the closet, and an earsplitting squeal came from somewhere deep in Carrie's gut. She jumped to her feet and while she was at it just kept going up. Nick grabbed her in his arms.

Junior fell over backward, fumbling for his gun.

"It's a mouse!" Nick shouted to head off the shootout. "She's just startled."

"Carrie, for Pete's sake!" Junior rolled onto his hands and knees.

Carrie whispered into Nick's chest, "God forgive me."

Nick felt kind of sorry for the little sweetheart, who labeled her greatest phobia a sin. That was quite a burden for someone to carry around. He held her close to help her bear it.

The mouse dashed between Nick's feet. The cat snarled behind his back. Nick turned with Carrie in his arms in time to see the mouse zip out the torn screen door on the porch with the cat hard on its heels.

Carrie's arms went around Nick's neck as she leaned to watch the chase. "I love that cat." She sounded almost reverent. True love had come to her while Nick held her in his arms. Too bad it was love for that mangy cat.

Out of the corner of his eye, Nick saw another mouse slip from the pantry into a hole at the base of the kitchen cupboards.

He didn't even consider mentioning it.

"How is it," he asked, pulling her attention away from the porch, "that you can touch a dead body, kneel beside it, and phone 911 all without turning a hair, but a little mouse scares you?"

Carrie said in a tiny voice, "It's a sin, that's all. It's stupid. I'm stupid."

"No, you're not."

"About mice I am."

Nick hesitated. She might be right.

The mouse and Grizzly vanished into the browning leaves of the lilac hedge at the back of the lawn. Carrie twisted in Nick's arms to look at poor Wilkie.

"It looks like you were the last one to see him alive, Nick. That makes you the prime suspect." Carrie narrowed her eyes at him.

Since she didn't show any signs of climbing out of his arms, he doubted she really thought he was a killer.

"You two get outside before you contaminate my crime scene." Junior glared at them. The sirens got louder.

Nick nodded.

"Wait." Carrie tightened her hold.

Stopping, Nick asked, "Why?"

Carrie pointed at the kitchen table. "Take me closer, please."

Ever the obedient pack animal, Nick complied.

Carrie leaned down, still with one arm clinging to Nick's neck, and signed the last complaint. "No need to hunt for the frying pan now."

Shaking his head, Nick carried his little armload of phobia outside.

She tapped him on the shoulder and arched her eyebrows. "You can put me down now."

The wind was sharp but nothing like the

wind that whistled through the skyscrapers in Chicago's fall and winter. Nick was grateful for his Windbreaker and wished he'd taken the time to carry her to her coat before they'd come out. But she had a thick sweater on that was the exact color of her eyes, plus blue jeans and black leather boots, so she'd be okay for a while.

Setting Carrie down on Bea's sidewalk, which was so old and broken that it was almost gravel, Nick followed her toward a rickety picnic table. She perched on the top. Paint chips sprinkled off the table, and Nick remained standing rather than get messy. A bit of snow lay on the shaded ground under the table, left over from an early snowstorm. A police car pulled up, its siren shrieking. A second siren fired up across town.

Carrie said, "Rescue squad."

Junior came out, and Nick was touched to see he'd grabbed a coat for Carrie, a denim jacket with brown fur lining. Junior handed over the coat just as the screaming squad car pulled up. Junior walked away to talk with his deputies.

The first curious Melnikite stuck her head out her front door. A second gray head soon followed, and then a third. A screen door slammed a block over.

Carrie started to follow Junior.

41

Junior glowered at her. "Stay put, Carrie."

Nick noticed a pouty bottom lip, but Carrie stayed. She shook the blue-jean jacket violently as if expecting a mouse to have taken up residence.

"Let me check." Nick relieved her of it.

She gave him that wide-eyed-wonder look again. Nick knew he had the social skills of a swamp rat. He'd never held one in his arms before. A woman, that is. He'd had a swamp rat or two in his grasp during Vertebrate Zoology in college.

To be or not to be a science geek or math geek, that was the question. Nick wanted to kick himself. Internal sarcasm with mutant Shakespearean quotes was a really bad indicator of coolness.

Dear God, could I be cool just this once in my pathetic life?

He ran his hands heroically down the sleeves and into the pockets, even squeezing the whole coat as if he could wring a mouse out of it. Then he handed it back. She practically glowed as she pulled it on.

Say something. *Let's run off and get married. Then I can protect you from mice for the rest of your life since I'll be living in your house.* He clamped his mouth shut for fear of what might come out.

How about dinner? Better. That didn't

make him sound like a complete moron.

Unless, when he actually asked, she said, "No, forget it. Ick. You're a complete moron."

But he'd saved her from two mice now. *Slayer of pint-sized dragons at your service.* And she was smiling up at him as if she liked morons.

He could do this. *How about dinner?* Five syllables. He took a deep breath. "How about —"

"Nick, I've got to ask you a few questions."

Nick's eyes shut along with his mouth. He turned to face Junior. His deputies were working at stringing up yellow crime-scene tape.

Junior donned a black down jacket he'd fished out of his cruiser. The coroner had to drive in from fifty miles away, so there was plenty of time for an interrogation. Swell.

"You know Carrie's right, Nick. You were the last person to see him alive."

"Oh, I was not." Nick's frustration with Junior's timing sounded loud and clear. *Okay, loser, mouth off to the policeman who thinks you killed a guy. Brilliant.*

Junior looked up from his notes. "How do you figure?"

"Well, obviously whoever killed him saw

him after me." Nick's was a logical, orderly mind — except about women. Then the swamp rat took over.

Junior shrugged one shoulder and arched his unibrow. "Good point." The interrogation went on, occasionally lapsing into gossip over Wilkie's many and pitiful indiscretions. Was Junior just killing time until the real policemen got here, or did he actually suspect Nick?

A cold chill danced down Nick's spine at the thought. In Chicago, he'd have called his dad, and Dad would have called in a high-powered lawyer. The closest thing Nick had seen to a high-powered lawyer in Melnik was eighty-five-year-old George Wesley, who handed out legal advice from his wheelchair in the assisted-living wing of Melnik Manor.

Nick wasn't going to call Dad or Wesley. He hoped that Junior just needed to feel productive. Or maybe he loved writing in his nifty pocket-sized notebook.

"Who had the most to gain by Wilkie's death?" Carrie muttered the question as if she were hoping Junior would think it had come out of his own thick skull.

A gray station wagon inched its way through the onlookers and then turned into Bea's driveway. Its tires crackled on the brightly colored fall leaves on the pavement. It pulled to a stop, and the driver's side door swung open. The words DODGE COUNTY CORONER were painted on the side.

Junior turned back toward Nick and smiled down at his shiny new notebook. "So, what *did* you have to gain by Wilkie's death?"

Nick groaned. "I had absolutely nothing to gain by Wilkie's death." He gave up on keeping his backside clean and settled beside Carrie on the picnic table.

The whole town was slowly but surely gathering in the street. Music was playing, and Nick thought he smelled hot dogs, like maybe the school's athletic booster club had seized on this perfect opportunity to raise money for new football uniforms.

"What a bunch of vultures," Carrie muttered.

"Now, Carrie, that's not fair." Junior licked the tip of his pencil. "None of 'em wants anything bad to happen. They just don't want to miss it if it does."

Carrie sighed, centered her elbows on her knees, and plopped her chin onto both fists.

Nick watched Junior's deputies gossip with the gathering horde. The whole house was surrounded by twenty-foot-tall lilac bushes, blocking the view of nosy neighbors. So the neighbors just came around the hedge.

The deputies, Hal and Steve, roped the town out and Carrie, Nick, and Junior in. With Wilkie.

Nick suspected that the tape came as standard equipment in a police cruiser and it'd been rolling around in Junior's trunk for years. No chance Junior had bought it. Why would he? There was no crime in Melnik.

A coroner in a white lab coat climbed out of the wagon.

Almost no crime.

"What did you say you had to gain by Wilkie's death?" Junior asked Nick, as if he wished he'd listened closer earlier — but, golly, that crime-scene tape was pretty and shiny, and who wouldn't be distracted?

"Junior, I did not kill Wilkie, and you know it."

"How do I know it?" Junior looked at his pad of paper as if dying to write down SOLVED.

"I wouldn't do a thing like that!" And *that* might be the weakest alibi ever given by a human being in the history of the earth.

Junior shrugged again. "True. Okay, who did kill him?"

Apparently it was enough.

Nick looked sideways at Carrie.

"Means, motive, opportunity." Carrie suggested.

Junior stood in front of them, too wise to risk his weight on the wobbly table.

A middle-aged woman gave a no-nonsense wave of greeting to Carrie, Nick, and Junior, went to the back end of her wagon, swung the tailgate down with a creak of unoiled metal, and busied herself inside the vehicle.

Junior scratched his spare-tire belly thoughtfully. "Well, his wife was madder'n sin at him."

Carrie perked up. The table creaked. "Why's that?"

"He got his girlfriend pregnant."

"Whoa." Nick clenched his hands between his splayed knees. "Good motive."

"Great motive." Carrie glanced at Nick just as he looked at her.

"Plus, everybody knows he liked to gamble. Spent time in Iowa at that casino. He might have owed someone money."

Geese high overhead honked as they passed by on their way south. The street held a growing crowd of snoops, all talking quietly behind the yellow crime-scene tape. Well-behaved snoops in Melnik.

Carrie waved at Dora, who'd brought a

lawn chair and perched it on the sidewalk across the street. Nick tried not to feel smug about the fact that he'd made the inside of the tape at gossip central, while Dora was cordoned out.

"Not a lot of loan sharks in Melnik, but it's worth looking into." Carrie nodded. "Anyone else?"

"Wilkie did a little time about five years ago." Junior flipped a page in his notebook. "Stole a bunch of riding lawn mowers from farm places in the area before we caught him."

"I remember that." Carrie sat up straight and punched her knees. "He got my dad's brand-new Snapper. Still, Dad's over it by now."

"Not much motive there." Nick rubbed his forehead.

"But Wilkie may have met some lowlifes in the pen. Maybe he still associates with them." Carrie chewed her thumbnail.

"Plus, his girlfriend was after him for child support." Junior jotted on his pad.

Nick grabbed Carrie's arm and pulled her thumb out of her mouth. "You've been touching things in there." Nick shuddered and shook his head.

Carrie glared at him.

He added, "Things mice might have run across."

Her face twisted with horror, and she turned and spit onto the grass. Then her hands tightly clenched against lapsing into her bad habit, Nick supposed, she turned to Junior. "So if child support is kicking in, the girlfriend already had the baby?"

Nick reached into his pocket and pulled out a wrapped alcohol wipe and handed it to Carrie.

She began by scrubbing her lips and teeth before she focused on her hands. It looked for all the world like she intended to scrub her skin off.

"No, Donette's still pregnant; she's just getting started early," Junior said. "And the rumor is, she wants more than money. She wants Wilkie to dump Rosie and marry her."

Carrie shook her head. "I can't believe it."

"That anyone would be so irresponsible?" Nick nodded in agreement. He reached for the wipe when the scrubbing stopped. Carrie handed it to him. He refolded it and put it back in the foil packet.

"No. Well, yes, that, too," Carrie said. "But what I meant was, I can't believe any self-respecting woman would get close enough to Wilkie to get pregnant. Eww."

Junior stuck his notebook into his shirt

pocket and pulled black leather gloves out of his coat pocket. "I think the key word is self-respecting."

"Let alone," Carrie went on, "want to marry the bum."

"It's one of life's little mysteries," Nick said. "There's someone for everyone."

Except him. There'd never been anyone for him. Until maybe now. He considered keeping Carrie's alcohol wipe and putting it into a scrapbook. Except that might qualify him as a stalker.

"True," Carrie stood from the table and blew on her hands, rubbing them together, as the coroner dragged a heavy white case in the shape of a toolbox out of her wagon. "I've known lots of slimeballs who are married."

Junior retrieved his notebook and poked at it with his pencil. "I've hardly ever known a slimeball who *wasn't* married."

"So are you listing suspects? A girlfriend and a wife. Loan sharks." Carrie added dryly, "My dad."

"Got 'em all." Junior tapped his shirt pocket containing the notebook.

"I'm Dr. Notchke." The coroner, a stocky woman in sensible shoes and an unfortunate pageboy haircut that made her face a perfect square, approached the table. "They sent me out from the Dodge County coroner's office."

The doctor and Junior went in the house together.

Carrie studied their retreating backs.

"You want in the house bad, don't you?" Nick couldn't remember the last time he'd enjoyed a woman's company this much. Her silly fear of mice, her amazing nerve around the corpse, her silky blond hair, that sassy mouth, and the dreams in her intelligent sky blue eyes.

Carrie looked at Nick, smiled sheepishly, and hunched one shoulder. He was really close. He leaned closer. Five syllables. Seven if he said her name first.

"Carrie?"

"Yes?"

"How about . . ." That sounded rude. He should have said, "Will you please —" No. Bad grammar. Learned that from the semester he considered being a novelist. *Would you like to have dinner with me?* Better. How many syllables? Nick started counting. *Would you like to —*

"What?"

He tried to say it, remembered his nose-hair problems, and forced his jaw to unclench. "Would you like to —"

"No!" A scream with the force of an

electric shock jerked Nick around.

"No, not Wilkie, not my Wilkie!" A painfully thin woman, wearing tattered blue jeans and a T-shirt that hung on her skinny body, fought against the grip of Junior's two deputies. Her limp brown hair flying, she collapsed, screaming with grief. She buried her face in her hands. A boy, maybe fifteen, dashed up behind the woman and fell to the ground beside her, nearly knocking her onto her side.

"Mom, Mom, it's got to be a mistake. It's not Dad!" The boy broke into sobs and flung his arms around the distraught woman. A girl around seventeen, wearing low-slung jeans and a tight, short T-shirt faded to a drab shade of army green, edged up beside the two.

"That his wife and kids?" Nick whispered.

"Yeah, he has two with Rosie." Carrie stood and dusted off the seat of her pants. "Shayla was born just after Rosie turned seventeen. Wilkie was twenty-four."

"That's statutory rape." Nick clenched his jaw.

"Only if someone presses charges."

"Wrong."

Carrie nodded. "Rosie was thrilled, and her parents didn't complain when they got married real fast. It was a huge scandal."

"As big a scandal as you pulling that chair out from under your friend?"

Carrie narrowed her eyes. "I won't dignify that with a response."

"Good for you." *Would you please have dinner with me?*

Say it. Say it. Say it, loser.

"I remember how happy Rosie was." Carrie shook her head and her hair swept back and forth, so close, so silky that Nick's fingers itched to touch it. Of course he didn't.

"And how sure we all were that she'd hooked a loser."

"Probably what she was fishing for." Nick shoved his hands in his Windbreaker pockets to control them. "Should we go help?" He took a step forward.

Junior loped out of the house in response to the screams.

"We don't want any part of Rosie's drama." Carrie caught Nick's arm. "Let Junior handle it."

"Wilkie's dead?" Another woman shoved through the crowd. Little more than a teenager, she wore a blue-jean jacket that was impossible to button, and a stained, white T-shirt stretched over her stomach. She was obviously pregnant.

The woman on the ground whirled on her

53

knees, and with a scream that would have humbled a horror movie actress, launched herself at the second woman.

Even pregnant, the new woman was tough. She sank both hands in Rosie's hair and screamed, "You killed him, you . . ."

Dora actually stood up from her lawn chair.

Nick raced toward them, leaping the crime-scene tape. Hal and Steve were there ahead of him, each grabbing a woman. The pregnant woman was giving Hal all he could handle, so Nick caught the woman's hand and pried her fingers loose one at a time from Rosie Melnik's hair.

Junior was one step behind him. "Break it up, you two."

Rosie shouted a string of words no woman should ever say, let alone in front of her children. She drew back her fist.

The pregnant woman bared her claws and yowled. For a second, Nick felt like he'd bought into a fight with Carrie's cat. Trying to protect the pregnant woman from Rosie's punch, Nick got clipped on the chin. Rosie didn't pack a lot of wallop. Nothing like Bea and her skillet.

"Donette, knock it off!" Junior used his significant weight to push between the women.

"She killed Wilkie!" Donette lunged, but the deputy hung on. "He was leaving her for me!"

"He was done with you, Donette." Rosie lashed out with her foot and kicked Junior in the backside. "You never meant a thing to him!"

"Both of you settle down," Junior growled in a tone that would have cleared the mice out of Carrie's house if they'd heard it.

The deputies tightened their grips on the two loves of Wilkie Melnik.

"You make me sick, Donette." Wilkie's daughter charged into the middle of the riot and jammed her hands on her hips. "I hate you."

Nick rubbed his chin, now puffy enough to match the bump on his forehead, and gazed at Carrie, who shrugged.

"Back off, Shayla." Donette yanked against Hal's restraining hold. "I was in love with your dad."

Rosie lurched toward her daughter and wrapped her arms around the girl. Shayla shrugged like her mother's arms were smothering her. "You were supposed to be my friend. Instead, you were hanging around with me to get to Dad. You're disgusting."

"I didn't go after your dad. He came after

me. We were in love."

"Dad didn't know how to love anyone. He used you because you're a —"

"Enough, Shayla." Junior cut her off. "It don't do no good to spread the hate around."

Junior turned to the deputy gripping Donette. "Hal, take Donette home."

Junior shifted his eyes to Donette. "I expect you to let this drop. Fighting don't solve anything. You come at Rosie again and I'll arrest you."

"You belong in jail." Rosie released Shayla and bent over sobbing. "You're a home wrecker and a murderer."

Nick tried to imagine two women fighting over him. It'd never happen in a million years. The many charms of Wilkie had escaped Nick.

Rosie threw her whole self into a weeping fury that struck Nick as more theatrical than truly sad. He wondered just how sorry Rosie was to see her lazy, drinking, cheating, gambling, ex-con husband dead.

Junior turned toward Rosie. "That goes double for you. Any more fighting between you two and you'll both cool off in a cell."

"Let's go." Hal forced Donette away from Rosie.

Donette resisted as Hal pushed her forward. "She killed him," Donette yelled over her shoulder, jabbing her index finger straight at Rosie. "She wanted him dead when he told her he was leaving."

"And Steve, get Rosie home."

"No!" Rosie made a quick move toward the house. "I want to stay. I want to see Wilkie!"

Steve caught her with the finesse of a nose tackle.

Rosie, held securely by Steve, twisted toward Donette. "You're the one who killed him."

The two women were dragged away weeping, occasionally bursting into screaming fits. Nick heard Hal shout in pain as he wrestled Donette into the squad car. Steve had to deal with the distraught son and hostile daughter, too. Once the cars pulled out, Junior returned to the house muttering. Nick heard the words, "Worthless Wilkie" but couldn't make out the rest.

Nick smoothed his hair and tucked his shirt back in, trying to recover from the catfight. He wondered how soon would be too soon to try asking Carrie out to dinner again.

Before he could ease into it, a vision in splattered primary colors burst from the crowd. Tallulah Prichard, president of the

Melnik Historical Society and keeper of All Things Melnik.

"Wilkie's dead?"

She wore a turban. Nick knew there were turbans, and he'd seen plenty of them in the news — in stories about the Middle East. But he'd never personally met anyone who wore one. Ditto caftans. This turban was bright red, and it matched a giant splash in her caftan.

Carrie muttered beside him, "It looks like a parrot exploded on her."

"Wilkie was going to be the master of ceremonies for this year's Maxie Parade." Tallulah flung her arms wide, playing to the cheap seats.

"That cannot be true." Carrie sidled closer to Nick — the better to whisper. "No one in their right mind would honor a loser like Wilkie Melnik."

Nick thought about the fact that he'd hired Wilkie and decided not to comment.

Tallulah wrung her hands together, rings flashing on nearly every finger. "He and his family were the last of the Melnik line."

"You know, no one in the town was very good to Wilkie," Carrie said under her breath. "Not that he inspired a lot of good. It's amazing that so many people are upset that he's dead."

Nick looked down at her. "If you're keeping score, there are about fifty people in this crowd and, so far, I've counted five that are upset — so Wilkie's not doing all that well."

"We've already got the float half built for the parade." Tallulah laid her hands on her face with great flourish, careful not to smear her substantial layers of makeup. "It's a giant mouse, and Wilkie was going to ride on its back."

Carrie shuddered and inched closer to Nick.

"It's a fake mouse, for heaven's sake," Nick hissed. "You don't get scared over Mickey Mouse cartoons, do you?"

"Mickey is a very obvious cartoon," Carrie retorted under her breath. "Tallulah will make the float look just like Maxie; you wait and see. Ick." She moved closer yet.

Nick knew there was some way to parlay her phobia into a dinner date if he could just figure out the right approach.

"A completely realistic six-foot-tall mouse. That is my own personal nightmare."

Her shoulder touched his and, so far, this was his best day in Melnik since he'd moved here.

Nick grinned and patted her on the shoulder.

Tallulah ranted a bit more. The crowd

went back to their own whispered reflections on the unfolding events while they munched on their hot dogs. All in all, everyone appeared to be enjoying themselves. A great day to be from Melnik, unless you were Wilkie or one of the four or five people who cared about him.

Then a hush fell over the crowd. Nick saw eyes focus on the house behind him. He turned to see the coroner emerge through the doorway.

The stout doctor walked down the steps. Junior appeared from the midst of the onlookers to meet her.

Carrie jumped off the picnic table and headed straight for them.

As repelled by murder as Carrie was attracted to it, Nick trailed along to talk to the officials. If he was going to be arrested, he didn't want to annoy them by making them hunt for him.

4

"Okay. The preliminary exam tells me that Wilkie died from a gunshot wound and he's been dead several days — I'll narrow that down." Dr. Notchke read from her notes.

"Gunshot?" Carrie heard Junior gasp. "I saw a bruise on his head — there was no blood."

Carrie hung back, afraid they'd clam up if she got too close.

"I didn't see it at first either," Dr. Notchke said. "The wound didn't bleed like it should have. Even moving the body doesn't explain the lack of blood on his clothes. In fact, I suspect an autopsy will show that someone shot him after he was dead. But for a preliminary cause of death, well, we can't discount that he's got a bullet in him."

"Why would anybody do that?" Carrie backed up enough to whisper to Nick. Her fingertips tingled, she wanted to take notes so badly. A leftover habit from working the police beat in Omaha. She didn't dare in front of the coroner, though. Besides, she didn't have any paper. She wondered if Junior had any to spare.

"Any idea about motive at this point?"

"Nick, get over here." Junior turned a dark expression on Nick.

Nick, his eyes wary, approached. Carrie tagged along. If they were going to tell him stuff, then she ought to get to hear it, too. He made room in the little circle for Carrie, which gave her an "us against them" feeling.

"What?" Nick shoved his hands in the pockets of his black Windbreaker.

"When did you last see Wilkie?"

"I told you I didn't do it. You can *not* believe —"

"Just answer the question." This was Junior in serious-cop mode.

"Fine." Nick sighed. "I hired him around noon on Monday. He worked for me the rest of the day." The crowd, still lingering two hours after the first siren had sounded, murmured into the fall breeze. More geese honked from a bedraggled V far overhead.

"Keep going." Junior wrote steadily.

"I already knew he was going to be trouble by the end of the day, because he was more interested in taking breaks than in working."

"Wilkie never was a hard worker." Junior shook his head in disgust at the ultimate Nebraska sin.

"Then he showed up an hour late on Tuesday. I told him we started at seven and I expected him to be on time."

Junior nodded.

"He didn't come in at all on Wednesday."

"Great-Grandma Bea died Tuesday night," Carrie interjected. The paramedics on the Melnik Volunteer Fire Department had shown up. Some had gone inside, but the rest waited, their blue jackets proudly sporting *MVFD*.

"Have you looked into Great-Grandma's death?" Carrie grabbed Junior's forearm. "It can't be a coincidence that both she and Wilkie are dead."

The chief's heavy brow furrowed. "I came over when your grandpa Leonard called 911. She was a hundred and three, and she . . ."

"Oh," Carrie cut him off, "so now it's okay to kill people once they're one hundred and three?"

"I didn't mean that, and you know it." Junior's cheeks turned red. "I just meant that she was old and unsteady. You know there were risks in her staying here alone. Leonard tried to get her to move in with him and your grandma, but she wouldn't budge. There was nothing suspicious about her death."

"Nothing suspicious?" Carrie planted her fists on her hips. "How about another body? That's suspicious."

Carrie looked at Nick for support.

"Seems suspicious to me." Nick moved closer to Carrie.

Carrie shot him a grateful smile.

"Well, I didn't know about this body until now, did I?" Junior shrugged and made a note. "I'll keep it in mind."

Carrie felt her blood pressure rising at Junior's dismissive tone. Given the circumstances, there was no way her great-grandmother's death was an accident.

"Go on, Nick." Junior looked up. "Is Tuesday the last time you saw Wilkie?"

Nick nodded. "I had cabinets to build. A big project. I told Wilkie to come to my place on Wednesday morning. He still hadn't shown up when I heard about Bea's death. I came over here as soon as I could to see Leonard. He was pretty broken up about his mom dying. I offered him all his money back."

Nick turned to Carrie. "I promise I tried

to quit. I'd see him on the street, and every week since he'd hired me, I told him I wasn't earning the money he was paying. But he'd say 'Keep trying,' and when I refused to take his money, he started depositing a check in my account at the bank. I even told the bank not to accept it, but your aunt Lucille is the head teller, and she just laughed at me and said, 'Learn to duck when you're around Bea.' "

Nick looked back at Junior. "I got the impression he wanted me to check on his mom. I know he didn't like her living here alone, and he was over here every day and your grandma called and stopped, and Dora and lots of others visited, but he still worried."

"That sounds like Grandpa." Carrie noticed Grizzly slip through the torn screen into the house. She hoped her scary new pet cleared out the mice and fast.

"And I think Bea kind of liked swinging her skillet and yelling at me." Nick shrugged one shoulder. "It seemed to make her happy."

"That sounds like Great-Grandma."

Nick focused on Junior again. "When I saw Leonard Wednesday morning, he told me it was time to earn my money. So I went to work. I called Wilkie again to tell him to come over to Bea's. No answer. I figured he'd already headed to my house so I went back home. Wilkie wasn't around. I gathered up the tools I needed to work here at Bea's and left Wilkie a note in my workshop, telling him to come on over. I never heard from him."

"He was already dead." Dr. Notchke consulted her clipboard. "I'll pin down the time of death better after the autopsy, but I'd guess he's been dead at least three days."

"You mean he's been dead since maybe Tuesday night, the same time my great-grandma died?" Cassie asked.

The coroner nodded. "Certainly when you were hunting for him Wednesday morning, he was already in the closet."

"So I've been working in the house with a dead body?" Nick grimaced at the thought.

The coroner nodded. "We're done here. You can take over, Chief Hammerstad."

"Thanks. Let me know when . . ." Junior fell silent as a paramedic emerged from the house. Wheels clattered as one husky medic lowered the white-sheeted gurney down the steps.

The crowd in the street fell silent. Wheels squeaked down the sidewalk, and the EMTs escorted the ne'er-do-well great-great grandson of the town's founders away.

Tallulah wept loudly. Dora stopped knitting. Carrie noticed Grandma Elsa and Grandpa Leonard Evans, her dad's parents, in the crowd. Grandpa Leonard, who'd been doing his best to take care of his uncooperative mother for years, nodded at her and gave her a little wave.

Most of Melnik quietly watched while Wilkie made a spectacle of himself one last time.

When the ambulance pulled away, Junior clapped the notebook closed. "We're done inside. The coroner's team did a sweep for fiber evidence. You can have your house back."

"Fiber evidence?" Carrie shook her head. "Great-Grandma's house is one gigantic fiber."

"Tell me about it." Junior walked away, snagging the crime-scene tape as he went. The crowd surged forward, Dora at the lead.

Carrie looked at the house and swallowed with a throat gone bone dry.

Nick rested one hand on her upper arm. "You don't want to sleep here. Besides Wilkie, there's the mouse situation."

Carrie didn't admit that the mouse situation bothered her a lot more than Wilkie.

"You can stay with your folks or at your grandparents'. All four of your grandparents live in Melnik, right?"

Carrie turned from staring at the house. "I'm looking for my backbone, okay? Don't make it harder by giving me plausible excuses."

Nick's eyes were warm with concern. "If you're really worried about mice, you stay with your folks, and I'll stay here a few days and make sure they're cleared out."

"You and Grizzly?"

Nick opened his mouth, but no sound came out.

"I didn't think so."

Nick cleared his throat. "No, you didn't give me enough time. I'll team up with Grizzly. You can even help me clear out a different bedroom than the one you were planning to use, if you feel like that's an invasion of your privacy."

"They're all piled to the rafters with junk."

"We've got a few hours of light left. We could clear one out before bedtime."

"We'll help." Dora invaded their conversation.

Carrie knew just how Atlanta felt when Ulysses S. Grant showed up.

"No!" Tallulah, playing the part of Robert E. Lee, shoved her way through the crowd. That wasn't hard. Everyone wanted her front and center where they could watch

68

the show.

Grandpa Leonard came up beside Carrie on the right while Nick stood on her left. Grandma Elsa was close behind her husband.

With a sigh, Carrie said, "Why not, Tallulah?"

"Bea Evans's house is a gold mine of historical information. She's got over one hundred years' worth of newspapers and artifacts in there."

"The main artifacts she has are ten thousand *Reader's Digest*s and *TV Guide*s," Carrie said, unable to keep the sarcasm out of her voice. "There's no treasure, Tallulah."

"Someone with the correct historical understanding needs to go through that house with a fine-tooth comb."

Carrie closed her eyes so she could roll them without getting caught. "And who exactly would that be?"

"Why, me." Tallulah touched her chest gracefully with five ring-spangled fingers. "Of course."

"Of course." Carrie folded her arms, hoping the body language would help. "The thing is, I don't have time to comb the fine teeth of my house. So we're not going to be careful."

Grandma Elsa eased up by Carrie. "If

69

something has been buried in that house for one hundred years, we can live without it forever. I say let's gather every trash can in town and fill 'em up."

Carrie smiled at the spry little woman who always had time for her youngest grandchild.

Tallulah's gasp of outrage was drowned out by the voices of a herd of bustling housewives, many of whom had been itching to get their hands on Bea Evans's house for years.

"How about a compromise?" Grandpa Leonard asked.

Carrie saw Grandma Elsa's eyes narrow. "Leonard, we're cleaning that house. Don't try to stop me."

Grandpa smiled and patted his wife's arm. "I was going to say, why don't we attack the first floor tonight? My mom kept the first floor pretty clean until these last five or ten years. So there's not going to be any ancient treasure down there." Grandpa smiled triumphantly, as if he'd just arranged world peace.

Tallulah launched the first attack of the cease-fire. "But she could have brought something down."

"No, she never went upstairs." Grandpa shook his head firmly. "She hadn't been up there in ten years at least, ever since she broke her hip. She refused to even try."

Then how'd she die by falling down those steps? Carrie didn't say it. It might be too much excitement for the more elderly Melnikites. But she didn't intend to let it drop.

Grandpa went on. "So, we just toss everything on the first floor and decide about the rest later."

Dora came up beside Tallulah. "We can't get more than that done tonight, anyway. So we'll help with the first floor to make the place livable, and if you want us to, we'll come back and help you with the rest of it whenever you say."

People started emerging from their homes all up and down the street rolling huge green trash cans. Sacrificing their own garbage space for her. Carrie choked up. Of course most of them were senior citizens and only threw one small trash bag away each week, but still, she appreciated it.

Dora laid her hand on Tallulah's exploded parrot shoulder. "And we'll include you, Tallulah. We'll let you examine anything we think is interesting for historical value. That's the best deal you're going to get."

Dora as peace activist. Dora should be turned loose on the Middle East. She'd straighten everyone out. If nothing else, she'd send them running to their own homes just to get away from her. Dora had some good qualities. She wasn't all bad.

"And since Carrie has that same slob gene Bea had, we'll keep at her to clear the place out."

Carrie clenched her fist to deck the old bat.

Nick rested his hand on Carrie's back, and she got control of herself. Trash receptacles rattled past them.

"This is going to be great," Nick said. "Fixing that majestic old house."

"Okay," Grandma Elsa rubbed her hands together as if she'd just scooted her chair up to a feast. "Let's go, ladies!" Carrie knew Grandma Elsa had been dying to clean up her mother-in-law's house for years. She was right behind Dora.

The whole town seemed to stream past Carrie, nearly knocking her into Nick.

"Be careful with the cat," she called after them.

Grandma Elsa looked back. "We'd never hurt your cat, Carrie. Shame on you."

"I'm not worried about the cat. I'm worried about you."

5

As the invading army of neat freaks filed past, Nick stayed at Carrie's side. "Your great-grandma's home is spectacular. Your family lived there?"

His reverent tone stopped Carrie from entering the infested wreck. It was possible she was looking for an excuse. "You must love big old houses."

"Sure." Nick shoved his hands into his back pockets. Carrie noticed that his shirt was neatly tucked in again under his jacket. He'd had a shirttail or two flying after the tussle with Rosie and Donette. His hair didn't show a sign of being mussed.

"I was an architectural engineer in Chicago before I moved here. Form and function was my job, but I was always more interested in form than function. I just love beauty in a building." His eyes wandered over the house. "It's why I quit. All those high rises, sheets of glass hung on load-bearing walls. I wanted to do something better, something that would make people stop and enjoy a building. My firm in Chicago sent me out to do some engineering work for Valmont, the irrigation company near here, and I loved the area. I fell in love with the houses in Melnik."

"A lot of them were built by my ancestors."

"You must be so proud of that." Nick's eyes sparkled.

She'd never given it much thought, but now that Nick mentioned it, she was proud of her forebearers. She was the first failure in the family.

"I'd gotten so tired of pushing for more beauty in the buildings my company designed. What I wanted took time and money. I was always in conflict with my bosses.

"Boy, I know how that feels." Carrie's ears were still ringing from her last conflict with her boss.

Nick's eyes sharpened as he watched her. "Trouble at work? I wondered why you'd quit your dream job to live in Melnik. I thought maybe you missed home."

Before Carrie could answer, Grandpa Leonard came sauntering back from the house. The fall breeze ruffled his comb-over, which was much thicker than Junior's.

Grandpa smoothed it back into place. "Listen, let me apologize one more time for not warning you before I sent you over and Mom crowned you with the frying pan. I should have warned you, but I just didn't think she was spry enough to get you. I underestimated her. Sorry."

Nick winced, but his smile held.

There were still people coming with cans, and Carrie saw a couple of ladies carrying casserole dishes. When the first filled trash can came out of the house, Carrie knew she'd procrastinated long enough. Trying not to think of mice, she headed inside. She sidestepped to let another garbage receptacle out as she crossed the porch with Nick and Grandpa right behind her.

When they got inside, the kitchen counter was already empty, and Tallulah was hugging age-yellowed copies of the *Melnik Bugle* to her brightly colored bosom.

Carrie felt funny watching all the activity, a beehive buzzing on the floor where only moments ago, Wilkie lay dead. No one looked interested in pausing for a moment of silence, though they probably would if Carrie clapped her hands and demanded quiet so she could ask. But instead, she decided to have her own.

She bowed her head and said a short

prayer for poor Wilkie. There'd been rumors about him all his life: hyperactive as a child back when they just called that being a brat; learning disabled in his teens back when they called that being stupid; shades of manic depression self-medicated with alcohol and drugs back when they called that being a moody drunk.

Had the new terminology done any good? Wilkie had precious little raw material, and what he'd had, he'd squandered.

God, Wilkie is Yours now; You know his struggles and his choices better than I can. Be with his family; heal the scars. Bless his wife and children. Bless Donette and the baby she's carrying. I miss my great-grandma, Lord. Hold her in the palm of Your hand and bless us all. Amen.

A hand rested gently on her shoulder, and she looked up.

"Thinking of Wilkie?" Nick asked, his eyes warm and kind.

"Yeah, and Great-Grandma Bea."

Nick nodded, but then Pastor Bremmen came inside with his usual energy and pulled Carrie away from her somber thoughts. "We just finished a Community Pastors' Meeting, and when we heard about this, we all came over."

He was the minister at the nondenominational Country Christian Church between Melnik and the neighboring town of Bjorn — one of four Swedish capitals of Nebraska, all self-proclaimed. Sweden had wisely not gotten involved. Carrie thought with a sniff of satisfaction that no one else claimed to be "The Home of the World's Largest Field Mouse." A true claim to fame, however horrifying.

Grandma Elsa slapped the lid closed on a bulging trash can. She backed up a step and eyed the messy kitchen. "How did we let this place go to rack and ruin so badly, Len?"

Leonard shook his head. "You know Mom."

Nick whispered to Carrie, "Did she use a skillet on everybody?"

"People she didn't know," Carrie said. "But not usually family."

"Everybody knows how Bea was." Carrie turned to see that her mother had shown up. Carrie gave her a hug.

Carrie saw Grandpa Leonard shake his head. Nick rubbed his.

More family appeared when Carrie's mother's parents, Grandma and Grandpa Anderson, came in the back door through the porch. No one had used Great-Grandma

Bea's front door in one hundred and three years.

Carrie's grandma Anderson was a classic Swede. Tall and round as a beer keg. Grandma Helga gave Carrie a hug that almost smothered her granddaughter. Grandpa Hermann, a head taller than his wife and as skinny as Grandma was stout, hugged her, too. They were farmers, thrilled when their daughter, the youngest of six — all girls — married a man who wanted to work the land. They'd taken Carrie's dad on as a partner and then retired and moved to town about ten years ago.

The kitchen kept filling with people. Carrie thought she should probably be directing them, but Grandma Elsa was already in charge and Grandma Helga looked eager to give a few directions. Mom was no slouch either, plus Tallulah kept shouting orders, and of course everyone obeyed Dora out of sheer terror.

Carrie had a dictator for every room on the first floor.

"Are you keeping anything, Carrie?" her mom asked.

"No."

"Don't throw any clothes away," Dora ordered. "I'm taking them to Second Time Around in Bjorn to sell. Just bag them and put them in my car. I've already opened the trunk."

Carrie mentally apologized to the young family who had started the tidy used clothing and furniture store. When they got hit with all this, they'd probably turn tail and run.

"Carrie's bedroom needs to be cleaned out." Carrie heard her mother issuing commands. "We'll do that before we tackle anything else so she has a place to sleep tonight."

"Strip the bed first," Grandma Helga ordered. "I've got Bea's washer uncovered. We'll get a load of laundry going so Carrie can sleep on clean sheets."

Carrie barely controlled a shudder at the thought of sleeping in the mouse-infested house.

"You don't have to stay here." Nick patted her back, which meant she hadn't controlled the shudder as well as she hoped.

"And before we go any further," Pastor Bremmen's booming voice quieted the crowd. "Let's say a prayer, remembering Bea and thanking God that Carrie's back."

Nick said, "Say a prayer for Wilkie's family, too, please."

Pastor Bremmen smiled. "Absolutely."

Everyone bowed their heads, and Pastor

Bremmen prayed for about ten minutes, a prayer that covered Bea, Carrie, Wilkie, his family, and the whole town. He then outlined the salvation message, threatened everyone there with eternal darkness, and offered a brief altar call. He finished with a flourish, and then everyone got back to work.

Carrie counted at least thirty people in her house. As she worked her way through the crush toward the living room, she found herself pressed against the curved railing of the stairway.

Above the chattering horde, Carrie heard a floorboard creak upstairs. It sounded for all the world like a footstep. They weren't supposed to be cleaning up there yet. She glanced around and realized she'd lost Nick in the chaos.

Carrie started up the stairs, making sure to be noisy to scare off any mice, although the talking and laughing in her home had surely harassed every rodent back into its hole — maybe even scared them into moving out.

Fat chance.

Someone came through from the kitchen holding a turkey sandwich. This was turning into a party. Another green trash can came wheeling in — this time through the front door. Viola Seavers pushed it as she bickered with her sister Alta. Carrie, who had never seen the front door to this house open, stopped on the bottom step to greet her.

"Put us to work." Viola quit complaining and greeted Helga. "We want Carrie settled so we can work her like a slave at the paper." Viola produced a key and handed it to Carrie. "Front door of the *Bugle*. Heard you were going to work with us."

Carrie took the presentation of the key to mean that she was hired. The ladies walked away from her, squabbling. Carrie went back to braving the upstairs.

The stairway was square at the bottom, with about five creaky steps coming down from a landing. Although the bottom was open, the stairs turned at the landing at a ninety-degree angle, and the steps went on up past an enclosing wall. When Carrie reached the second floor, she heard the strange creaking again, this time from the third floor.

Carrie hadn't been up to the third floor since she was about ten. Inhaling the stale, musty air of the second floor, she approached the narrow doorway straight ahead, her hand trembling.

Grizzly dashed up the stairs, and Carrie

felt better. She gave the cat a few seconds to scare all the mice into their holes, and then she ascended, step by creaking step. The murky staircase was so narrow that she could touch both walls with her hands hanging at her sides. The air was thick and laden with dust and ancient neglect. Carrie breathed through her mouth to keep from sneezing. She swallowed and tasted dirt.

Her head emerged into a full third floor. Three rooms off the hallway stretched the length of the house opposite where she stood, and two more were behind her. The hall was stacked high with a lifetime of junk.

A flash of movement made Carrie jump. She grabbed the walls to keep from tumbling back to the second floor. After her first frightened reaction, she got mad. "Who's here? What are you doing up here?"

Tallulah jumped from behind a stack of boxes. An armful of papers slipped from her grasp and spewed in a graceful stream to the floor, kicking up dust as they skidded in all directions.

Grizzly, startled by the raining papers, jumped with an unearthly yowl from behind a cardboard box to the top of it. Rotten with age, the box broke, and Grizzly scrabbled for a foothold as old clothing spilled from the box. The cat vanished into one of the rooms on Tallulah's left that stood with its door slightly ajar. Carrie could see footprints in the dust going in and out of several rooms.

As the papers settled, Tallulah, usually a flurry of motion and color, stood frozen like a multicolored deer caught in the headlights of an oncoming semi. One paper floated nearly to Carrie's feet, and she saw what looked like a legal document. Tallulah wasn't just going through old newspapers.

"Carrie, I d-didn't expect you to come up here."

Since she'd been ducked down behind boxes, Carrie doubted that.

"Were you planning to steal those things?" Carrie nodded at the mess scattered on the floor, covering the little bit of a walkway Great-Grandma had left.

"No! Steal? Carrie, don't say that! I — I wouldn't steal anything from you. I was just worried that things of historical significance might be thrown away."

"You were there when they decided to leave the upper floors alone, so you knew nothing would get thrown away up here. And if your intentions are so honorable, why did you hide from me when I came up here?"

Tallulah's mouth opened and closed

goldfish-like, but she couldn't seem to think of a good answer.

That's because there wasn't one.

Then Tallulah squared her shoulders and took on an offended look. "Well, I was just curious. I'm shocked that you'd doubt my word."

"Let's go downstairs."

"Of course. Glad to. After you?" The Melnik history buff made a grand gesture toward the steps.

Carrie came fully up onto the third floor and crossed her arms. "No, you first."

Tallulah gave the floor a look of such blatant longing Carrie couldn't even pretend Tallulah was just snoopy. The woman wanted something from this house, and she wanted it badly.

Eyes locked on Tallulah, Carrie didn't even blink, afraid Parrot Woman would slip a few papers under her caftan. Tallulah went back to her usual dramatic self and flounced past Carrie.

Carrie intended to have it out with Tallulah, but the woman charged down to the first floor so fast that Carrie couldn't catch her.

Her jaw tight with annoyance, Carrie realized that although she'd only learned she owned Great-Grandma's house today, she already felt possessive of the old wreck.

6

Carrie gathered Tallulah's papers, wondering if a mouse was going to dash out at her from somewhere. Grizzly peeked out from the bedroom door. "Hi, guy. Welcome to the family."

Glancing at the old documents, Carrie didn't see anything that jumped out as important, but she wanted to decide what papers to share with the town, and she couldn't do that until she had time to go over them carefully.

Grizzly hissed and slashed a paw at her and then ducked back into the bedroom.

The exact temperament Carrie wanted in a cat.

Carrie, filled with dread, knew there was one place the papers would be safe.

The Dead Zone.

With a little shudder, Carrie went back to the second floor and approached the room on the west end. She twisted the knob. It was stubborn and so were the rusty, squealing hinges, but she wrestled the door open and stood in the Dead Zone. Deer heads sporting massive antlers, an antelope, a big-horned sheep, a regal elk, a shaggy buffalo, a black bear, a wolf, a coyote, and even a massive moose head. Living creatures that some Supermannish dose of testosterone must have poisoned her ancestors into believing was art.

On wooden display stands with bases that resembled miniature columns from the Roman Coliseum stood pheasants, grouse, a wild turkey with its tail feathers splayed, and every imaginable breed of goose. Carrie looked at the whooping crane with wings extended as if caught in a mating dance. Two bald eagles; one with wings closed as it dove in for the kill, one with wings wide, its beak spread in a grim smile as it soared on an imaginary breeze. Both birds fell into Great-Grandpa's clutches before anyone noticed that they were almost extinct.

A fox seemed to skitter along the floor, as if frozen in mid flight. A white ermine, a deep brown mink, and a dozen other furry, ratlike critters crawled along the floor. Fish of every size and color were mounted and left to collect dust as they hung on the walls. A full-sized buck, doe, and fawn stood in one corner. That spotted baby especially horrified Carrie, to think of her great-grandpa wanting that little still life.

Her great-grandpa had been in his eighties when she was born and had no longer gone upstairs much, abandoning this room to the moths. But Carrie had come up here with her cousins whenever they could, especially to stare at the greatest prize of all.

A life-sized grizzly bear stood on its hind legs, its mouth wide open as if frozen forever in a sharp-toothed growl and its claws slashing the air.

Carrie forced herself to enter the room, clutching the papers against her chest like a security blanket. As children, there'd been a strange kind of thrill in coming here with her siblings and cousins and spooking themselves half to death. The thrill was definitely gone.

The single bare bulb swung quietly as she pulled the string that ran from it to an eye-hook by the door. That moving light danced over the animals, making their eyes come to life. Shadows made the bear's claws appear to rise.

Knowing exactly where she wanted to hide the papers, Carrie picked her way through the muddle of Great-Grandma's life savings of trash to a swan, standing with its neck curved down, looking depressed. Who could blame it?

She tilted the graceful bird up and slipped the papers under its substantial wooden base.

With the papers secure, Carrie picked her way out of the room to find Nick in the hallway.

He smiled. "I lost track of you."

Carrie decided that someone else knowing about the papers might not be such a bad idea. "I've got something to show you in the Dead Zone."

"That's the Dead Zone?" Nick peeked past her shoulder.

She turned back and was glad for his company as she led the way into the room.

Grizzly the cat sauntered into the room dragging a stuffed fox.

"Yuck." Nick crouched beside Carrie.

He snagged the fox and began a tug of war that struck Carrie as really brave, considering the noise emanating from Grizzly's throat.

Nick chose that moment to rest one big hand on the feline's head and rub the course, matted fur with a gentle caress. Grizzly twisted his head as if to get closer, and Nick scratched the cat behind his ears, murmuring something Carrie couldn't hear. The demonic growl changed to a purr.

"Quite an inheritance, huh, Nick? Do you like trophy animals?"

"Sure. What's not to like?" Nick won the tug of war with Grizzly. He held the poor battered fox in his hand.

Carrie glanced back and saw Hal, Junior's deputy, just outside the door to the third story, almost as if he were about to head up the stairs. Her gaze met his, and he looked away and then went downstairs. "I hid some papers in this room. I want someone else to know about them in . . . in case something happens to me."

"Nothing's going to happen to you, Carrie."

"Well, somebody put Wilkie in that closet."

"Whoever did it had a problem with Wilkie, not you."

"They might come back. They might be after something in this house."

Nick set the fox at the feet of the huge bear. "Carrie, I was an architectural engineer before I came to Melnik."

Carrie scowled and jammed her hands on her hips. "What does that have to do with anything?"

"My job was to make a building work."

"Work? What does that mean?"

"I didn't design the buildings. I made sure that the blueprints were feasible, the service elevators were adequate to meet the needs of the structure, the wiring met codes, and there were enough bathrooms to provide service to the projected number of occupants of the offices or stores on each floor. There are hundreds of little details, especially in a big building and with so many building codes. It was complicated and tedious."

"That's very impressive." To her own ears, Carrie sounded completely unimpressed. "And it sounds like a really great job. High-paying, too."

"I did okay."

"And you gave it up to repair porches in Melnik?"

She might as well have added, "Stupid" after that question. She hoped Nick hadn't heard it.

"My work was mathematical. Very detailed and orderly. I employed logic."

Now Carrie knew where he was going. This wasn't just a walk down memory lane. She sighed and checked her fingernails for dirt. Whoa — there was a lot of it.

"When a one-hundred-year-old woman falls, especially in a town with no crime like Melnik . . ."

"You're forgetting Wilkie."

"Listen, I'm not saying you're wrong. Something happened here, and I'll help you track down any answers you need. But I'd hate to see you get hurt."

Her head came up and her brows arched. "That's my point. Whoever killed Wilkie might come after me."

He shook his head. "I don't mean your being in danger. I mean in getting your *feelings* hurt. It sounds like Wilkie had plenty of enemies. Logically it would seem that none of them would turn their attention to you or your great-grandma."

His brow furrowed as he studied her. She wasn't sure how she felt about him showing this much concern. Kind of warm.

"Nick, I confided in you because I thought you were the one person in this house who might believe me. It's a small-town trait to not believe what's in front of your eyes if it doesn't fit in your tidy little life. You're not a small-town guy."

"I want to be."

"Why? What can you accomplish in a place this small? I mean, you can help people one at a time, and there's nothing wrong with that."

"There's everything right with that."

"But it's so much better in a city. Bigger

92

communication, bigger jobs, a bigger church that can provide a real mission; it takes . . ."

"It takes God, Carrie. And God always reaches one person at a time. That's the only way a soul can be saved."

With a huff of anger, Carrie snapped, "Tell that to Billy Graham. He'd have been a great, great pastor of a small-town church, but there was more to do. God called him to it. And God has called me."

"Called you away from Melnik?"

"Of course called me away from Melnik."

Nick seemed to shrink — or maybe just shrink back from her. "Okay, let's clear this up about Wilkie and your great-grandma. Where do you want to start?"

Nick's warmth was gone.

She thought again about the break-in. "I'll start by writing a news story for the *Melnik Bugle.* I need to shake a few people up."

"Why?" Nick caught her hand. "Why shake people up in this nice, quiet, little town?"

What was quiet worth if it was only a mirage? She tightened her jaw and said what she needed to say. "Because I think someone in this nice, quiet, little town killed my great-grandma."

7

Carrie heard scratching in the walls. Of course, between worrying about mice and murder, she was going insane. So the scratching might have been her imagination. Grizzly also yowled from time to time. Carrie was rooting for him.

She survived the weekend by mostly staying at her parents' house, eating with them and going along to church. Despite her mom's urging, Carrie went back and faced that house to sleep every night. On Monday morning, she shook all her work clothes thoroughly. No mice fell out. Then she pulled them on quickly and brushed her teeth as fast as possible, grabbed her purse and coat, and sprinted outside. If she didn't see the actual rodents, she could pretend they didn't exist.

Denial was a beautiful thing.

Glancing back at her new home, she shuddered. "You chicken. You can't let mice scare you, Cindy Lou Who came downstairs Christmas morning and found the Grinch stealing Christmas. And he was a hairy, creepy creature. But was Cindy Lou afraid? No!" She spoke to God through the canopy of Great-Grandma's huge maple trees. "Lord, I'm sorry. I know they're more afraid of me than I am of them."

And that was a cliché that Carrie hated almost more than any other in the world. She hated it especially because it was so stinking true.

She walked to work, leaving her ten-year-old rust bucket Cavalier behind, wishing God would heal her of this strange fear. Yes, she'd admitted years ago that it was going to take a miracle.

She turned at the corner that took her toward Main Street. She'd need to pass the lifelike statue of the giant rodent Maxie the mouse, preserved forever in granite on the corner of Third and Main. Three-foot-tall, disease-bearing vermin was a questionable decoration for the sidewalk in front of the town's only grocery store, but oh, well.

Nick drove up in his black Ford truck. He smiled and pulled to a stop. She walked out on the street toward him, knowing that the chances of an oncoming car were slim.

"Did you get through the night okay? No

mice?" Nick leaned farther out the window to talk. The sharp November breeze tousled his hair like fingers running through it. He smoothed it back.

Carrie had already learned he didn't like to be messy. "I didn't see any. But I . . . uh . . . didn't check the mousetraps you set in the pantry."

Nick rested his elbow on the open window. Even the hair on his forearm looked combed and neat. He wore a knit shirt just like before, only red this time, with black thread in the "OC" logo just above his heart.

"I'll do it for you and reset them if I find anything."

Her smile widened. "Between you and Grizzly, I almost feel safe."

"Almost?"

"What can I say?" Carrie shrugged and studied her toes. "It's a phobia."

Nick chuckled. "See you later."

Carrie nodded and stepped back so he could drive away. She headed on to work. She rounded the corner onto Main Street, giving the Maxie statue a wide berth, and was caught by the drab block of old buildings.

Her eyes slid down the row of stores, mostly brick, mostly two stories, mostly empty. Their facades squared at the top, even though the buildings had peaked roofs.

It hurt Carrie's heart to see it. Despite wanting to get away from Melnik, Carrie loved her hometown and hated to see it folding up. She arrived at the *Bugle* office at eight a.m. and let herself in. Viola pulled up in her drab, orange Park Avenue and parked so crookedly that she took up all three diagonal spaces in front of the building. It didn't matter. Except for one car parked in front of the grocery store, the parking spaces along Main Street were empty.

"Hi, Viola."

"Hi, honey. Bright and early your first morning. Good girl."

Carrie pushed the door open with a flourish. It screeched as if it were desperate for attention.

Viola followed Carrie inside, sat at the closest of three desks crammed into the little L-shaped room, and shut her purse in a drawer by her right knee.

"What do you think of the old place?"

Carrie was torn between dismay and wonder. This was the newspaper business at its most basic. Also its most depressing. You didn't need a ten-story building, the latest technology, and an army of reporters to put out a good newspaper. But it sure helped.

Viola's desk stood on Carrie's right. The

other two desks were bunched in behind that. Shelves lined two walls, all stacked with oversized books that held bound copies of the *Bugle,* going back over a hundred years. The whole town's history was in those yellowed pages, and no one could look at them because the paper was too fragile to touch — although honestly, no one needed to look at them. Everybody knew the town's history by heart.

"Thanks for stopping by Friday night, Viola. I really appreciate all the help."

Viola waved her words away. "It was the best party in town. I wouldn't have missed it for the world. You'll need to put a thank-you note in the *Bugle* this week. They cost six dollars unless you want to get wordy."

"Thanks." Carrie should say she was happy to be here, but she just couldn't wrap her tongue around a blatant lie like that. She caught sight of the equipment, and her stomach twisted. "Uh, how old are these computers?"

Viola wrinkled her nose and her glasses jumped up and down. "Pretty bad, huh? I've got one at home that's a hand-me-down from my granddaughter's college years, and it's ten times fancier than these."

"Are they Windows 98, at least?" Carrie saw the disk slot on the closest computer and suppressed a gasp. It was for the old five-inch floppy disks.

Viola snorted. "They were all old when I started fifteen years ago."

"Are we online?" Carrie knew the answer before she asked the question. These computers were too old to have modems.

"Nope. Your desk is the back one."

To Carrie's left in the short end of the L-shaped room, a rack of wooden easels lined the wall on two sides, each supporting a sheet of paper the size of a newspaper page. The words *Melnik Bugle* were a bold masthead on the first sheet. The other seven were mostly blank, although Carrie recognized a few small ads scattered near the bottoms of some of them, ads that appeared in the paper week after week, never changing. The last two pages were covered with fine print with the words "CLASSIFIED ADS" across the top.

Predictable, eternal, boring. Carrie couldn't read them from where she stood, but she knew in general what they'd say. *Kittens, free to a good home. Garage Sale.*

Carrie suppressed a sigh because Viola was a nice lady and it wasn't her fault Carrie was a failure at age twenty-two.

Viola rose, drawing Carrie's attention away from personal failure to focus on the disaster of the out-of-date newsroom. "C'mon, I'll show you how to run these dinosaurs. We live in a kind of constant fear that something will break, because no one makes parts for these computers or the printer anymore."

"New computers don't cost much."

Viola laughed as her trim form led the way to the back desk. "You either have to make enough money on the paper to finance it yourself or get the new Gunny to kick in. Good luck with that."

"Old Man Gunderson should have invested in capital improvements if he expected his business to have any market value."

Viola gave her a pitying look. "Well, he never planned to sell it, I'm sure. Gundersons never sell anything. He wasn't interested in the market value of anything, only rent money. And now he's dead, so he was right not to put money into the business, I expect."

The place smelled like ink and something else Carrie recognized as intrinsically the *Bugle,* but she couldn't identify it.

"Pay attention, because formatting is a sixteen-step process. You'll catch onto it."

"Can't you just create a master copy and reuse it?"

Viola shooed Carrie into her desk chair. "You're welcome to try, although again, if you break it, we're doomed. And we've never failed to get out an issue of the *Bugle* in one hundred and seventeen years, so you don't want your name on *that* disaster."

Viola plunked some scraps of paper down in front of Carrie. "These are stories that have come in. Since we change employees so often, we've written down all the formatting steps, but I expect you'll have questions, anyway." Viola pointed to a half-buried page of tired-looking paper taped onto the desk. "It's all there. For now, just get the story typed into the computer, and we'll work through the formatting later. Can you type?"

Carrie nodded. "I'm fast and accurate."

"Accurate enough not to call Stuart Piperson 'Stupid Person'?"

Carrie looked up, and they both started laughing at the same second. All the tension and defeat and sense of failure dropped from her and, for now, Carrie could enjoy what was best about Melnik. Everybody knew about the typo in last week's paper. Mixed with the horror of such a thing appearing in print was the laughter, and once the shouting was done, there was the understanding that it was, indeed, just a funny mistake.

Poor Stu. But eventually even he would laugh.

Viola was mopping her eyes, and Carrie had just turned to the Jurassic Era Computer. The front door screeched like a rabid parrot, slammed against the bookshelves behind it, and, in another rabid parrot imitation, Tallulah came flying into the *Bugle,* dressed in full plumage.

"Carrie, you have to help me save Melnik!"

8

"Tallulah!" Carrie jumped to her feet. She had to admit that drama queen Tallulah looked distraught even for her. Sniffing the air for smoke, Carrie wondered if even now a fire was burning down Main Street. "Save Melnik?"

"This is the fiftieth anniversary of Maxie being declared the World's Largest Field Mouse." Tallulah flailed her arms and nearly knocked her bright pink turban off her head. She grabbed for it before it could roll away. "I need a book written about it before the festival. And now that Wilkie's dead, I don't have any true founders to honor."

Maxie. Of course.

Carrie realized that she was the drama queen here, worrying about fire when it was only about that oversized rodent.

The only disaster at the moment was Tallulah's fashion sense.

"Wilkie's got two kids, Tallulah," Viola

said. "Ask them."

"I already did. I've been after them for months to ride on the float, but they were both angry at their father and refused. And of course there are no other direct descendents."

The door screeched open again. Donette came in, her stomach preceding her.

Tallulah turned when the door alerted her to the newcomer. Her greedy eyes locked on Donette's baby bump. "When's that baby due?"

Donette stopped short. Her hand went to her stomach. "About two weeks."

Tallulah clapped once, loud, as if a bolt of lightning had zapped her with inspiration. "So it'll be born before the festival?"

Donette's chin wobbled, and she covered her mouth. "Yes, but Wilkie won't be around to meet the baby."

Carrie hurried past the insensitive history freak, went to Donette, and wrapped an arm around her. "I'm so sorry, Donette. I'm praying for you."

"Don't bother." Donette jerked away from Carrie.

"You and your baby need a church family, Donette." Carrie hated to see the hardness in Donette's eyes. But girls Donette's age didn't go for guys like Wilkie if they didn't

104

have lives that made them hard. "More than ever with Wilkie gone."

"No, we don't. We have each other." Donette's voice broke. "I'm going to love him enough for Wilkie and me both."

"We can help you. We can —"

"Him? You know it's a boy?" Tallulah raised her hands in triumph. "The name will survive."

"Wilkie's got two kids." Viola exchanged a glance with Carrie. "One of them is Kevin, a son. The name is already going to survive. Refusing to ride on the float isn't the same as not existing, Tallulah. Don't you think you're being a little thoughtless?"

Remembering the fight between Donette and Rosie and Donette's claws, Carrie didn't think bringing up Wilkie's other kids was a good idea. She didn't want to have to call the chief to pull Donette off Viola.

Carrie rested a hand on Donette's trembling shoulder. "Finding out about God would be the best thing you could do for this baby. You'd never be alone if you had God in your life."

Donette scowled at Carrie and then tried to burn Viola to the ground with her tear-filled eyes. "I'd be proud to have my baby on the float, Tallulah. Thank you for asking."

Carrie sighed, determined to try again with Donette. But she wasn't ready to hear it now. *Please, God, give me the right words at the right time.*

"You can ride right there on Maxie's shoulders." Tallulah framed her fingers into an open-topped square as if she were a director, laying out a scene before the cameras rolled.

"You know the float is going to be a giant replica of Maxie, right?" Carrie shuddered as she told Donette. Carrie wasn't the only person in the world with a mouse phobia. "A realistic replica. You're riding a room-sized rat."

"Maxie — is — not — a — *rat!*" Tallulah's voice went so *Exorcist,* Carrie watched close to see if her head would spin around. "He is absolutely, unequivocally, fully tested and certified to be of the species *Peromyscus.* Field mouse!"

Tallulah spoke Latin. How was Carrie supposed to respond to that? *E pluribus insane-um?*

Besides, Carrie knew Maxie's scientific classification as well as any Melnikite. Animalia; Chordate; Vertebrata; Mammalia; Rodentia; Sciurognathi; Cricetidae; Sigmondontinea; Peromyscus. She'd had to learn it to pass the fourth grade.

"Rat jokes could ruin us. If Maxie is a rat, then he's not so big anymore, is he? He's not important. Melnik isn't important. *I'm not important.*" Both fists in the air, Tallulah was one sunset, a silhouetted tree, and a handful of gnawed onions away from bursting into the "As God as my witness, I'll never be hungry again" speech from *Gone with the Wind.*

"Everybody knows how you feel about mice." Tallulah jabbed an index finger at Carrie. "Just because you're afraid of a precious little animal doesn't mean . . ."

Carrie gave Tallulah a minute or two to rant. When she ran short of breath, Carrie jumped in. "So what did you mean when you said I have to save Melnik?"

Tallulah, caught off guard, actually quit yapping. For a second. She got over it fast. "I need someone to write a book on Melnik's history and get it published in time for the Maxie Mouse Golden Anniversary Festival."

"You know, Tallulah, we've always included Maxie in the *Christmas* festival in Melnik, and it's fine to play Maxie up big, but it is *Christmas,* you know. Our Savior's birth? Salvation? The Virgin Mary and the Little Town of Bethlehem? We don't want to lose track of what's really important here."

Tallulah swelled up with indignation. Her face picked up the lovely fuchsia shade of her turban. "We've renamed it to fully take advantage of this historic occasion. The city council approved the change. It could attract state and even national media. I expect the *Melnik Bugle* to embrace the change."

Take another breath, please, Tallulah.

It wasn't to be. "This celebration could be just what we need to put Melnik on the map once and for all."

Tallulah apparently didn't need air.

"I demand that the full power of the *Bugle* be brought to bear to promote this."

Power? The Bugle?

"Done correctly, this could attract businesses and new residents to Melnik."

Carrie tried to figure out how she was going to put a picture of Maxie on the front page of the paper without looking at it or touching it. The phobia stuff wasn't just something she did as a hobby. It was full-time.

"This will be Melnik's finest hour. This will be the defining —"

"Tallulah!" Donette yelled. "Enough already. Carrie just started this morning. Viola and I know all about the Golden Anniversary. Carrie isn't going to fight you on it. I'll be glad to be in the parade. It will be a

tribute to my love for Wilkie."

Viola and I? Carrie barely caught that because she was focusing on Tallulah, despite her better judgment. "You know the festival is usually held in City Hall, too. A parade in December is kind of a bad idea." And wasn't Carrie just snowing on Tallulah's parade with that reminder. "It gets cold in Nebraska in December, you know."

"Macy's does a Thanksgiving Day Parade in New York City every year." Tallulah wasn't going to let a little thing like reality stop her. "People just wear coats. We'll be fine."

"New York and Melnik?" Carrie rolled her eyes. She just couldn't control herself. "Is it worth pointing out the difference?"

Tallulah seemed to run on some recorded speech she'd downloaded from her brain-pan to her mouth. She turned, vampire-like, on Carrie, the fresh blood in the group.

"I have compiled data on Maxie, and I want a book we can offer to the media and sell in a booth set up in the City Hall for after the parade." Tallulah looked so sincere that Carrie knew that what was coming next was a lie.

"The reason I was so interested in your great-grandma's old papers is because I believe there are photos of the original ceremony when Maxie was first placed in Maxie Memorial Hall."

"Where?" Carrie, Viola, and Donette all said it at the same time.

Tallulah beamed and pointed at the building straight across the street from the *Bugle.* "I've approached the city council to officially rename City Hall as Maxie Memorial Hall, since it's housing Maxie's shrine. Isn't that nice?"

The shrine was a cheap, rectangular fishbowl. Carrie didn't mention that fact.

"Going back to the first part of that, what you really want is my permission to snoop through all my great-grandma's papers, right?" Carrie had worked in the city too long. She'd forgotten that straight-talking and Melnik just didn't mix.

"Well, of all things, Miss Big City Newspaper Woman. I was *not* asking for that."

Another lie. "That's good, because the answer would be no."

Tallulah's jaw tightened perceptibly.

"And there's no way to get a book written and published that fast. Maybe we can print up something here at the *Bugle.* Pamphlets or something." Pamphlets with mouse pictures prominently featured. Carrie closed her eyes in dread.

"Pamphlets? I want a book! Hardcover.

110

We'll sell them to Melnik tourists."

Melnik . . . tourists? Those were words that could not coexist in a sentence. The woman wanted something out of Great-Grandma's house, and Carrie needed to find out what. It might genuinely be about Maxie, but it might also be related to Great-Grandma's and Wilkie's deaths. But how in heaven's name could Tallulah be involved in either death? The woman was obsessed with Maxie, but she wasn't a killer.

"Tallulah, bring me whatever research you have. I'll do my best to put it into some form for a book. I'll also promise to search Great-Grandma Bea's house. I —"

"Now, Carrie, I don't mind —"

Carrie raised her hand like a cop stopping oncoming traffic. Tallulah closed her mouth.

Hand signals. I'll have to remember that.

"I said I'd do it."

The rabid parrot's eyes narrowed until Carrie feared she might be pecked to death. Tallulah crossed her arms in a huff, emphasizing a generous belly the caftan covered nicely. Dora ought to look into a caftan.

"If I find papers that have any historical significance, I'll make sure to go over them with you. That's the best offer you're going to get. I don't want anyone taking important papers out of *my* house without me know-

111

ing about them." Carrie thought that was the first time she'd called the house hers. She kind of liked the sound of it. She had a house. A mouse-infested, filthy, falling-down house, true. But a house nonetheless.

Tallulah opened her pink painted lips to complain.

The door screeched and Clara Wickersham came in, dragging her rolling cart. Staring at her feet, Clara mumbled, barely audible, and what was audible didn't make a lot of sense. But everybody knew that's just how Clara was, and it was no big deal.

"Anybody want a pie? No one goes hungry in Melnik. Not while Clara Wickersham has breath in her body."

"I'll take one." Carrie interrupted when Clara's singsong-ranting broke off so the woman could suck a breath into her body. Carrie's offer distracted the poor woman from the mumbling story, the same story she repeated over and over again to her shoes. Or maybe it wasn't the same story. Carrie didn't listen, so she couldn't be sure.

Everybody knew better than to actually eat Clara's pies, but Viola, Tallulah, and even Donette piped up. "I'll take one."

They had to be sold for Clara to pay her bill at the grocery store, which was sky-high because of all the baking she did. Dreadful, dangerous baking. It was every Melnikite's duty to buy a pie.

Clara began pulling pies out of her cart. They were all squashed because she stacked them five deep. "Thistownwouldn'tsurvive. NotifIdidn'tseetothings."

Carrie clenched her teeth at the sucking sound made as Clara pried the pies apart.

She faithfully produced twenty-five pies for the town of Melnik every Monday. Her family, five grown children, took turns staying with her on the weekends, often luring her into visits at their homes scattered across the state. And the town did its best to pull her into activities, to save themselves from buying pies every day. The routine had settled into a Monday bake sale.

"Wildcatsrunninglooseeatingpieleftand-right."

Her children didn't want her locked up. Clara had been like this for the last twenty years, so she obviously had the skills to survive. And the citizens of Melnik helped by pulling together, buying her pies, and then discreetly disposing of them.

"I'm not going to let some oversized mouse get the upper hand." Clara handed out a green bean pie to Viola.

Viola waited until Clara turned her back and then lifted a tater tot up off the top of the pie for the others to see.

Turning back to her metal cart, a low mesh basket with a handle so it rolled, squeaking along behind her, Clara continued her sanity-challenged food distribution and storytelling.

"NotwhileIhavebreathinmybody,ohno. IseewhatIsee. Ido."

Carrie fought down a grimace when Clara gave her a hamburger meringue pie. It had been underneath Viola's and Donette's, so it really looked bad.

"It'sthatMaxieandhisCommunistfriends. They'rebehindallthetrouble.Anddon'tthink-Idon'tknowit."

Taking the pie, Carrie felt the pinch of handing over her last five dollars in cash. Tallulah gamely accepted something that smelled like it might be mostly lard, looking like she'd be willing to start in on the argument with Carrie as soon as Clara left.

"NowaythatGundersonboygetsapie. Noway. Nohow. Giantmice. Whoeverheardof suchathing?"

Carrie caught enough of that to agree with Clara, but she didn't say so, afraid the crazed but harmless — well, harmless if you didn't count her cooking — woman would linger.

From here, Clara would go across the

street to Jansson's Diner. Olga Jansson was the best cook in town. One cup of Olga's coffee and you were hers for life. She was the best cook in town, but she'd still buy one pie, give Clara a slice of safe pie along with a cup of coffee, and then shoo her on her way before quietly discarding the ghastly baked offering.

Everybody knew the drill.

"Somepeoplethinktheyownthistown. I've-gototakecharge."

Clara talked her way out the door.

"We'renotsafeinourownbeds. Communists everywhere."

Carrie didn't even consider discussing the fall of the Berlin Wall with Clara. The Communists weren't really that much of a threat anymore.

Carrie, holding the door for Clara, saw Marlys Piperson duck behind a minivan parked outside, pulling Jeffie into a crouch beside her until Clara moved on. Marlys obviously wasn't in the mood to buy a pie. It was the only time Carrie had ever seen Jeffie obey anyone. Carrie had personally signed a petition asking Boys Town to drop their age limit and let the child in.

Marlys, the town's postmistress, then headed for the *Bugle* and, bless her heart, thwarted Tallulah's nagging because she wanted to gossip about Edith Eskilson misspelling her husband's name.

Tallulah apparently got sick of waiting to rant some more and went on her melodramatic way. Marlys ran out of steam and went off with Jeffie in tow to gossip about Edith elsewhere.

Donette settled into her chair, and the other shoe dropped for Carrie.

Viola and I? Donette clearly included herself in the *Bugle* staff.

"Uh, do you work here?" Carrie asked Donette.

"Sure. I just started a couple of weeks ago."

"Oh, sorry. I didn't know. Aren't you supposed to be in school?"

"I quit. My name's in the paper every week. Everybody knows I work here."

Everybody knows. Carrie sighed. They should just go ahead and carve that right into the WELCOME TO MELNIK sign out by the Highway 77 turnoff onto Main Street. Right next to the five-foot-tall painting of Maxie — which, Carrie had long believed, did more to scare people away from Melnik than to lure them in.

"Sorry. I never read the masthead."

Donette frowned. "The what?"

"The what?" Viola asked.

116

Something not everybody knows. "That's the list of names and job titles of those responsible for producing a publication: editors, writers, designers, art directors, sales representatives, publishers, lawyers, and support staff. It usually runs someplace in the first few pages."

"Oh, we've got that." Viola turned back to her typewriter. "I just never had a name for it before. Guess you learned that in newspaper college, huh?"

Journalism school. Carrie was too tired to define yet another term. "That's right."

"Well, knowing what it's called won't help you get the paper out." With those words of wisdom, Donette began clicking away on her keyboard.

And wasn't that just the truth. All the "newspaper college" in the world wasn't going to help her figure out how to work this antiquated piece of junk. Bill Gates would probably be horrified if he knew this old computer was still in use. She sighed, wondering when she would find out the computers had to be stoked with coal. She might as well put her name on the masthead: Stupid Person.

Carrie fought with the balky computer mouse and the Jurassic Era machinery, rehearsing a "You need to go back to school" speech for Donette.

As she typed, Carrie planned how to deal with the news of Wilkie's death in the paper. Poor, dumb Wilkie, the serial statutory rapist. First his wife, now Donette. Had there been others?

She had to make the article show some respect. His family deserved that even if he didn't. Some in town would think that death was an inappropriate topic for the *Bugle*. There was a tendency to avoid anything resembling news in Melnik's fourth estate. But Carrie was determined to print the truth. And she was going to kick over rocks until something crawled out that told her what happened to Wilkie and Great-Grandma Bea.

9

Carrie wrestled with her computer as Viola and Donette whipped out copy. They were living proof it was possible to master the system, so she clung to hope.

Viola announced that she was taking a lunch break.

"Can I go with you?" Donette asked in a shaky voice.

"Sure, I'll buy you and that baby lunch."

"Thanks, but you don't need to do that."

That was most likely not true.

They both turned to Carrie.

"I think I'll keep typing." Carrie wanted time alone to work on the Wilkie story.

"Take a break sometime." Viola slipped on her light blue cardigan. "This place'll make you nuts if you don't get out of here for a while."

Too late. Carrie smiled. "Okay."

Donette followed Viola out, and then the door swung back open and Carrie heard

Donette call out, "I'll be over to the diner in a minute."

"Uh, what you said earlier?" she asked Carrie.

Carrie tried to think of all she'd said earlier, most of it insulting to Donette, Wilkie, Tallulah, and last — but certainly not least — Maxie Mouse.

"About not being alone if I had faith in God?"

Carrie's stomach twisted as she realized Donette wanted to know more about God. *Give me wisdom, Lord.*

"Yes?"

"What's that mean? How is God with me? I don't get it."

Carrie rose from her chair and circled the desk, making her way to Donette's side, praying every step. "It's hard to explain what it feels like to have God in your life unless you've experienced it." Carrie settled onto a corner of Viola's desk. "But He's with me all the time, Donette. Someone to lead me, Someone to talk to. You're not alone if you have Him."

Donette rested both hands on top of her stomach. "I get so lonely sometimes. Mom's gone with her boyfriend most of the time. Dad's long gone. Wilkie . . . having him in

120

my life was so much better than being alone."

Carrie wasn't sure how plainly to speak. Donette was so defensive about her relationship with Wilkie. "But he left you, too, didn't he?"

Donette bristled. "He didn't mean to. He loved me!"

"But that's the thing about love between people. Maybe Wilkie would have left Rosie and married you."

"He would have!" Donette backed toward the door and reached for the knob.

"But losing someone you love can happen to anyone. When you put your faith in Jesus, He never leaves. That's what makes it so wonderful. God has offered this gift to everyone. All you have to do is reach out and take it."

Donette stared at Carrie for a long, quiet moment. At last she nodded. "I know I need something. I want my baby to grow up and amount to something. I want a better life for him than the one I've had, and now he won't have a father, just like me."

"He can have a heavenly Father, Donette. That gives a baby a really good start in life."

"I want to change. I know I shouldn't have been with a married man. But he loved me, and he was so unhappy with Rosie. Even

Shayla hated Wilkie. He couldn't get his own daughter to love him. Wilkie and I needed each other." Donette pulled the door open. Carrie stood and took a step toward her, not wanting to let her go when she seemed so open to God.

Donette held her hand up. "Stop for now, please. Let me think about what you've said. Maybe . . . maybe I will go to church with you Sunday."

Carrie wanted to grab Donette and hold her until the girl had made a real commitment, but no one could be forced into believing in God. It was a choice Donette had to make for herself. Carrie nodded. "I'd be glad to talk with you more anytime you want."

"Thanks." Donette left, shutting the squeaking door behind her.

Carrie prayed as she returned to her desk. She talked to God a long time before she went back to work. The prayers and Donette reaching out renewed Carrie's spirit enough that she could treat Wilkie's death with respect but also with honesty. She decided to keep the article to herself until the last minute, knowing that whatever she wrote would cause trouble.

As she clicked away, polishing and revising the story, she heard a soft *thunk* and glanced sideways. A door behind her, one she had assumed was a closet, rattled on its hinges as if shaken by the wind. Wind? In a closet?

She printed out her Wilkie article, walking around her desk to get the story as it rolled out of the massive, decade-old machine. She took it to her desk and settled a stack of books on top of it so no one would notice it and snoop.

The closet door thumped again. As she faced the closet, imagining mice big enough to shake a door . . . her stomach growled, reminding her that she'd missed breakfast and couldn't afford lunch.

Another *thud* in the closet stopped her hunger pangs. She was busy working up the nerve to touch the knob when the usual murderous scream came from the front door's hinges. Carrie turned to see Nick.

He gave her one quick nod before he began studying the source of the noise. "This is awful. We've got to fix this door."

We? Carrie bit her tongue. Maybe efficient, order-loving Nick would fix the door because it offended his sense of decency to exist in the same town with those rusty hinges. With luck, he'd be done before she told him this was another job that offered no hope of pay.

Nick crouched down, vanishing behind Viola's desk. Honesty overcame avarice. "I don't have to look at the *Bugle* accounts to know we can't afford you. This place runs on a shoestring."

Nick stretched his neck so he could smile at her. "A badly frayed shoestring." He turned away. Swinging the door back and forth, he listened to the squeak as if he were a doctor with stethoscope in hand.

"Don't worry about it. It's on the house. Give me ten minutes, an oil can, and a smoothing plane, and I can minimize the noise problem and save a lot of wear and tear on your doorjamb and hinges."

He stood and turned, apparently to fetch the oil and his tools, and then caught himself. "I didn't come in for that." He shut the door, flinching against the noise. "I heard you were working through lunch, and I came to see if you wanted a break."

Carrie didn't even ask how he knew this. She shot an arrow prayer to God for her finances, because she wasn't going to let Nick pay. "I've got plenty to do here, but I'm hungry. I'd be delighted to take a break."

Nick smiled again and lifted up a white paper sack. "I've got subs from the Mini-Mart." The corners of his eyes crinkled in a way that told Carrie he smiled a lot.

Well, maybe she'd let him pay this once. She headed toward Nick and free food. "Did you find any mice?"

Nick's smile faded.

"Nick, what happened?" Dread scampered mouselike up her spine.

"I've considered all the ramifications." His eyes leveled on her like he was a gunslinger. "I've decided not to tell you."

Carrie felt her hand creeping toward the buttons on the collar of her knit shirt. "Why's that?"

"I told you I worked a lot with math, logic, analysis, right?"

"Yeah, on the skyscrapers in Chicago. What does that have to do with my mice?"

"I've analyzed the situation and concluded that the most effective way to handle it is to refuse to discuss it with you. Think about it logically. If I found a lot of mice, that would be bad, right?"

Carrie inhaled long and slow and crept backward a step. "You found a lot of mice? How many? What if . . ."

"I didn't say that." Nick raised his hands as if he were trying to keep a maniac calm.

Carrie could almost hear him thinking, *"Step away from the detonator. No one has to get hurt here today, ma'am."*

"If I found *no* mice in your traps, then that would be *really* bad, right?"

Carrie quit backing up. She advanced on Nick and caught two fistfuls of his neatly pressed logo shirt. "You didn't find any? You know there are mice. That means they're all still in there. That means —"

"I didn't say I didn't get any, now did I?" Nick gave her a pathetic failure of a reassuring smile. "And if I say I got a few, well, you'd know that's not all, so you'd —"

Carrie buried her face in her hands. "That house is still full of mice. No way there were only a few. I can't —"

"And that" — she felt Nick pat her on the shoulder gingerly, like he was afraid to make any sudden moves — "is why I'm not going to talk to you about mice. Because nothing I say will be useful. Right?"

Lifting her face, Carrie grabbed his shirt again and twisted the fabric tight to his neck. "Tell me!"

"So, forget about the mice." Nick spoke through his tightly squeezed throat. He put his hands on hers gently, like a caress, but he was really trying to save his miserable life. The jerk. She had to know.

"I can't!" She shook him.

"I've dealt with them for today."

Carrie felt light-headed. How wonderful

to have someone to deal with the mice.

"And I'll deal with them tonight before you get home and again tomorrow after you leave for work and every day until there aren't any mice anymore. Not to say there are any, but, well, just forget about them. They're not your worry. I will assume complete responsibility for your mice."

"You will?" Carrie thought she heard music, maybe an angel playing a harp. Maybe a choir singing "The Hallelujah Chorus."

"If you see one, call me, any time of the day or night. I'll come and protect you. I'll even get a whip and chair in case there are any Maxie descendants in the mansion."

"You mean you found oversized mice?" She didn't mean to strangle him, but with a phobia, sometimes these things just happened.

"I did not say that." He used two fingers to gently raise her chin. "I said I'm in charge of the mice. Okay?"

Carrie almost threw her arms around his neck she was so grateful. Still, a morbid part of her couldn't bear to be kept in the dark. "Tell me! How many did you find?"

"No. Leave them to me. Please?" Nick raised and lowered her chin a couple of times as if forcing her to nod in agreement and somehow, probably because she was a lunatic, she felt like she did agree.

"Okay."

"Good girl."

"Thank you."

"You're welcome."

"If only I don't see them. I'm pretty good at living in denial if they just stay inside the walls. You can't believe the extent to which a human being can lie to herself."

Nick smiled more generously. "And I've thought about it, and being afraid of mice isn't a sin."

"Is, too." She'd thought about it a lot more than he had.

"Is not. God loves you, and He made you just the way you are. I've decided that you're so close to perfect, God had to give you this one little quirk to make it so the rest of us won't spend our lives feeling inferior."

Carrie went all melty inside. "Wow." To combat becoming a puddle at his feet, she teased him. "Great line."

But it was such a sweet thing to say — she knew that the extent to which she was charmed sounded in her voice.

Nick caressed her chin with his thumb. "It *is* a great line. I've been working on it all morning." He smiled. "I thought it came out okay." His thumb stopped. "So, you don't have a phobia. You have a gift. Embrace it and respect it."

"You really are my hero." A soft, tender part of Carrie's heart got a little softer as she looked into Nick's kind eyes and clung to his poor shirt. She already knew he hated wrinkles, but he didn't make her let go. Their gazes locked. The moment stretched.

Nick glanced down near her lips — maybe it was his thumb he was looking at. Then he seemed closer and sweeter. "Carrie, would you like to . . ."

The door smashed open. Carrie jumped away from Nick but without letting go, so she dragged him back a few feet from the door.

Shayla Melnik stumbled as she came into the *Bugle* office. She caught herself and looked around, wild-eyed, until she found Carrie. She shoved herself off the door and knocked past Nick as a sob wrenched from her throat.

Carrie kept one hand on Nick's shirt, afraid to take her eyes off the distraught girl.

Nick shifted closer. Carrie felt safe just knowing he was there.

Red blotches and swollen eyes told Carrie that Shayla's tears had been flowing for a long time. Last night the girl had been furious. Now grief had finally hit.

"I've come because I need help." Shayla hurled herself into Carrie's arms, knocking her a step away from Nick, tearing Carrie's hand loose from the mooring to her hero. But Nick was here. Nick met Carrie's eyes over Shayla's heaving shoulder. Carrie arched her brows and, feeling like she had little choice, wrapped her arms around Shayla.

Between broken sobs, the girl said into Carrie's neck, "I need you to save me."

"Uh . . ." Carrie's mind went blank. "Okay."

Nick shook his head frantically. "Okay" might be a bad thing to say, but Carrie didn't try to get away. Shayla's grip clearly said that would be a waste of time.

Nick looked outside the door, as if he expected someone to be pursuing Shayla. He closed the door, jerking his shoulders as if the squeak gave him an electric shock.

"Save you from what, Shayla?" Nick asked the obvious question.

"Save me from going to jail."

"Why would you have to go to jail?" Carrie's heart turned over for the young girl, so distraught at losing her father. A man she obviously had just realized she cherished.

130

"Because I killed my lowlife, scum-sucking, dirtbag of a father."

10

Breath whooshed out of Nick's lungs. He watched Carrie stagger and ram into the wall as if she'd taken a hit. Shayla clung like a scared house cat.

Carrie widened her eyes at Nick, silently asking what to do.

He wanted to intervene and put himself between Carrie and Shayla. He'd offered to do it for mice. He'd better be doing it for a murderer. He held back, giving Carrie a reassuring nod that he was here if she needed a rescuer. He lifted the phone and gestured at the keypad.

Carrie shook her head.

Violent sobs shook Shayla; then she released her death grip on Carrie's neck and sank to her knees as if she were begging. "Everybody knows you're really smart. You solved a bunch of crimes in Omaha, right?"

Carrie shook her head. "I worked the police beat. Not the same thing. Although I did some investigative reporting. Not successful at it, really."

Nick caught Carrie's muttered protest, but Shayla didn't. He'd heard Carrie solved crimes, too. Everybody knew what a great investigative reporter she was. Then why did she quit? What did she mean by "Not successful at it, really"?

Just because you inherit a house doesn't mean you have to live in it. Nick didn't like unsolved puzzles. He wanted things in balance, like a correctly completed algebraic equation. And this didn't balance. Why would Carrie give up her dream job? Then he remembered that she was leaving again — maybe not right now, but that was her goal. She couldn't have been clearer Friday night in the Dead Zone.

"You can help me. I didn't plan to do it. Well, I did, but I didn't mean to do it. Well, I did mean to, but not ahead of time. But well, a little bit ahead of time. But not . . ."

"Shayla!" Carrie cut off Shayla's ranting.

Shayla looked up from the floor and seemed to get a grip on herself.

"Get up." Nick stepped closer, moving slowly, trying not to set the poor kid off again. He reached down. "Tell us what happened, and we'll help you."

Shayla looked over her shoulder through

stringy, dishwater-blond hair stuck to her tear-soaked face. "Where'd you come from? Now I've confessed to you. Now everybody will know."

"I won't tell." That, Nick realized immediately, was a stupid thing to say. Not telling was aiding and abetting. Accessory after the fact and . . . what else? There'd been a semester he'd spent studying law. He remembered some basics.

The white of Shayla's blue eyes had been bloodshot into a road map. Her shoulders trembled with another hopeless sob.

"Well, I will." Carrie pulled Shayla's attention back.

"No!"

Nick's muscles tensed as he prepared to pull the girl off Carrie.

"Yes. You can't keep this to yourself. We'll talk it through, and then you and I will go see Junior."

"He's a sick, stupid jerk." Shayla howled to humble Grizzly.

Nick stepped closer. "Junior's not so bad."

I meant my dad!

Nick decided to quit talking.

"He got my best friend pregnant. I hated him. I shouldn't have to go to jail. Someone needed to do something about him before he hurt anyone else!"

134

All the starch went out of Shayla. "But I can't quit thinking about pouring that antifreeze in his beer can." Shayla looked up. "He was already so drunk, the big perverted dope didn't even realize he was drinking it."

Nick came around beside Carrie so Shayla could see him and not be startled again. She didn't seem to be able to keep a thought in her head — except for the one about killing her dad.

Carrie slid an arm around Shayla and supported the poor little murderess while she stood.

Nick put a hand under one of Shayla's arms. They steered her around Viola's desk and eased her into the wheeled chair behind it.

Carrie knelt in front of Shayla. "Okay, start at the beginning."

"There's nothing to tell. I hated him. I poisoned him."

Carrie tilted Shayla's chin so their eyes met. "Why?"

"Donette was pregnant, but I didn't know my dad was the father. I caught them together, and Donette laughed. She told me they were in love."

"When was this?" Nick inserted quietly,

hoping he wouldn't stop Shayla from talking.

"Tuesday night. The night I killed him. Dad had — he had . . . he said my cat, MacGyver, was going to have kittens, and he threatened to poison her. He said he was going to put antifreeze in MacGyver's food and she'd die before we had six more cats eating us out of house and home. I was scared to death because the cat left footprints all over Dad's pickup that morning. Like that stupid pickup wasn't a piece of junk! Dad was so mad, I thought he'd kill MacGyver with his bare hands. He ended up hitting me when I tried to stop him."

Shayla rubbed her hand over her face as if remembering the pain.

Nick saw the faded yellow of an old bruise at her temple.

"Dad had a bottle of antifreeze when he got home that night, and he said the cat was going to die. I started yelling, and when he started in on me again, I ran out, hoping to find MacGyver and take her to Donette to protect her until Dad calmed down."

"I couldn't find the cat for a while. When I finally did, I went to Donette's mom's house — she still lives with her mom — and caught her and Dad . . . together. He ran out the back door, but I saw him. Donette just laughed and told me that the baby she was expecting was Dad's." Shayla ran both hands through her hair, distraught, staring at the floor as if a crystal ball was unfolding the events of last Tuesday.

Shayla looked up from the floor, her face pale except for vivid circles of violent red high on her cheeks. "Donette spent the night with me a lot. I thought she was my friend."

Nick's heart ached for the devastated young girl.

"I took MacGyver to the park and let her go. I knew she'd come home, but I needed a few minutes alone with Dad first. By the time I got back, he was back home, and he'd finished off a six-pack and was halfway through another one. Just like always. He didn't even act like anything had happened. Maybe he thought I hadn't seen him. He hollered at me to get him a beer the second I stepped in the door and . . . I don't know . . . him and Donette . . . MacGyver . . . He slaps me and Mom around every time he's drunk. He grows marijuana in the basement and sells it to little kids. I saw that gallon of antifreeze sitting right by the refrigerator. I just snapped! I cracked open his beer, swallowed most of it, and then filled the can with the antifreeze and gave it to him. He was so drunk, probably on some drugs, too, that he'd have swallowed sand if it had poured out of that can. He drained it and then finished off two more and left. I never saw him again."

Shayla threw herself back into Carrie's arms.

Nick sighed. Well, the crime was solved, but it was a terrible shame.

Carrie held the weeping girl, rubbing her back. Nick stepped close and gingerly rested one hand on Shayla's shoulder, hoping that would help calm the poor kid. As he continued his awkward attempt to comfort the little homicidal maniac, the door in the far wall shook. A draft — something else to repair in this historic old building. As the sobbing died, Carrie gripped Shayla's shoulders and pushed, lifting the girl away from her until their eyes met.

"We need to tell the chief. You're a minor, this is a spontaneous act, not premeditated — uh, not premeditated much. We'll fix it." Carrie nodded.

Shayla nodded her head while she sniffled.

"Let's go." Carrie slung her arm around Shayla, and Nick let them outside.

The inner door shuddered again, and Nick glanced over his shoulder. He knew the layout of these old Main Street build-

138

ings enough to realize that the door didn't lead to the alley. Instead, it opened into a big, vacant room that had once been a mechanic's workshop. He'd need to check with Sven Gunderson, who had inherited most of Main Street when his father died, and make sure there weren't broken doors or windows that allowed weather to further damage the beautiful old wreck of a building.

Nick ushered Carrie and Shayla through the door of the cop shop, just a half block down the street from the *Bugle.* He'd been in Melnik long enough to know that everybody who saw them would start talking and filling in blanks. Those guesses would be passed on as pure facts. Any questions would be answered by leaps in logic that would have humbled an Olympic pole-vaulter. Normally, that made for some seriously twisted gossip. Unfortunately this once, the wildest thing they could guess at would be very close to the truth.

Junior looked up from his computer, where Nick suspected he was playing solitaire. Why not? There was no crime in Melnik.

"I killed my father." Shayla broke into sobs again.

Almost no crime.

Junior's eyes widened. He rose from his desk.

"She didn't kill him," Nick said quietly.

Carrie turned to him. "Yes, she did."

"Yes, I did," Shayla wailed between sobs, her face buried in her hands and her whole body shuddering.

"It took me a minute to think of this, but it wasn't enough." Nick quickly explained to Junior about Shayla's confession. "I've heard enough about antifreeze poisoning to make me doubt that a beer can full of it would kill a man."

Junior beetled his unibrow. "Wilkie was drinking heavy. Alcohol can make poison react differently."

Nick exchanged a doubtful look with Carrie, and he was honored by the quick nod of her head and the trust he saw in her eyes. Shayla was innocent, probably.

Shayla's whole body had straightened, her tears had subsided, her terror replaced by hope. "You mean I didn't kill him? I might be innocent?"

"Probably." Junior shook his head. "But shame on you for trying to kill your dad, Shayla, honey."

Shame on you — Shayla's punishment for premeditated murder. Not a bad system if

140

you were a murderer. For every potential murder victim, it was kind of scary.

"Well, okay." Shayla started backing toward the door. "Guess I'll go now. I'm on my lunch break from school. If I hurry, I won't even be late for fifth period."

"Hold on just a minute." Junior looked torn. Tardiness? Homicide? What was an overworked policeman to do? "You're not going anywhere except to jail, Shayla. We're not going to just take Nick's word. We have to have that autopsy report back first and see the cause of death." He pointed a beefy index finger at the chair directly in front of his desk in the tiny office. "And even if it turns out that you didn't kill him, he made you killin' mad."

"I don't know . . ."

"You may know others he's made that mad. You have information — without knowin' it — that could turn up a killer." He jabbed his finger at the chair again. "Sit!"

She did. Then Carrie sat in the chair next to her. Junior grabbed a folding chair leaning against the wall beside his desk. Nick took it and placed it next to Carrie's chair. All three of them sat like well-trained basset hounds. Very law abiding, Melnikites, even the murderers.

141

Nick noted how tiny and bare the office was — just room for a small metal desk painted we-have-no-imagination gray; a beige, cloth-upholstered rolling desk chair for Junior; and the two chairs in front for Hal and Steve. In fact, if they didn't position the two chairs correctly, they'd block the door to the outside. Nothing on the wall but a couple of pieces of printer paper. Both looked like they had a week's worth of work schedules on them. There was also a wooden and brass plaque that said "OUTSTANDING COMMUNITY SERVICE," with Junior's name, Roland Hammerstad, engraved below. In a town where everybody knew everything, Nick realized he'd never heard Junior's real name before. Oh, the older folks probably knew Junior's father and, using "Junior" as a clue, knew Junior's name. But anyway, according to the plaque, Roland Hammerstad was a man of honors in a teeny office.

Of course, why would there be a bigger office? There wasn't any crime in Melnik.

"I wanted him dead because he got my friend pregnant. Donette's a jerk, but she's still in high school, which makes my dad a child-molesting pervert. And he cheated on my mom, and he hits me and my brother and my mom, and he spent every night drunk, and there's that weed growing in the basement."

Almost no crime.

Junior cocked his head at her. "Now, first, are you eighteen? Because if you're not, we need to get your mom in here. I can't question a minor without a parent or guardian present."

Shayla nodded her head frantically. "I'm eighteen." Then she shook it, just as frantically. "But if I didn't kill him, we don't need to let Mom know."

Junior rubbed his chin. "Honey, you're not walking away from this. You've confessed to attempted murder, and I'm going to arrest you. Maybe Nick's right and your poisoned beer didn't kill your dad. But we can't be sure without talking to the coroner. For now, your confession is enough for an arrest. We'll have to talk to a judge before you can make bail, and out here that's gonna take at least overnight. And then you or someone is going to have to come up with bond money. It don't matter anyway. You know this is Melnik. No sense in even trying to keep a secret in this town."

Shayla got a mulish look on her face. "I'm moving away as soon as I graduate, and I'm never coming back."

Nick had heard Carrie say almost the

same words about Melnik. Shayla and Carrie, kindred spirits — except for the antifreeze.

Junior ignored Shayla's declaration of independence. "Just tell me what you told these two."

"*Fine!* I'm already eighteen, just last month, so let's get this finished and get me locked up." Shayla retold her story, and it didn't get better.

Nick reasserted that the quantity of antifreeze made it unlikely Shayla had administered a lethal dose.

Shayla was considerably less devastated by the time the interview was over.

Suddenly the police station door slammed open, and Rosie Melnik charged into the room, literally breathing fire.

Nick could actually feel her rage heating the room. She took a long drag on her cigarette, and it lit up bright. She dragged it out of her mouth, tossed it on the floor, and left it to smolder. Nick fought down the urge to grab it, extinguish it, and dispose of it properly.

"You killed your own *father?*"

Shayla rose from her chair and backed toward Junior's desk. "Mom, I —"

"Shut up!" Rosie charged toward Shayla. Nick jumped in between the young girl and her enraged mother. Rosie shoved her hands into her lank hair. Her skin, sallow and pitted with acne scars, flushed a blotchy red and her teeth bared; Nick saw she was missing a couple of important ones right up front.

Junior dodged in front of Nick and grabbed Rosie's arm. "She didn't do it. Now settle down."

Rosie turned her fire on Junior. "I heard she did. I heard she confessed."

"Where did you hear that?" Carrie asked. Nick felt more than saw Carrie move to Shayla's side.

"This is Melnik. Everybody knows." Rosie's T-shirt hung on her emaciated body. She shoved Junior's shoulder as if she needed to rough *someone* up.

"No, Rosie," Carrie said. "Not everybody knows. Who told you —"

"Shayla did not kill her dad," Junior interrupted. "I don't care what you heard, it's wrong. She did break the law, though. I'm locking her up, and you'll have to call the county courthouse about arranging bail."

Rosie glared past Junior, Nick, and Carrie to Shayla. Nick shuddered at the rage.

"You can rot in jail for all I care." Rosie jabbed a finger at her daughter. "And if you do get out, don't come crawling to me looking for a roof over your head. Just stay away from me."

Rosie whirled, wrenched the door open, and charged out of the building, slamming the door viciously.

Dead silence was broken only by Shayla's devastated sobs. Nick turned to find Carrie hugging her. He offered the girl a handkerchief.

At last Shayla swiped a hand over her face and straightened her shoulders. "She always picked him over me and Kevin. I used to try to protect her when Dad started in on her, but sometimes she'd hit me, too, like *she* was protecting *him*. Maybe jail's a better place for me now."

Jail. A better place than home. Nick sighed. It wasn't much of a jail, either, reachable through a door in Junior's office. It was actually more of a steel shed with a chain-link fence — no great security there. But most of the people who did time were sitting out traffic fines they couldn't pay, so they weren't apt to attempt escape, knowing they'd just have to come back later and sit longer.

"Your mom'll calm down. And we know you probably didn't kill your dad, so she'll figure that out pretty soon. Nice catch on the antifreeze, Nick. I've got just a few more

146

questions, Shayla." Junior studied his faithful notebook.

"Forget it. I'm done talking." Shayla grabbed the doorknob and snarled at Junior, as if he'd done something wrong instead of her. "Is the jail unlocked?"

Junior nodded. "Wait a second. I'll come with you."

"I'll get there myself. Just stay away from me." Shayla slammed the office's side door after storming through it. A perfect imitation of her mother's exit. Nick heard the *clank* of the cell door as it shut.

"Nice to see she's got all her anger issues under control." Carrie stared at the door to the county jail.

"Is there another door out of there? She could have slammed the door without going in and just kept walking." Nick rubbed the back of his neck and then smoothed his hair, worried that he'd mussed it.

"I think she's smart enough to stay put."

"Let's hope she's smart enough to quit trying to kill people, instead of smart enough to get better at it." Carrie laid her hand on Nick's upper arm. "You probably saved her by knowing all that about antifreeze."

"I took a semester of animal husbandry in college when I thought I might want to be a veterinarian." Nick gave a very sweet, humble shrug. "Pets accidentally drinking antifreeze happens a lot."

Carrie almost sighed out loud. It was the kind of modest shrug she expected from a hero. He was the real deal. She knew it, and unless she was mistaken earlier — before Shayla had burst in — he'd almost asked her out. Who was she kidding? He'd almost kissed her. She needed to get him alone and give him another chance.

"Anyway, Shayla couldn't have been convicted." Junior pulled an official-looking stack of papers out of his desk drawer.

"Why not?" Carrie saw the letterhead, DODGE COUNTY CORONER, and forgot about Nick. She leaned forward, hoping to read the report upside down.

"Because even if she'd given him enough, it wouldn't have had time to kick in. Antifreeze kills you slow. Something else got him long before he'd have died of poison."

"Of course," Carrie nodded. "When she first started confessing, I didn't even think of that. The coroner said that Wilkie was shot."

"He was shot." Junior kept skimming the paper that listed possible murder weapons. "But they haven't pinpointed that as the cause of death yet. How about your great-grandma's lethal skillet?"

Carrie twisted her fingers together. "I'm never going to be able to fry an egg in that thing now."

"The skillet isn't likely," Junior added. "Although it's kind of hard to say what combinations went together to finish off Wilkie. Poison, bullet, and skillet aren't the only possibilities."

"What else?" Nick asked. "Maybe I should start a spreadsheet when I get home."

"He was also smothered." Junior pointed to a spot on the paper with his beefy finger. "Again, there are doubts about that being the ultimate weapon. These results are preliminary; no tox screen yet. They don't have a thing in here about antifreeze. Who knows what all else he had in his system."

"Smothered?" Goosebumps erupted on Carrie's arms, and she began rubbing them. "I remember now. There were short, mousy gray hairs on his mouth."

Nick gave her a sympathetic look and glanced at her arms.

"That's right. The autopsy isn't finished. But it's looking like Wilkie might have been smothered." Junior gave Shayla's chair a dark scowl.

"S-s-smothered?" Carrie knew what was

coming, but she couldn't deal with it.

"Yes, almost certainly smothered to death by a . . ."

"No!" Carrie knocked her chair over, jumping to her feet.

". . . really large mouse."

11

Nick heard Carrie's head crack against the glass in the door. He rushed over, to be handy in case she needed to jump into his arms.

Her eyes were so round and dilated that he could almost see into her brain. She had no color in her face. Her breathing was short and rapid. He could count her pulse by a throbbing vein in her forehead. Her white-blond hair trembled so violently, it seemed alive. But this was Carrie, the mouse-ophobe. She was doing pretty well.

He watched her closely as Junior stationed himself on Carrie's other side.

Nick asked him, "Are you done with us?"

"Sure." Junior sorted through the file and extended a few pages toward Carrie. "You want the part of my report I can show you? There's mice stuff in it."

Carrie's quaking hand reached past Nick. "I–I–I'll take it."

There was something illogical in being proud of someone just for picking up a form that *mentioned* a mouse, even if the mouse was a murder weapon. And Nick hated illogic.

"You must want a look at that thing really bad." Junior snickered.

Some of the color returned to Carrie's cheeks. "I know it's stupid to be afraid of mice. Okay?"

"Especially the *word* 'mouse' written on paper."

"I've just got this image, this horrible image." The paper crinkled up into a ball in Carrie's hands. "Of a huge mouse stalking Wilkie, holding him down, pressing his sharp clawed paws over his mouth." Carrie backed into the door again.

"You know, if a mouse really killed Wilkie," Junior was torturing Carrie — deliberately in Nick's opinion — "then we've got no murderer. It's more of an animal attack, like if a bear came after you. Or if you hit a deer driving down the road and crashed and died. No crime there. Of course, there's no reason to think the mouse was big. It'd only need to be big if it attacked Wilkie while the poor guy hid in the closet or if it stuffed him in the closet afterward. And that means this new, supersized Maxie Mouse tried to cover its . . . uh, mouse tracks, you might say — which means it knew that what it was doing was wrong, so there goes its insanity defense. We have to assume . . ."

Trying to stop Junior, who was enjoying himself way too much, Nick said, "Common sense tells us that a mouse couldn't smother Wilkie, which means someone had to *use* a mouse to . . ."

"Eeek!" Carrie screamed and jumped.

And just like that, Nick had an armful of soft, vulnerable woman. He'd been trying to help. But now that he thought about it, using a mouse as a murder weapon might rank up there with Carrie's worst nightmares.

"Forgive me," Carrie whispered.

Nick hugged her. "You want me to take that paper? Maybe if it wasn't so close to you . . ."

It was trapped between their bodies. Carrie had her hands full clinging to Nick's neck. "No, I'll keep it."

Junior groaned and then reached for the doorknob to help Nick out. "The really weird thing is, because of the reputation of this town and the fairly strange mode of death, I've decided we need to do genetic testing on Maxie. I mean, where in this town would you go if you wanted to kill a guy and needed a mouse as a weapon?"

Carrie buried her face in Nick's shoulder with a whimper. "How about my house? It's full of mice."

Junior pulled the door open. "But they're not handy like Maxie. My gut tells me someone took Maxie out for a . . . walk." Junior covered his mouth while he chuckled.

Suddenly, the smile vanished from Junior's face. He quickly but silently shoved the door closed, pushed Nick against the wall with Carrie still in his arms, flattened his back against the other side of the door, reached out, and flicked the dead bolt.

"Peoplewon'tstarveinthistownaslongasI'm-around,oh no."

"I already bought my pie from Crazy Clara this week. I'm not buying another one. This job doesn't pay that well, my youngest needs braces, and I'm just not doin' it!"

The door knob rattled. "Giantsizedmice-runningwildkillingfolks."

Carrie lifted her head off Nick's shoulder. "What did she say?"

"Shh!" Junior waved his hand at her.

Clara turned from the door, exited the building, and pulled her squeaking cart on down the sidewalk.

Junior pulled a handkerchief out of his

154

back pocket and mopped his brow. "Nasty business, those pies."

Opening the door, Junior peeked left and right and then slipped out into the outer hallway where he could get a better view of the street.

"What did Clara say?" Carrie asked again.

"I'd be glad to keep carrying you," Nick said. "But people will see us when we walk down the street. Dora, you know. I don't mind. But maybe you'd rather walk."

Carrie nodded then relaxed her death grip on Nick's neck.

Junior returned. "Coast is clear."

"Are you done with us?" Nick set Carrie down with regret.

Junior laughed. "Except for comic relief."

Nick glared at Junior over Carrie's bowed head.

Junior held up one hand, as if vowing to quit having fun at Carrie's expense. "I've authorized the tests on Maxie. Apparently they can make an exact match even with a mouse. We'll know for sure, but it's slow. I couldn't convince them it was a priority."

Carrie buried her face in her hands. "DNA testing on a mouse? Only in Melnik."

Nick lifted Carrie's chin. "Try to stop thinking about the mouse and think about how many people had access to that glass case in front of the Historical Society Museum. If we pinpoint Maxie as the, uh . . ." Nick almost said *culprit,* opened his mouth to say *murder weapon,* then finally settled on, ". . . you know . . . we can narrow the list of suspects. It's a great lead. Way better than if it turns out that someone killed Wilkie by whacking him with that frying pan."

"Except someone *did* whack him with the frying pan, despite whatever . . . *method* finally did him in." More color returned to Carrie's face.

Nick could almost feel her spine stiffening.

"So narrow the list to whoever had access to the museum and Maxie's case, throw in motive, and the crime is solved."

"Shayla obviously had one." Carrie held up one finger. "And Donette and Rosie and Kevin."

"Not a long list." Nick smiled, hoping to encourage her and distract her from mice at the same time. "It should be easy. This is a sweet little town. How many potential murderers can there be?"

Carrie had a list as long as her arm by the end of the day. Everyone in town hated Wilkie Melnik, mostly for very good reasons.

Life couldn't get much more interesting — for Melnik. As for anywhere else on the planet — well, don't ask.

And then, back at the office, she met her new boss.

The door screeched worthy of a haunted house, and a wizened old man came in. No one Carrie had ever seen before, and she'd seen everybody.

"You're my editor, right?" The man, tall and gaunt, bent with age, balding and gray-haired, his face plowed deep with grouch wrinkles, advanced on her desk with surprising speed.

"I'm Carrie Evans, and you are . . . ?"

"Sven Gunderson." The man slammed his fist on Carrie's desk.

Carrie jumped to her feet, startled but not really afraid. She could take him. Of course, he seemed to be furious, so he had rage on his side.

Gunderson wore a threadbare brown suit that hadn't been in fashion . . . well . . . ever. Carrie knew he was rich. Everyone knew the Gundersons were the wealthiest people in Melnik. Like slumlords, the family had bought up most of Main Street three generations ago and held on tight, letting buildings fall into disrepair and charging exorbitant rent. People had tried to buy lots and backed off due to sticker shock.

No cabal of earnest citizens had been able to disabuse the Gundersons of their strange notion that in the great mysterious "someday," downtown Melnik would be worth a fortune. Meanwhile, Main Street buildings deteriorated and no new businesses took on the onerous monthly lease rates.

"I own the *Bugle,* and I'm going to make some changes around here. I'm sick of the way my father ran this newspaper."

Carrie stiffened, wondering if she was going to be fired before the end of her first day of work. That was fast even for her. And since when had Sven's father ever "run" the newspaper? He'd collected rent and left it to succeed or fail on its own.

"Mr. Gunderson, I just started this morning." She went for a little reverse psychology. "I absolutely understand if you want to bring in your own editor."

"I'm not here to fire you. I'm here to tell you what's what." Sven bent vulture-like over Carrie, across the desk. His nose even looked a little like a beak. His dark, beady eyes, shining through gold-rimmed glasses, made him look like he'd feed on the dead.

"This paper is gonna change." He hammered the desk again. "Just because Melnik is small doesn't mean we can't tell the truth.

I'm going to blow the lid off this town."

Carrie sincerely hoped he didn't break anything he pounded on, because she had a bad feeling about him paying to replace it.

In an effort to placate him, she said, "It just so happens that I agree with you, Mr. Gunderson. I want to write a real newspaper. Right now, I'm finishing a story on Wilkie Melnik. I don't intend to offer platitudes or whitewash the events surrounding his death." On the other hand, there was no sense in humiliating Wilkie's wife and children. Or upsetting his girlfriend, who had a bad temper and worked five feet away.

Gunderson grunted and fished a piece of paper out of his brown suit pants. "My family goes back as far as the Melnicks. I consider it an injustice that this town bears the name Melnik instead of Gunderson."

Carrie didn't mention her family's deep roots. No sense in throwing gasoline on Gunderson's fire.

"Wilkie Melnik was a liar and a thief, and I want him exposed. Dying doesn't end all the wrong he's done." He slapped the paper on her desk. "I want this story in the *Bugle* this week."

Carrie had a nostalgic moment dwelling on the old "Don't speak ill of the dead" rule. Those were the days.

"I'm not going to let the truth die with Wilkie Melnik." Gunderson's fists curled.

Carrie hoped he was going to slug only her desk. "Let me print up what I've got for you to read. I'll go over your notes and add them to my story."

"I don't have time to sit here and do the work of my editor." The man had an almost deranged gleam in his eyes. "You put that information in *my* newspaper word for word or find yourself another job."

Gunderson turned and stormed out of the building, slamming the door so hard that the glass rattled. Carrie's heart pounded with fear, and her face burned with barely controlled anger.

She reached a trembling hand toward Gunderson's exposé on Wilkie, sinking down into her chair. She started to read and knew her career as a small-town journalist was over.

She crumpled the pages of half truths and character assassination and tossed them in the trash.

Like poor dead Wilkie didn't have enough trouble. The article she'd been planning to write was tough enough. But this? Out of the question.

She'd never print such hogwash. So Gunderson would fire her Wednesday afternoon at about three, when the *Bugle* hit the stands. Two days from now.

One issue. Even for the revolving door of the *Bugle,* this had to be some kind of record. She could see it now: *Carrie — the World's Largest Failure.*

Maybe they'd stuff her and put her in a case right next to Maxie.

That's why she believed in God, to avoid something like that. Because spending eternity next to a mouse in Melnik was Carrie's very own personal definition of eternal darkness.

12

Nick squeaked the *Bugle* door open. Carrie knocked page six of tomorrow's paper onto the floor and shrieked. She sounded a lot like the door. She whirled around, her eyes wide, clutching her chest.

Great, scare her to death, doofus.

He'd spent Monday and today on her house repairs — and dealing with all those mice. It'd kill her if she knew.

Last night there had been another cleaning party, but tonight she'd had to work, so she would be going in that house alone. Nick had kept at the repairs, hoping to protect her from facing the mice by herself. And it had gotten later . . . and later . . . and later.

He could see the lights of the *Bugle* office from her house — if he stood at the third floor window on his tiptoes and watched the reflection in the insurance office across the street from the paper. So he'd work a while and then jog upstairs to check. The light at the paper just kept burning. Before jogging up and down the stairs gave him a heart attack, he broke down and went to see her.

"Sorry." He held up his hands, glad to surrender. "I saw the *Bugle* lights still on, and I thought I'd check. It's almost midnight. I was afraid something might have happened to you, like you fell into the wax machine and were now The World's Largest Pair of Red Wax Lips."

Don't mention lips, idiot.

"I can leave if . . ."

"Stay!" Carrie strode across the room. It looked to Nick as though she didn't run only because there wasn't time to pick up speed.

She wanted him.

Nick smiled. "I can help with the paper so you can get out of here, or I can fix this door."

"Come and see what I've got." Carrie reached his side and grabbed him by the sleeve of his Windbreaker. "Then the door would be great. I'd let you help with the paper, but I'm figuring it out as I go along, mostly thanks to Viola's notes. I can't imagine explaining it to you."

She sank her nails into the fabric of his

jacket, and Nick had the strange sensation of being taken prisoner. The woman was definitely glad to see him.

"Okay, I think I've finally gotten it all laid out." Carrie pulled him to the first oversized sheet of paper. The front page lay slanted backward at a forty-five-degree angle on the wooden easel. Seven more stands just like it lined two sides of the little nook of the L-shaped *Bugle* office. The third side was a flat table that lit up under white glass. The easels had sheets of paper on them about the size of one page of a newspaper. All of them were covered with newsprint and pictures.

THE MELNIK BUGLE blazed across the top of the front page just like it did every week. Under the banner was a picture of Wilkie Melnik that looked about fifteen years old. Below Wilkie's picture, the headline read "DESCENDENT OF MELNIK FOUNDER DIES."

"This was the best picture of Wilkie I could find." Carrie tapped on what looked like a blown-up picture of Wilkie taken out of a crowd scene.

Nick studied the picture. "He's got an I'm-up-to-no-good smile on his face."

"Yeah, he was born with that smile. It's a shame we don't have something a lot less honest to put in the paper." Carrie looked sideways at Nick.

He caught her glance, and they both grinned.

"So, how'd the story come out?"

Carrie clenched her jaw. "I'm dreading the moment Donette reads it. I know she'll say that I am betraying her child's ancestry and denying the little tyke of any hope for a full and happy future."

"Wow. Not very nice of you."

Carrie snorted. "Viola voted for not even mentioning Wilkie's death except for a tasteful obituary. Her position was that everybody knows already anyway."

Nick leaned forward and read. Carrie leaned in by his side, going over the article again herself. She smelled great for a woman coated in wax and ink.

After several minutes, Nick straightened. "There's nothing in there to offend anybody. You didn't make reference to Wilkie's problems. You just wrote the facts."

"In Melnik, people don't like facts; they like puff pieces. They like 'Don't speak ill of the dead.' I believe Viola said those very words to me seventeen times."

Nick frowned, skimming the article again. "Where in there do you speak ill of him? You don't mention the illegitimate child

165

with his daughter's friend. You don't mention his battered wife and children, his substance abuse problems, his time in the state penitentiary. You even leave out his threats against his daughter's cat."

"I said he was found in my great-grandma's pantry." Carrie tapped paragraph two. "I didn't pretend he died peacefully in his sleep."

"Everybody knows where he was found. What's the harm in mentioning it?"

"What indeed?" Carrie crossed her arms. "And yet I know I'm in for trouble."

Nick noticed that her fingertips were black and there were smudges on her cheeks and her arms. She'd really dived into the paper. "So when this comes out, will Donette and Viola quit in a huff?"

"We'll see."

"Well, try to hang on to them. You might have to stay even later into the night if they quit on you. So, what's left to do before you can get out of here?"

"I've got to double-check that all the ads we sold are on the pages." Carrie held up a clipboard. "Viola went over it, and I'm sure it's fine, but she said to double-check, so I will. Then I have to blue line it and I'm done."

"Blue line?"

"See those faint blue lines on the paper?" Carrie pointed at the large sheets covered in news.

"Yeah." Nick leaned close.

"I put the whole sheet on the light table." She pointed at the flat, glowing, glass-topped table. "And use those lines to make sure everything is perfectly straight."

Nick ran a finger over a square yellow Post-it Note stuck on the paper slightly below the photo of Wilkie. "What's that for?" He reached for the edge of the note.

Carrie slapped his hand. "Don't touch it!"

Nick jerked his hand back. "Why not?"

"Because it's a picture of Maxie. I can't stand to look at it."

Nick fought down the urge to laugh. He stared straight at the paper, not wanting Carrie to see him.

"Oh, just go ahead. Laugh all you want. I can't stand that awful little rodent staring at me. I had a fight on my hands there, too. Viola wanted the picture three columns wide. I refused because I didn't have a Post-it big enough. Ick. A huge close-up of a mouse on the front page? Why don't I just post a huge 'Stay Out' sign out by the highway? A mouse is *not* the symbol a town should adopt for itself. I'm not even going to be able to read the front page tomorrow with him on there."

Nick patted her arm. "You're very brave to give Maxie a front-page story when you hate him so much."

Carrie rolled her eyes. "I'm a ridiculous, stinking coward, but I still put him on the front page because it's the right thing to do."

Nick nodded. "That blue lining thing sounds a lot like something I did when working with blueprints. Show me what you want to do, and I'll help you."

"Really?" Carrie laid her hand on Nick's arm.

He leaned down. "Sure."

"Thanks. I know it's late. I really appreciate the help."

Nick felt his face heat up and hoped the rather dim wattage of the *Bugle*'s lighting system covered his embarrassment. "I . . . uh . . . the real reason I stopped in was because I was wondering if . . . if maybe you'd like someone to go into your house ahead of you tonight? There was still a crowd there working on Friday and you weren't home all weekend."

"Yeah, I was. I was gone a lot during the day, but I came home at night."

"Oh, I'm sorry. Were you all right?"

"All right for a lunatic. I never saw any mice."

Nick smiled. "All that cleaning must have scared them away, but tonight, well, if you don't want to go in alone . . . I could help."

Carrie's hand tightened on his bicep. The melting look of gratitude in her eyes almost made him lean in and kiss her. He backed away before he could do anything stupid. Or would it be smart? He almost asked her out, but the dark circles of exhaustion under her eyes stopped him. "I'll take that look as a yes and get to work."

"Thanks. You really are my hero." She smiled and lifted the front page off the easel then slid it onto the white glass of the light table. She reached for the little switch under the table and flicked it on and off to demonstrate it to Nick. The whole top of the table lit up, leaving the faint blue lines on Carrie's newspaper page clearly visible.

"See, with the light on you can see right through the paper. Then we can make sure the stories we've waxed and stuck on are perfectly straight."

Nick edged in next to her, really close, as she showed him how to make sure each story, picture, and ad on the page was perfectly straight.

He hoped Carrie would decide that she'd

like a hero around her all the time. But he kept that to himself. For now.

Carrie dropped off the *Bugle* at the post office at noon on Wednesday. The paper normally went out closer to three p.m., but they pushed extra hard this week because of Wilkie's funeral in the afternoon.

She delivered the bulk of five hundred copies to the mail, tied together in bundles of about fifty each. Then she dropped more bundles off at Jansson's café, the Mini-Mart, and the grocery store.

She regretted being fired, but she knew it'd be coming just as soon as the newspaper hit the streets.

She'd ignored Gunderson's warning, just like she'd ignored Viola and Donette, and written Wilkie's story her way. And she'd paid tribute to the upcoming Maxie Christmas Festival, set for mid-December and now only six weeks away, without being snide but without slavering either. Which meant Tallulah would be gunning for her.

At least she'd go down in flames on her own terms.

And wouldn't that just look great carved on the brass plate by her shrine in Maxie Memorial Hall. Right below the words, "World's Biggest Failure."

She stepped out of the post office, pressing on her aching back. A bright yellow cottonwood leaf fluttered down at her feet, as dead as her career. The massive tree flanked the corner by the post office, and a soft November breeze rustled in the branches and made the leaves glisten like raining gold.

A perfect fall day to be unemployed.

Dora drove by in her 1975 Chrysler New Yorker, the cruise ship of automobiles. Dora got about four car lengths to the block and four miles to the gallon. No clue what it looked like at the beginning of its life. But now the New Yorker was a solid red shade of rust. A nice contrast to Dora's general grayness.

Dora waved, not watching the quiet street for way, way too long. The car began driving toward Carrie, who stood on the sidewalk waving back. But Dora finished trying to read Carrie's mind and turned to watch where she was going before anyone was killed.

That defined success anytime Dora got behind the wheel.

Carrie drove straight home. She'd walked to work today but found out it was her job to drive the *Bugle,* in its waxy, one-step-up-from-chiseled-in-stone condition, over to

Gillispie to be printed. The Gillispie newspaper owned the only printing press in three counties. She'd loaded the newspaper into its oversized wooden suitcase last night and stopped by to grab it this morning and drive to Gillispie. Inking a paper was similar to coloring in first grade — finding scratches in the negative they'd made of each page.

She watched while they attached her negatives to the massive wheels of the press, ran them off onto newsprint, and folded them on the spinning, room-sized press. Then she'd loaded them into her car, drove back to Melnik, slapped five hundred mailing labels on the papers with help from Viola and Donette, and reloaded them into her car. She began her deliveries at noon and was done at twelve fifteen.

Also, done forever.

13

The autopsy went into extra innings.

The funeral morphed into a memorial service — so Wilkie wasn't required to attend — because the Melnik ladies already had their casseroles done for the dinner.

Nick picked Carrie up at one fifteen on the dot. Not a minute early, not a second late. The man liked order. Carrie suspected that her chaotic house was driving him nuts.

She scaled his truck, careful of her black rayon sheath. She'd added a thin silver belt; small, silver hoop earrings; and black pumps — two-inch heels, closed-toe shoes — not a strap to be found anywhere. The funeral uniform she'd learned from her sorority sisters. She had her hair pulled back in a French twist, but wisps of blond already escaped.

"Did you catch any mice this morning?"

"You look nice." Nick smiled as he ignored her question, the traitor. He knew she needed the information to guard her sanity. He wore a black suit that made his chocolate brown hair more milk than dark. A crisp white shirt fairly glowed behind the thin diagonal stripes of his red and blue tie. A gold tack held his tie in place, as if even in this Nick was afraid to be out of control. He looked great. But he was still a brat about the mice.

"You've got to tell me how the mouse hunt is going." She pulled her seat belt across her body, clicked it sharply, and then turned to glare at him. *I have to know!"*

"So, did the paper go out?"

Carrie's jaw clenched. She considered not telling him just to get revenge for his stubborn refusal to tell her about his mouse-catching escapades. But what else did they have to talk about for ten minutes until they got to the little country church?

"Fine! Be that way."

Nick grinned.

"I'm going to be fired."

Nick jerked his head around, and his brows slammed together. "Did someone come in and yell at you?" He looked for all the world like he'd hunt them down and pound them. What a sweetheart.

Then he shook his head. "No, they couldn't have. No matter how many typos there were or how badly you insulted some-one, the paper hasn't hit the street yet."

"Well, technically it has. I mean, just a few minutes ago. People snag it pretty fast. But it's not for something I put in the paper; it's for something I left out. Gunder-son came in to see me the other day."

"He's back in town?"

"Yes, Sven Gunderson is back. He came in with this really nasty smear piece on Wilkie. Plenty of it true, lots of it rumors, none of it necessary. Gunderson told me to run his story or get out. I smiled nice and he left — I hadn't seen what he'd written yet. I figured I could weave enough of his info into my story to make him happy."

"And . . ." Nick pulled off the highway and drove down the gravel road to Country Christian Church.

"It was awful. No way I could use that stuff. I mean, my piece wasn't exactly a whitewash. I certainly didn't tap-dance around the fact that Wilkie was murdered. But I didn't start guessing at possible mo-tives."

"Well, no, of course not. You mean Gun-derson did?"

Carrie nodded as she remembered some of the things in Gunderson's story. "He speculated on people in town who had motives. By name. He talked about Wilkie being a drunk and a doper. He said that Wilkie sold grass to kids."

"But there's no proof of that."

"There was no proof of most of what Gunderson gave me." Carrie looked at the charming little clapboard church just ahead. She'd been baptized, gone to Sunday school, attended the youth group, sung in the choir, watched two of her older sisters get married, and seen her great-grandma and other ancestors buried in the backyard cemetery there.

It was home in the way all of Melnik was. Small and boring but part of her. She loved to visit. She just didn't want to live here. This was her past.

Her future lay elsewhere.

"And when he sees you've left it out, you really think he'll fire you?"

Her very near future.

"He was breathing fire in my office. He was dead serious. I'm done."

"We'll talk to him. He'll listen to reason. A young man like that shouldn't be so stubborn." Nick turned into the church's crushed-rock parking lot. The tires crunched, and the cold wind blew dirt past the windshield.

"Young? Where'd you get the idea that

he's young?"

Nick pulled up beside a line of three late-model sedans.

"Uh, I guess from him being known only as a son. A son sounds young."

"Well, he's old. Old Man Gunderson was in his nineties, remember. Sven is midsixties at least. And he's so grouchy it's like his face has been cut into these grim, deep lines. No, I'm sure he means what he says." Carrie swung down from the truck and trudged across the graveled parking area.

The church lot was lined with sugar maples, their leaves a brilliant orange-red, dipping and swaying in the breeze. The three cars, parked side by side, formed a line close to the back door of the church. The cars would belong to the serving committee that Carrie was here to help. A bevy of ladies were already hard at work an hour before the service.

Carrie led Nick to the back of the building. He pulled the heavy wooden door open for her. The church basement steps went down on her left, and a ramp to the sanctuary went up on her right. Carrie and Nick went down.

The basement was cool, but it was nothing compared to the blast of pure ice awaiting Carrie at the bottom of those steps.

"How could you do that, Cindy Lou?" Dora plodded toward Carrie, wiping her hands on her apron.

"D–do what?"

The plump tyrant made a fist, and Carrie took a half step back until she bumped into Nick's solid form. She heaved a sigh of relief that he was there. She might need rescuing from more than mice today. The whole white knight thing must be exhausting for him. Dora, Melnik's answer to the CIA, wore bright green — a terrible fashion choice considering that she'd just had her hair tinted an amazing shade of bluish purple. She wore fluorescent green polyester slacks decorated with small white flowers and a solid green tunic top that reminded Carrie of something she'd seen growing in Great-Grandma's refrigerator.

Carrie had badly misjudged funeral styles in Melnik.

A gnarled finger waggled in front of Carrie's eyes. "You young whippersnappers don't know it isn't right to speak ill of the dead."

Uh-oh. The Wilkie story.

"I'm ashamed of you, Carrie Evans." Another lady, this one adorned in a pumpkin orange blouse sprinkled with appliquéd fall leaves, marched out of the kitchen with

178

her hands jammed on her ample hips. A third woman stormed straight at Carrie.

Dora quit talking, obviously too busy recording the attack with her eagle eyes and steel-trap brain.

And if Carrie once in a while wished that steel trap would snap shut on Dora's . . .

"I never thought I'd see the day . . ."

Carrie noticed quiet Bonnie Simpson neatly slipping brownies out of a pan onto a plastic platter that looked like crystal. Carrie tried to remember the last time Bonnie, ten years older than she was and a fixture at all community events, had actually spoken to her. Bonnie kept her head bent, her thick round spectacles focused on her work, her blue jumper concealing any hint of the woman's size and shape. No yelling from Bonnie. Carrie decided Bonnie was her new best friend. After Nick.

Nick rested his hands on Carrie's shoulders, and for a second she enjoyed the support. Then it occurred to her that she was the only thing standing between Nick and these furious women. Was he protecting her? Or using her as a human shield? She couldn't decide.

Heavy footsteps pounded down the wooden stairs. "Carrie, I am shocked, do you hear? Shocked."

Carrie whirled around at the deep voice coming from behind. Nick stepped out of the kill zone.

Chicken.

Pastor Bremmen, his face normally the very image of love and forgiveness, had a vein pulsing in his forehead, his jaw clenched, and his cheeks florid.

"All right, hold it!" Nick's voice boomed into the crowd.

Silence fell on the basement.

"I read that story. She was fair to Wilkie."

Nick had obviously gotten the message loud and clear, too, without Wilkie's name being mentioned once. And he'd stepped in to protect her. God bless the man.

"You're all overreacting. Now Carrie might not have . . ."

Pastor Bremmen slapped a folded-up newspaper against Nick's chest. "You call this *fair?*"

Nick unfolded the paper. Carrie looked around his arm and then flinched when she saw Maxie staring at her. Nick must have felt her reaction, because he quickly flipped the paper over and folded it so Maxie didn't show. There was a mug shot of Wilkie in prison garb with a number across his chest.

EX-CON MURDERED screamed in bold, underlined forty-eight-point type across the top of Wilkie's photo.

Nick swiveled his head around to look at Carrie.

She looked up, afraid he'd start yelling at her, too.

"I did not write that." Carrie swept the foursome with her gaze. "You have to believe me. I . . ." She looked back at the text. Where had this come from? She racked her brain to figure out how this switch could have been made and then realized that she'd never really looked at the paper this morning, avoiding that awful Maxie. She'd figure out who and how later, but the responsibility was all hers.

As she scanned the story, "who" became immediately obvious. *Gunderson!*

This was his lurid tale of rumors and half truths, every sin, real and imagined, Wilkie had ever committed, in painful detail.

Nick spoke up. "This is a story Sven Gunderson wanted run about Wilkie. Carrie refused. He must have . . ."

Carrie's nails dug into Nick's forearm. Their eyes met. He fell silent.

Carrie looked at all these old friends and her heart twisted. These ladies and Pastor Bremmen loved her. But she knew her place in this fiasco.

"This is a mistake."

"Sven Gunderson did this?" Pastor Bremmen thundered.

"It's *my* mistake. I didn't mean for this story to be in the *Bugle.* But I'm the editor. Whatever comes out in the pages of the *Bugle* is my responsibility." She *should* have double-checked this morning. That stupid mouse! This was all *Maxie's* fault.

"This is all my fault. It won't happen again." Carrie looked from one lady to another, until finally she turned to face Pastor Bremmen head-on. She might as well face it. In Melnik there was nowhere to run. "An article retracting this and printing the truth will be in next week's paper."

Too little, too late.

Pastor Bremmen still looked grim. "This is going to hurt a lot of people." In all honesty, it'd only *hurt* four. Maybe five since Shayla was still living in the county lockup for trying to kill her dad. Shayla was probably hurting pretty bad these days, but it wasn't about grief. Not even close.

Junior had sprung Shayla for the funeral. The plan was for her to sit through the memorial service, far away from her mother since Rosie was still in a rage, and then Shayla would have a nice lunch and go back to jail. Junior wanted to let her go but for now, since the poor little confessed-but-probably-innocent murderess had nowhere to go, he was using the jail like low-rent foster care.

But judging from the lynch mob in front of Carrie, these citizens of fair Melnik didn't have to be hurt to be appalled. And they especially didn't have to be hurt to come and scold her. They'd be openly furious, but they'd quietly revel in the gossipy pack of lies. It pinched to know that more copies of the *Bugle* would sell this week than ever before.

She turned and wanted to beseech these ladies not to hate her and to not enjoy the pain she'd caused. "I'm terribly sorry. I should have given the paper a final look before I took it to the printers."

It occurred to Carrie she might *not* be fired. Of course, by the time she was done with Gunderson, she *would* be fired. Her termination would result from screaming at the boss, not for disobedience.

Nick patted her shoulder. She gave him a grateful look and then turned to Pastor Bremmen. "Would it be all right to say a few words of apology at the funeral, Pastor? I never intended to inflict more pain on this family, and I want to say so publicly."

The road-flare red of Pastor Bremmen faded, and the usual kindness Carrie depended on returned to his eyes. "I'll ask Rosie. We'll go by her wishes."

Carrie nodded. "Now, ladies." She turned to face the septuagenarian hit squad. "Do you forgive me enough to let me help in the kitchen, or am I banished?"

14

Far from being banished, after the funeral Carrie had been given hard labor. And Nick wasn't sure why, but it appeared he'd been sentenced along with her.

He rinsed the one thousandth plate — or was it the one millionth? — while Carrie scrubbed. Wilkie had quite the turnout.

The church had used all their paper plates and china and still the food line stretched up the stairs and into the parking lot. So Nick and Carrie washed. As the day wore down and the food ran out, the crowd thinned.

They worked silently as long as there were women bustling in and out of the kitchen. But at last even those faithful ladies began to untie their aprons and go home.

"At least they forgave you, Carrie." Nick glanced over his shoulder. There were still a few people left, but they were busy in the social hall.

"I don't think this exactly qualifies as forgiveness. They just see fresh meat. Someone young to do the heavy lifting. That's Melnik for you."

"I love this." Nick grinned at her. They stood shoulder to shoulder by the double sink, their hands in hot water — not unlike Carrie's whole life. "I mean, I don't love that you've become a Melnik pariah. I love helping. This is the purest form of Christian service."

Carrie pulled the metal strainer to let the water go. "You see that dreary dishwater being sucked down the drain?"

"Sure."

"That's my life, Nick." She faced him and a hank of her fine hair hung in one eye. She blew it away and glared. "And washing dishes is not the purest form of Christian service. Washing dishes is what got Martha in trouble with Jesus."

Nick tried to accept that Carrie hated living in Melnik. He'd found his home here. He'd found the direction God had for his life. So where did that leave them?

Looking back at his rinse water, he scooped out a fistful of silverware and changed the subject to keep himself from begging her to love this town. "You were so brave up there during the funeral. It was the most courageous thing I've ever seen, the way you stood there and let everyone have their say and didn't complain."

Carrie reset the drain plug and let fresh hot water spray into her sink. Nick caught the scent of lemons as she added a generous squirt of soap. Suds bubbled in the sink.

The door between the basement social hall and the kitchen swung open, and a woman Nick knew in passing came in. "Hi, Marian." Nick lifted his dish towel in greeting.

The woman carefully scraped the plates and stacked them on Carrie's left, perfectly positioned to wash. Nick noticed a nervous glance between Marian and Carrie.

"Uh . . . Nick?" Carrie said.

"No, it's okay." Marian blushed, and the dishes clattered as she set them down and fled the kitchen.

Nick slipped a plate out of the rinse-water side of the double sink with a quiet splash and set it on end in the drainer with a soft click. "So, Gunderson really changed the . . ."

"Nick!"

"What?"

"Her name's Bonnie."

"Whose name?"

"Bonnie's."

"Who's Bonnie?"

Carrie closed her eyes. "You embarrassed her half to death. *Marian* isn't her name, it's *Bonnie.*"

Nick's brows rose nearly to his hairline. He looked over his shoulder through the opening above the countertop that separated the kitchen from the hall. "I'm sorry. I'd heard her name was Marian."

Carrie turned around and looked through the same window. "And there are still a few plates on the table. Bonnie never left anything undone in her life."

"I've been calling her Marian for six months. How come she's never corrected me?"

"Do you talk to her often?"

"Well, no."

"And you heard her name was Marian from Dora, right?"

Nick turned back toward the sink. "Right."

"That's because Dora calls her Marian. As in Marian the Librarian. It's from *The Music Man* or some old movie. Just like she calls me Cindy Lou, as in Cindy Lou Who, from Whoville."

"Marian seems so shy. I must have embarrassed her every time I've talked to her. I need to apologize." Nick straightened away from the sink, intending to run after her right now.

"Relax. I'm the one who embarrassed her. She knew I'd tell you. She didn't mind. Just like I don't mind being called Cindy Lou ... much."

"Well, I have to find her and tell her I'm sorry."

"That won't be hard. She works at the Melnik Historical Society Museum, which also contains the closest thing Melnik has to a library. She's the curator and librarian. Thus the nickname."

"Okay, I'll make it right." Nick went back to his wiping with a decisive nod.

"Nick, listen, I really appreciate the kind words about taking abuse. I feel like I took a beating, but it needed to be done. Since the whole town showed for the funeral . . ."

"Mainly because of your story."

Carrie gave a short, humorless laugh. "Yeah, hoping for fireworks. Anyway, I'm hoping I let them get it out of their system. I'm hoping it'll minimize the long, drawn-out, behind-closed-doors whispering campaign that would have normally followed."

Nick shuddered. "Well, you took it like a . . ."

"What?"

Nick was tempted to just go ahead and drown himself in the rinse water. "I was going to say 'You took it like a man.' "

Great, insult her.

"You like doing this, huh?" Carrie handed another plate to Nick. She was fast. It kept him hopping.

Nick lifted one shoulder. "Yes, I like this. It feels like I'm God's servant. He tells us to comfort those who mourn. This is a way to do that. And we don't ask for thanks."

"The family always comes in and says thank you."

"Yes, but the service committee doesn't quit if no one comes in."

"True, but they gossip about them."

"Well, we don't insist they pay."

"Actually, a donation to the Women's Auxiliary is expected."

Nick glared at her.

Carrie grinned. "Sorry. I agree with you, actually."

"So you're just arguing with me for entertainment?"

"Of course. This is a great ministry. But nothing like what a big church can offer. In my church in Omaha we had a casserole committee to prepare meals, freeze them ahead, and deliver them. But we did more than that. There was also a grief counselor on staff. We had someone coordinating the funeral, and using memorial money, we funded Sunday school classes and Bible studies for new widows, parents without partners, and a singles ministry. Even those were targeted — some for traditional singles, others for divorced singles, and still others for people who'd lost a spouse, parent, or child. We did so much for so many in that church. But in Melnik there aren't enough people, so everyone gets lumped in together or forgotten, with nothing available to meet their needs."

"But here people actually know each other by name." How could she not know what she had in this little town? It was filled with people that cared so much for her. "They can give Rosie Melnik a hug and tell her they'll stop by. They can show kindness to Shayla and Kevin as they pass them on the street. They can be a support system for Donette, now and when the baby comes. This is a *real* church. The reason grief counselors and casserole ministries and funeral coordinators exist in huge churches is because no one does that stuff, because no one even knows each other."

Nick quit drying to stress his point. "I moved away from Chicago, and I've never heard a word from my church there. There's no one to notice I'm gone. We had six services on Saturday and Sunday and a nine-piece praise band that recorded albums. We supported a dozen churches in Africa and sent mission teams to build churches and hospitals there every summer. And that's all wonderful, and I don't disparage the work they do. It's a beautiful ministry. But I could go weeks without seeing anyone I knew well enough to say hi."

Nick looked back at his water. "I wish I'd thought to bring a casserole to the funeral."

"Can you cook?"

"No."

"Then thanks for not bringing one."

Nick laughed. He couldn't help but like her. But why would she be interested in a man who wanted to stay in the very place she was itching to leave? A man who was such a dope and so out of the loop that he'd called a nice lady by the wrong name for six months? But that was the whole point, wasn't it? Yeah, he'd done it wrong for six months with Bonnie, but in Chicago he would have never even discovered his mistake.

"I can learn. Living in Melnik will *make* me learn. Maybe I can take food to the Melniks' home." Nick went back to work feeling good about his decision, as if the Lord Himself had put the idea in his heart.

"I'd better phone Rosie and warn her that

192

she might have another Crazy Clara pie-type situation on her hands."

"Hey! You take that back!" An aging china plate slipped through Nick's hands and landed flat on the water, splashing his pristine suit. "I'm a much better cook than Clara." He snagged a nearby dish towel and dabbed at his shirtfront.

Carrie splashed him deliberately, much more dramatically than the plate had. Nick's jaw dropped. "I can't believe you did that."

He made a move toward the water with the flat of his hand.

Dora lumbered in. They both went back to work while Dora told Carrie to stand up straight so her stomach didn't pooch out. She also advised Nick to start dyeing the gray out of his hair and to use a better deodorant.

She launched into the pros and cons of mouthwash just as Tallulah came into the kitchen breathing fire. "Carrie Evans, you have destroyed Melnik and ruined my life's work. The Maxie Festival will be a disaster, and the governor will never come."

Nick braced himself to step between Carrie and Tallulah. Sure, Carrie was tough, but she had to be exhausted after the funeral inquisition.

Before he could protect her, he remembered that this was her town. She was used to it. Carrie belonged in a way he never would. And she didn't even know to be grateful. He went back to rinsing dishes. When Dora had been insulting him, he'd almost felt like a true Melnikite. But now he was back to being an outsider, the loser, the fat kid who spent recess dodging bullies and class time showing up those losers, which only bought him more trouble. He'd never found his place. His home had been nice with three equally geeky brothers and a sister, all younger, and his kindly college professor parents who thought all two hundred pounds of his five-foot-two eighth-grade self was wonderful. But he hadn't been able to take his family to class.

He'd grown past six feet without gaining an ounce, but the awkward nerd was still alive and well. Despite his fumbling attempts to find himself in college and his pivotal role in the engineering firm, he had never fit in. Then his brothers, one by one, had moved out of Chicago. His parents had retired to Florida and left him their big house to live in alone. The solitary life had almost crushed him.

He had hoped he'd finally found a home in Melnik. And now here was Carrie, the prettiest thing he'd ever seen, and all she wanted was to get away from Melnik and — by extension — him.

Nick sighed and took over washing so Carrie could defend herself, something she was perfectly capable of except when it came to mice. *Thank you, God, for mice.*

"How did I destroy Melnik, Tallulah?"

"By assassinating the character of our favorite son."

Nick thought that Wilkie had done a fair job of that without any help from Carrie.

Once Dora and Tallulah wound down and left, Nick and Carrie finished cleaning the kitchen. They headed up the stairs, Carrie clicking off lights behind them with a familiarity for the building that made Nick envious. The rest of the church was dark. As they got to the top of the murky basement steps, Donette stepped out of a dark corner.

Carrie squeaked. Not quite her mouse eek, but close.

"Thanks a lot, Carrie." Donette sneered the words. "You've taught me what it means to be a Christian."

Nick glanced at Carrie.

Carrie's eyes widened with regret. "I'm so sorry about that story. It wasn't supposed to end up in the paper."

"All you are is a nasty gossip. I don't want to be like you ever!" Donette whirled and shoved the door open.

Carrie ran after her. "Donette, wait. Please, let's talk about this."

A rust-bucket Pontiac was sitting in front of the church door, headlights blazing and motor running.

"Hurry up. I'm tired of waitin', babe." A man who must have been one of Wilkie's bum friends from the memorial service swung the passenger's side door open. When the dome light came on, Nick saw the guy leering at the very pregnant Donette. A cigarette hung from the corner of his mouth. Acid rock music, oldies from this guy's era, blared out of the radio.

Donette stalked straight for the car. Carrie ran after the girl. Donette reached for the handle just as Carrie caught her arm. Nick was close enough to see Donette's eyes brim with tears.

"Donette, don't leave. Be angry with me if you want, but don't blame my mistake on God. Talk to Pastor Bremmen." Carrie lowered her voice so Nick could barely hear. "Don't leave with this guy."

"If I don't want to spend the rest of my life alone" — Donette jerked free — "I'm going to have to put up with a few things I don't like."

The distraught girl climbed in. The car

tore out of the parking lot, spitting gravel.

Nick prayed for Donette as his heart broke for the defeated look in Carrie's eyes.

"She listened to me, Nick, when we talked about God. Letting that story get published wrecked her chance at finding Jesus."

He urged her toward his truck and helped her inside. "You can't take that on yourself. Donette has to make her own choices. And it was Gunderson, not you."

"I'm responsible. And I'd have caught that story if I wasn't such a coward."

He climbed in, released his parking brake, and started his truck, easing over the crunching gravel onto the dark road home. His headlights cut through the setting darkness. "Do not *ever* call yourself a coward again in my presence."

"Is this about my mouse phobia not being a sin?"

"It's about Donette, Tallulah, Rosie, Pastor Bremmen, the funeral committee, and everyone else in town."

"I know. I stood there and took it like a man." Carrie shoved her fingers into her hair, wrecking what little was left of her neat hairstyle. "I'm going to do some serious payback when I get my hands on Gunderson."

"Sneaking in there and switching the

stories late last night was so low, I just can't believe it." Nick pulled his car out onto the road. They were the last ones out of the church. He flicked on the heater as he drove. "Did you really look at what he wrote?"

Carrie nodded, crossing her arms over her seat belt. "Pure yellow journalism at its worst. And what really kills me is, he left *my* byline on it. I deliberately used a byline because I knew there would be trouble and I wanted it to land on me, not the paper. He could have put his name on that story, but noooo, there's my name, Carrie Evans, front and center. He did the whole thing at home, too. The font isn't right on the article. It doesn't match the rest of the paper.

"And he must have cut that picture off a wanted poster. Then he snuck in there, waxed it, and put it on the page. I already had the page packed up, so he had to hunt through the case and find it. What a jerk! And I didn't notice it because I didn't want to look at Maxie when I was inking the paper, so I skipped the front page. I'd have noticed that headline and picture if I'd so much as glanced at the paper."

"Why would Gunderson have a wanted poster on Wilkie?" Nick knew a lot of town gossip, but . . . "I've never heard of Wilkie being on the *run* from the law. If he had been, they might have hung one in the post office. But he'd been arrested. So it must have been a mug shot. Where would Gunderson get that? Would Junior have one? But Junior would have mentioned it if Gunderson had asked for one."

Carrie scowled at the scenery. "I can't decide if Gunderson has some grudge against Wilkie or if he's just got twisted ideas about the newspaper. Gunderson never should have included all that about Shayla and her confession. I can't believe Junior would tell him all that. I'm going to have a talk with Melnik's loose-lipped chief as soon as I'm done with Gunderson."

"When are you going to go after him?"

"Just as soon as I get out of this stupid dress." Carrie looked at Nick.

"No one in town has mentioned seeing him but you. He may not be that easy to find." Nick pulled up beside Carrie's house.

"He can't hide forever."

Rounding the truck, Nick opened her door before she could reach for it. She dug in her little black joke of a purse and found her keys. He took the keys and unlocked the outer door to the porch. He'd installed the sturdy lock without being asked. He

crossed the porch. Carrie followed, stomping until the floor shook.

"What's that for?"

"To scare the mice away."

Nick nodded. He banged long and hard
on the inner door with the side of his fist.
Glancing over his shoulder, he asked,
"Enough?"

Carrie smiled. "Yeah, thanks."

He unlocked the door, and Grizzly shot
past both of them to beat them inside.

Carrie sighed audibly. "If the stomping
and banging doesn't shoo them away, the
cat will."

Nick flicked on lights as he tramped
around the kitchen into the bathroom,
bedroom, and the living room. "You know,
this place is looking pretty good."

"Thanks for all the traps you've emptied."

Nick came back in from the living room
smiling. "Nice try. I'm not telling."

That growling noise Grizzly was famous
for came out of this cute little woman —
who needed his protection — since she was
all alone — late at night — with the man
she'd called a hero.

Say something, loser. Ask her out.

He'd almost kissed her earlier, and she
hadn't been running when they'd gotten
interrupted. Of course he was so clueless

about women he might not have noticed she was about to run. He took a step toward her, fully expecting to trip over a shoelace even though his shoes were slip-ons, or spill something on her even though there were no liquids within ten yards. She didn't back up. In fact she seemed to inch forward. So he'd invite himself to stay a while.

"I've got to go."

Idiot!

Her face fell. "Uh . . . okay, bye."

The good-bye kiss was a classic. Maybe that would be the right way to go. "I've got a full day of work planned for tomorrow." He stepped closer, no disaster yet. "Here at your place."

"With the paper out, I should be home for a change, although I've got a Community Club meeting tomorrow evening to cover for the *Bugle.*"

"I'll bet the *Bugle* work will keep you busy all the time."

"Yeah, there's a 4-H Club meeting on Friday afternoon and a Senior Citizen's fund-raising dinner on Saturday at noon. And there's a mission dinner at the Missouri Synod Lutheran Church after services on Sunday — plus the Catholics are having a Thanksgiving program on Sunday evening, and I need pictures. And I'm sure that

201

people are going to want to drop by and yell, so that will keep me occupied. I've also got to hunt down Gunderson and strangle him, and go have a nice, sharp talk with Junior for giving Gunderson that information and the picture. Plus, I think I ought to visit Shayla in jail, if she's still speaking to me, and try to find Donette and beg her forgiveness — and I'd like to take a casserole to Rosie. But aside from that, I want to spend the day going through the upper floors. To see what I've inherited." She shuddered. "Besides mice."

What Nick wouldn't give for a sword, a shield, and a year's supply of D-Con. "I can help you go through the upstairs if you want. Maybe you'll find some things that will give you a jump-start on Tallulah's book."

"And maybe if there are mice" — she twisted her fingers together and her voice got small and high-pitched — "you can scare them off for me?"

Nick nodded, finally close enough to touch her. *Please, God, make me cool. Give me some sweet talk. Give me some poise. Heal me of my dork gene.* But instead of reaching for her, he raised his hand and held out her keys.

"Thanks. I'll appreciate the help." She

lifted her hand palm up. He rested the keys on her fingers.

Help me say the right thing, Jesus.

He could think of nothing. He sighed, dropped the keys, and turned to go.

A mouse zipped out of the living room. Grizzly, a shaggy yellow blur, howled in hot pursuit.

In one split second Nick went from walking away empty-handed to holding an armful of warm, soft, clinging, shrieking woman. He looked down, and her eyes, scared, embarrassed, desperate, met his. God hadn't sent a *mouse,* had he? Because this sure seemed like an answer. But would God do such a thing? Would the heavenly Father use a mouse to get Nick a girlfriend? Did God think he was that pathetic?

The mouse seemed to be living proof that He did.

If God, in His infinite wisdom, did such a thing, it would be wrong of Nick not to respect the holy Lord's decision.

"Forgive me." Carrie seemed to be asking it of him, not God, this time.

Nick thought that was progress. "What did I tell you about being afraid of mice?" He hugged her closer.

"That God gave me this one flaw." Dejected, Carrie rested the side of her face against his shoulder.

She fit perfectly. She smelled like wax and ink and whatever wonderful thing she'd used on her hair. "Because you're so close to perfect."

She raised her head, her blue eyes glowing.

He lowered his head. She reached up and met him halfway. Maybe he'd said the right thing at last.

The kiss lasted only a moment. Nick pulled back and saw Carrie's eyes flutter open. Now he'd ask. Now he'd say, cool as Brad Pitt, "Carrie, would you like to have dinner with me?"

Of course she'll say yes. She wouldn't kiss me if she wasn't willing to have dinner with me. Surely a kiss was further along the relationship curve than dinner.

He knew just what to say. In his head, he was smooth, brilliant, and suave. "Would you like to . . ."

"Let me go!" Carrie pushed at him, struggling to get out of his arms.

"B-but, I didn't say anything stupid yet!" He must have a stupid vibe in addition to his stupid mouth. He let her go, suddenly feeling as if he were an attacker she wanted to escape.

Carrie charged toward her stairway.

"There's someone in my attic."

Nick heard the creaking overhead, realized what she'd said, turned, and ran after her. If there was a robber or a murderer up there, Carrie would probably be fine. But there might be mice.

15

The intruder dropped all efforts at stealth. Footsteps pounded overhead. Carrie's feet hammered as she raced upstairs with Nick trying to keep up. The attic door crashed open before she rounded the staircase landing.

Nick, just a step behind her, saw a pair of feet vanish to the left of the stairway. Another door slammed shut.

"He's in the Dead Zone." Carrie scrambled faster, Nick keeping pace.

Carrie raced for the door and slammed it open. A man dressed in black and wearing a black ski mask swung his leg over the window, an armload of papers clutched to his chest.

"You get back here!" Carrie took two running steps and launched herself at the man, knocking him into the window frame, and the two of them tumbled back into the room. The papers the burglar clutched went flying. The man grunted as he rolled sideways, scrambling, shoving at Carrie, knocking over a lineup of small fur-bearing creatures. Carrie wrestled with him, clawing at the ski mask.

Nick jumped into the fray as the man twisted loose from Carrie and rammed into the grizzly bear.

"Look out!" Carrie scrambled backward, knocking small animals aside as she dodged the falling behemoth. Nick leapt back just as the bear landed on the man, caging him, its extended paws on either side of the intruder's head and its gaping fangs stopping inches from his face.

Nick reached between the bear's teeth and the crook's face, snagged the ski mask, and yanked it free.

Deputy Hal froze.

Then he raised his hands like he was preparing to put his arms around the bear's neck and accept a big, toothy kiss. "Okay, I'm not running. You caught me."

Nick looked at Carrie and realized that her last-minute dive for safety had nearly buried her in dead animals. A raccoon perched on top of her head as if auditioning for a coonskin cap. She hoisted herself up, resting on her elbows. A mink, a badger, and an otter sat on her lap. A fox and a family of coyotes lay across her nylon-clad legs, and a baby fawn had tipped forward and rested its muzzle on her shoulder. It was almost like wearing a fur coat. Only icky.

He was also pretty sure he saw a couple of sharp teeth peeking out from under her backside. Carrie must have sat on a poor, dead predator.

Brushing all those long-dead remains aside with barely a glance, Carrie rose from the furry rubble. Nick wondered why those animals didn't scare her like Maxie the mouse did. He turned back to the trapped, defeated Hal.

The papers he'd been carrying were strewn across the floor. After thwarting the Cleaning Brigade Friday night, Carrie had let them have at the Dead Zone on Monday. It was clean enough that, except for a few neglected corners, the papers were all that was scattered. If you didn't count the corpses.

Carrie rose to her feet shedding fur like a mammal in the spring. "What are you doing in my house, Hal?"

Nick noticed a wolverine peeking around Carrie's waist, its teeth sunk into her dress, hanging from her . . . self. He quickly plucked it loose. Carrie never took her eyes off Hal.

"I admit it." Hal looked up, his expression as sick with fear as if the bear had growled at him. "I killed Wilkie."

He lowered his hands, twisted his head sideways, and buried his face in his palms, his shoulders trembling. "Just call Junior and get him over here."

"Go call." Carrie glanced over her shoulder at Nick.

The only phone was downstairs. Nick had a cell phone, but it didn't get a good signal in Melnik. And Nick wasn't leaving her up here alone with her second confessed murderer of the week.

"What possible motive could you have for killing Wilkie?" Carrie asked.

Hal clenched his fists and looked up. "He killed your great-grandma."

Carrie gasped. "You saw him?"

"I saw him standing over her body holding a skillet. When I saw what that lousy scumball had done, I just lost it. I grabbed him, and we struggled. I started out planning to arrest him, but while we were fighting, I remembered all he'd done to my mom."

"Your mom?" Carrie dusted away the mink fur that had shed onto her dress.

Hal ignored her, the better to continue confessing. Nick wondered where Carrie got this gift. The woman could give pointers to a priest.

"I saw your defenseless grandma laying there, dead. I — I wrestled the frying pan away from him and just hit him. Hard. Once. That's all it took. He collapsed onto the floor right next to Bea." Hal began pushing at the bear gingerly. Nick bent down to help, and Carrie chipped in, grabbing a fistful of fur. They managed to free the deputy from his bearskin prison. "Your great-grandma was already dead, Carrie. I checked. I'd have saved her if I could. But I couldn't help her, and I hated him enough that I hit him harder than I should. I'm guilty."

Hal rolled onto his knees and stood, his eyes locked on the floor. "Just go call. I'm not running anywhere. Get it over with."

Nick remembered Shayla locking herself in a cell and wondered if they could just send Hal over to the jail to turn himself in. Even the murderers in Melnik were a polite bunch.

"Uh . . . did you put him in the kitchen pantry?" Carrie asked.

Hal looked up, surprised. He obviously hadn't thought of that. "No."

"Did you, at any time, try to smother him with a mouse?" Nick tossed that question in but regretted it when Carrie shuddered.

Hal's lips curled in horror. "Hey, I may be a murderer, but I'm not gonna do anything as creepy as *that.* I'd never touch a mouse. I hate mice."

Carrie straightened, and her expression lightened. "Really?"

"Oh, yeah. It's something I can't control."

"I know."

"It's so stupid. I hate myself for it."

"I know."

"It's a phobia."

"I know."

Nick interrupted before they exchanged Facebook names. "I don't think you're guilty, Hal. Wilkie may have regained consciousness and hid in that closet, or someone may have come in and finished him off." With the mouse. Nick knew better than to say that out loud. "And then stuffed him in the pantry. But either way, the autopsy hasn't confirmed that he died of a blow to the head." Nick remembered the gunshot wound and definitely decided to create an Excel spreadsheet when he got home to keep track of the possible causes of death.

"I saw the autopsy," Hal said. "I know it's not settled, but it'll turn out to be me. Wilkie might have been wounded, and he might even have come around after I whacked him, but I know that blow to the head at least contributed to his death. I killed him. I *know* it!"

"You don't know it," Nick said. "I'm pretty sure it'll turn out to be something else."

"Really?" Hal perked up. "Uh, can I go then?"

"No!" Carrie and Nick spoke at the same instant.

"So what were you doing in here tonight?" Carrie crossed her arms, looking like a stern mother, even though Hal was probably older than her.

Hal shoved his hands into his back pockets and scuffed one toe on the floor. "Sorry about the breaking and entering. I . . . uh . . . I thought I'd maybe left a clue behind or something."

Since the whole town had spent two days cleaning this house, Hal included, Nick very much doubted Hal was worried about dropping an incriminating matchbook. Nick wondered what the guy really wanted. He also wondered how Hal happened to be here to find Wilkie standing over Bea. Maybe they'd find out when they went through the papers he'd been carrying. "*Sorry* is not going to cut it. We're still going to have to call Junior."

"I thought you said I probably didn't kill him." Hal scowled at Nick. "And anyway, I didn't mean to kill Dad, exactly. But I sure meant to belt him with that skillet. I'll gladly confess to that."

Carrie's jaw dropped open. "Did you just say Wilkie is your dad?"

Nick rubbed his still-puffy forehead. "That Maxie Mouse float they've got planned to carry Wilkie's family?"

Carrie looked away from Hal. "Yeah, what about it?"

Nick started mentally sketching out alterations. "It's going to need a sidecar."

16

"I can't believe Junior isn't going to charge him with breaking into my house." Coffee sloshed over the rim of Nick's cup when Carrie smacked it down on the table in front of him.

He didn't complain.

He was too afraid.

"Well, there is the murder charge." Nick had shown up early, determined to work quietly outside Carrie's house. He'd let her sleep in but be close if she needed him. He'd listened for *eeek*.

No eeks, but she had eventually come out and invited him in for coffee. He was pretty sure that meant she didn't consider him a stalker.

"Yeah, but the murder charge is weak, and you know it. He's claiming self-defense, even that Wilkie resisted arrest. Hal should have been arrested for burglary. That, we *know* he did."

"At least he's locked up." Nick mopped up the spilled coffee with his own handkerchief. He hated messes. "He won't be breaking in here, at least for a while."

Carrie looked up from her cup as she stirred in a spoonful of sugar. "Shayla was flirting with him through the bars until Junior told her that Hal was her long-lost brother."

I'd like to flirt with you. No, don't say that. If Nick lived to be one hundred and three, he'd still always be a fat, awkward, nine-year-old brainiac who got bullied every day at recess.

"And what's Shayla still doing there, anyway?"

"You heard Junior say that she won't leave." Nick sipped at his coffee. "What's he supposed to do? The door was standing open when we got there. Like he's hoping she'll wander out and he can slam the door quick with her on the outside."

"She doesn't have anywhere to go." Carrie lifted the cup for a sip but set it back down with a sharp click. "And Junior arrested Hal but he didn't *fire him.* If they call what Wilkie did resisting arrest, Hal may get a commendation."

"Too bad about that confession." Nick hoped he didn't slip up and confess all the stupid thoughts that rattled around in his head. Carrie had a way about her, so he'd have to be on his toes. "I bet Hal's kicking himself for that now."

"I think the bear scared it out of him." The woman who would let a mouse scare her into anything shook her head in disbelief. "Hal could be awarded right there in the cell."

Discussing their kiss over a cup of coffee would have been way more fun than talking about Hal. But, ohh, no. "People don't get fired all that easily in Melnik. I've noticed that."

"And then, when I threatened to press charges for burglary, Junior went all 'You're just like your great-grandma' on me. How am I supposed to respond to that, huh?"

It really had backed her down. Nick decided it was the perfect threat. *You know, your great-grandma hated me. You don't want to be just like her, now, do you?*

"And what was Hal after, anyway? I need to go through those papers he left and the ones I got away from Tallulah and everything else on the upper floors. I need to do it right now, today, before anyone else comes. Someone else may have *already* come. I may have missed out on clues that would give us a motive for murder because

216

I'm so . . . so stupid . . . so afraid . . ." Carrie looked up from the cup she hung on to for dear life.

Nick's heart turned over. She wanted to be strong. She wanted to be completely self-sufficient. She wanted to wade in and investigate patricide and burglary and trespassing and not talk about important stuff like kissing. In fact, right now, as her knuckles turned white and she braced herself to ask for his bodyguard services, it was only nasty little rodents keeping him in her life.

God, it wouldn't be sacrilegious to stop by the Maxie shrine just to say thanks, would it?

She got up from the table, tiptoed across the kitchen to the coffeemaker as if the mice were floodwater that was coming up around her ankles, and poured herself another steaming, rich-smelling cup. The aroma almost covered up the years of musty neglect, overridden with Pine Sol and Lemon Pledge — the Melnik ladies' weapons of choice in their war on grime. And by *almost* Nick meant *not at all.* The place smelled terrible. But it was better than before.

She turned with the pot in her hands. "Want more?"

"Not yet, thanks."

She replaced the carafe and tiptoed back.

He noticed she sat facing the pantry. Her feet were below the table, but he could hear her twisting them around the chair rungs to get them off the floor, and she glanced at the pantry door compulsively, watching for mice. Like they didn't come from all directions. The woman had denial down to a science.

"I tried to call Gunderson last night and again this morning. All I've got on him is his father's phone number."

"He'll turn up." Because he couldn't stand to watch her try to be brave a second longer, he offered what she was too ashamed to ask for. "I don't have any pressing work. I'd be glad to take a day off and sift through the upstairs with you."

Carrie's shoulders slumped on an audible sigh of relief. "Thank God, uh . . . I mean, good, thank you, and God, too . . . uh, I mean, okay. When can you start?"

Nick saw a mouse skitter along the wall behind Carrie's back, and he was very, very careful not to react. It vanished under her refrigerator, only about three steps behind Carrie's chair. If it kept coming her way, maybe he could get his hands on her again. But that seemed so low-down.

"Right now sounds great. Let's go."

He scraped his chair backward, making a

racket to scare off the rodent invader. Carrie arched one of her pretty blond brows. Great. He'd acted like a clumsy dork instead of mentioning the mouse. Why not mention it? Why not get her to jump again? Maybe he could reenact last night. Maybe this time no intruder would interrupt him before he could say, "Would you like to have dinner with me?"

Help me, God. Please un-dork me now. I've suffered long enough. The people near me have suffered long enough.

Carrie refilled their cups. Nick saw the mouse slip under the pantry door. He had five traps in that area alone. He was almost sorry that God had seen fit to keep Carrie focused on the burning liquid she was dispensing. Except for third-degree burns for both of them when she jumped into his arms with two blazing-hot cups of coffee, he'd enjoy getting ahold of her. He took his cup and followed Carrie upstairs.

They paused to grab the papers Carrie had taken back from Tallulah and Hal that she'd hidden under a trumpeter swan, species *Cygnus buccinators,* kingdom Animalia, Phylum Chordate, class Aves, order Anseriformes, family Anatidea, genus Cygnus.

Nick, thanks to the semester he spent studying endangered species when he wanted to try to save the planet, had memorized that and a thousand other useless facts that he now couldn't forget. He still wanted the planet to be saved; he just decided he'd repair woodwork until someone came up with a good idea first.

Grizzly climbed the steps, moving with heavy, plodding footsteps that didn't become a feline. Nick wondered if the cat had actually nailed a mouse yet. Carrie took the papers out of the Dead Zone and closed the door.

"Let's keep Grizzly out of there. Those poor animals have suffered enough."

Somehow that seemed like Nick's fault, too.

Carrie perched herself on the top step and began sorting through the papers. There really was no place for Nick to sit other than right beside her. And the steps weren't all that wide.

She shoved half the papers into his hands. "These look like legal documents." She tapped on the top paper she held in her lap.

"This is the deed to this house." With a soft crinkle of yellowed paper, she flipped to the next one.

"Wow." Nick was instantly fascinated by what he held. "This is the layout of the house. I wonder if there's a blueprint somewhere. Chances are, there isn't. Back then a builder like your great-grand-father . . ." He paused and looked at her. "Or was it your great-great-grandfather?"

Carrie grinned. "Two greats at least. The Evanses built this for my great-grandpa's parents. Great-Grandma moved in when they were married and lived here with her in-laws and some of their children because Great-Grandma Bea had younger brothers and sisters. Then the two of them had kids. This house used to be bursting at the seams with people. It's a shame it's such a huge, empty hulk now."

It was a shame. A crying shame. You should marry me. We could fill it with kids.

Nick shook his head to clear it and started looking at the papers she'd handed him. He focused on them quickly before he jammed his size twelve steel-toed Red Wings right in his stupid mouth.

"This is a copy of . . ." Nick fished in the inside pocket of his black Windbreaker for his glasses and shoved them on to make sure he was reading it right.

"You wear glasses?" Carrie stared.

Nick flinched. *Nick the Wonder-Dork.* Might as well admit the whole truth. "Yeah. I used to have these really thick glasses all the time. I had LASIK surgery so I wouldn't

221

need them, but now for really fine print I have to have reading glasses."

"Tortoiseshell rims?"

Nick shrugged. He hadn't thought much about the rims. They'd just felt good on his face.

"I like them." She seemed to be studying the glasses closely.

She was just being polite. Since glasses had been the bane of Nick's existence all through childhood, he could only imagine how stupid she thought he looked. Or worse yet — how smart.

To make her quit staring, he shook the paper. "Now why would your great-grandma have a copy of the last will and testament of Rudolph Melnik?"

"What?" Carrie looked away from him.

Nick breathed a sigh of relief.

She grabbed the paper out of Nick's hand and stared at it.

LAST WILL AND TESTAMENT — in bold writing across the top of an oversized piece of parchment paper. The words, written in heavy ink, possibly with a quill pen, swirled as elaborately as if this were the Declaration of Independence.

Below those words in smaller but equally elegant cursive: RUDOLPH MELNIK.

Then Carrie looked up at Nick with wide,

suspicious eyes. "Do you think this is what Hal could have been searching for? Did he somehow think there was a way to claim the property because he was related to Wilkie?"

Nick shrugged one shoulder. "I don't see how. Whatever Rudolph Melnik . . . where does he fit into this mess, anyway?"

"He's the son of the first founder. Rudolph was the one who consolidated the family's wealth. He bought property and worked like a fiend getting rich."

"Fiend, huh?" Nick curled his mouth into a grimace. "That just an expression?"

"Great-Grandma Bea knew him. 'Worked like a fiend' were her words exactly. Great-Grandma said he'd have worn a crown if he thought he could get away with it. She said he thought he deserved to own the whole town. The Melniks donated a fair share of Main Street to the city in order to get the town named after them."

"But regardless of what Rudolph had, the generations that followed lost everything."

"A lot of it to Gundersons. They now own a good chunk of the old Melnik family holdings."

"How'd that happen?"

"Wilkie was the lowest the Melniks sank. But each generation seemed to be a little more interested in lazing around. A few get-rich-quick schemes and way too much time with a whiskey bottle frittered away the family fortune."

"So what difference does a . . ." Nick pulled the paper around so he could see it. "Fifty-year-old will have?"

Carrie shook her head. "Beats me. This is from the stack that Tallulah had. What does she want it for?"

"Just for the historical record, maybe. It probably should be in the Maxie Museum."

Carrie snorted. "It's the Melnik Historical Society Museum. It's about more than Maxie."

"From what I've heard, Carrie, it's mostly about Maxie."

Carrie nodded and rubbed her head as if it ached. "You know these probably all belong in the museum."

"Right next to Maxie?"

Carrie glared at him through narrowed eyes. "Don't even suggest it. What I wonder is, would they like this will to be kept there? I should go over and show it to Bonnie."

Nick flinched. "I forgot to apologize to her. I need to do that. If you want, I'll go and show it to her, apologize, and scope out any other historical papers that might help us find some answers."

"Well, I'm not ready to hand them over yet, but you can look around the museum and ask Bonnie if the historical society might want these papers."

"Okay, I'll handle it."

Further examination of the stack that Hal and Tallulah had gathered amounted to yellowed newspaper clippings, including the momentous announcement that Maxie had been admitted to the Guinness Book of World Records.

"It was exactly fifty years ago this December." Carrie studied the story. "They featured Maxie in the Melnik Community Christmas Pageant that very year. No one took it too seriously. Grandpa Leonard said it was just for fun, a no-big-deal claim to fame."

As they set the papers aside, Nick, his hands so grimy he could barely stand it, said, "The rest of the second floor is pretty well cleaned by now."

"If you don't count those flea-bitten dead animals."

"You know, those could actually be worth some money. You want me to list them on eBay and see what happens?"

Carrie's eyes lit up. "You think I can convert those disgusting beasties to cash? Really?"

"We won't know unless we try."

"Well, okay." Carrie turned and glared at the Dead Zone door. "I'd part with them for the cost of shipping, so don't play hardball if you get any bids."

Nick laughed. "Your mom and grandma and the other ladies saw to this floor. But they haven't touched the third floor. I think we have to turn our attention there if we want to uncover anything really old." Nick looked up the narrow stairs, a funnel leading them straight to Mouse Heaven. Except he suspected that Carrie would die before she admitted there could be mice in heaven.

He felt Carrie tremble. "There's an attic, too, above the third floor."

"What a great house. I'll go first." He would have rubbed her back to comfort her if his hands had been clean.

"Let's just get it over with." Her head hanging, she plodded toward the stairway as if her feet weighed one hundred pounds each.

17

"Forgive me." Carrie clung to Nick's neck, feeling like a fool.

"I'm starved." Nick held Carrie in his arms.

"Let's quit." Carrie smiled, although she kept her eyes fixed on the stunningly neat piles of paper Nick had lined up on the floor. She'd seen about fifty mice today and she'd spent a good part of the day jumping and screaming. She just hoped she'd seen the same mouse fifty times, rather than seeing fifty mice. And heaven only knew where Grizzly had gotten.

"You know, I just used to scream. This jumping into a man's arms thing is new."

"I'm glad I can help." Nick scanned the floor then sat her down next to one of the stacks of interesting papers they'd found.

He'd been a perfect gentleman, and Carrie liked perfect gentlemen. She did. She especially liked gentlemen who wore tortoiseshell glasses. She'd just found that out about herself today.

But there might be some room in the perfect gentleman's handbook for a very polite kiss shared with the woman he'd spent a large part of the day holding. Especially since she hadn't exactly fought him off the other time he'd kissed her.

Oh, wait. She had kind of fought him off. Hal's fault. Maybe she should make sure he hadn't taken that personally. She looked deep into his eyes. He looked so gorgeous in those glasses. "Nick . . ."

Nick's arms didn't slip away like they had the other forty-nine times. Instead, he turned her to face him. Pulled her closer. "Would you like to . . ."

"Carrie Evans!"

Carrie dropped her forehead against Nick's strong chest. The stack of papers at Carrie's feet slid sideways, knocked over by the booming sound waves coming from below. Carrie gasped as they slid dangerously close to the box of Christmas ornaments they'd found. All she'd seen was dust-laden junk. Nick assured her that, once cleaned, the delicate glass baubles would be spectacular. He'd promised to chop down a pine tree and help her decorate for Christmas.

The sliding pile missed the ornaments, which was lucky because Tallulah was here, which left no time to pay attention to anything else.

Footsteps stomped upward. So much for knocking.

"We could hide," Nick offered.

"She'd just go through my stuff." Carrie spoke into his perfect green knit shirt, the logo in place, the fresh smell of laundry detergent still there even after a day in the grime. She sniffed quietly so he wouldn't notice. "There's no escape for us."

"We're up here, Tallulah."

After Nick hollered, Carrie sighed.

Nick patted her on the back. "I wonder what took her so long."

"It's Thursday." Carrie straightened. No sense putting off the inevitable. "Everybody knows that Tallulah drives to her sister's house in Bjorn to get her hair done on Thursdays. Her sister's a beautician. They have lunch and go visit their mother in the Bjorn Elderhostel all afternoon."

"Elderhostel? What is that?"

"The nursing home. Bjorn is the Swedish capital of Nebraska."

"I noticed. They're eyeball deep in Dala horses over there."

"Yeah, you can't move in Bjorn without

tripping over a lutefisk and falling into a bowl of muesli."

"As opposed to Melnik where you can't move without tripping over a . . ."

Carrie slapped him on the chest. "Don't say it!"

"I'm warning you, Carrie. I have pull in this town." Tallulah sounded like she'd gained the second floor and was heading on up, wheezing but determined. "I can make or break that newspaper with a snap of my fingers."

Nick's eyebrows arched. "True?"

"Nope. She's not even from Melnik."

"She moved here recently?"

"Yeah, she and her husband moved here in a snit from Bjorn when Bjorn's fire department didn't put out the fire in their garage fast enough to suit them."

"But she's not married, is she? I've never seen her with her husband."

"He died the year we celebrated Maxie's fortieth anniversary. I remember because I think Tallulah threw herself into that and created the historical society out of grief."

"Ten years? And they lived here how long before that?"

"Oh, twenty years or so."

"And you say she moved here recently? Thirty years ago is recently?"

"Well, yeah. I mean, her roots aren't here."

Nick's whole face just fell.

"What?" Carrie tried to think what Tallulah moving here from Bjorn could possibly mean to him.

"I'm never going to belong."

"Sure you are." *The poor sweet dummy. Why would anyone want to belong in Melnik?* It did occur to Carrie that maybe she wasn't a good judge of that since she, of all people, belonged up to her eyeballs. "Tallulah belongs . . ."

"You're darn right I belong!" Tallulah's vibrant pink turban broke the plane of the stairway opening.

Belongs in a loony bin.

Tallulah's mouth and the caftan of the day followed quickly behind the turban.

Nick leaned forward just a bit. "She got her hair done? Why?"

Carrie fought back a giggle. "Hi, Tallulah. Didn't like the article about Maxie or Wilkie in the *Bugle* yesterday, huh? And you didn't quite feel you'd made yourself clear after the funeral?"

That set Tallulah off. By the time she quit ranting, Carrie felt like her ear had been chewed off. The whole town was ruined. The governor would never come — *like there was a ever a chance that he would —*

231

and Tallulah's lifework was destroyed by a flick of Carrie's poisoned pen.

Carrie kind of liked the way that rolled off Tallulah's tongue. The woman had a bit of poetry in her obsessive-compulsive soul.

A lightbulb went on in Carrie's head. She snapped her fingers. "I'll tell you what, Tallulah. Why don't you start writing a column for the *Bugle*?"

Tallulah fell silent. *Thank you, God, for minor miracles.* Although *minor* might be an understatement. Parting the Red Sea was one thing, but making Tallulah be quiet, well, that was heavy duty.

Tallulah stood stone still, although Carrie thought the turban vibrated a bit.

Tallulah's shock passed, and she flung her arms wide. "I'll do it!"

Big surprise. Carrie nodded, accepting that she'd opened her mouth and now had to live with the results of having a foot inserted. Why not let Tallulah rave about wonderful Maxie from now until the festival? It'd save Carrie having to give the disgusting rodent much thought.

Tallulah clasped her hands in front of her with a loud clap. "Finally, someone who fully understands the true greatness of Melnik will have a hand in reporting the news."

"You can write an article a week, do a big buildup for the festival. Then after that, if you're still interested, you can write a column focusing on the town's history in any way you see fit. Or you can put in a report of the Historical Society's meetings, if you want. Just send in the minutes of the last meeting. Whatever you think is appropriate."

Carrie knew, way down deep inside, that Tallulah's definition of appropriate and Carrie's definition of appropriate were two very different things. Carrie made a mental note to put Tallulah's byline in big letters.

Tallulah went off on another outburst, this one overjoyed. Carrie tuned the woman out so thoroughly she barely registered Nick saying, "No, we're going to handle that."

"But if I'm writing about Melnik history, all these papers would give me a wealth of information. They would be in far better hands."

Tallulah trying to get her hands on Great-Grandma's stuff again. What is going on?

Tallulah might have harassed Great-Grandma this same way, not that Great-Grandma harassed worth a hoot, what with that cast-iron skillet handy. Tallulah couldn't have anything to do with Bea's death, could she? She wouldn't have, for example, sent

Wilkie, her favorite Melnikite, in here hunting around, which resulted in Great-Grandma confronting Wilkie, possibly with that blasted skillet in her hand. Which Wilkie took away from her and . . .

Carrie narrowed her eyes and studied the flamboyant woman. Was she obsessed to a degree that crossed over to dangerous? Would Tallulah have sent in Wilkie? Then, when Bea ended up dead, would Tallulah be treacherous enough to keep quiet about her part in it? Could Tallulah have been here? Might Wilkie, stunned from Hal's bonk on the head and maybe dopey from Shayla's antifreeze, have called the lady who sent him and asked for help?

Someone had smothered Wilkie, and Maxie Mouse had almost certainly been involved. Who better to have access to Maxie than Tallulah, the mouse-obsessed historian? Carrie would bet anything she had keys to both the museum and Maxie's cage.

Maybe. And maybe — instead of journalism — I should try fiction. A cozy mystery, maybe, about a town full of crazy people planning to spend Christmas worshipping a mouse instead of the baby Jesus.

Nah, who'd believe it?

"Of course you could go through them.

They'd still be yours, Carrie. You know, these should be in the museum. We could . . ."

"Not now, Tallulah." Carrie held up her hand. "*I'm* going to go through these things. I promise to be careful and treat them respectfully. But they're mine. I decide what I share with the world. Chances are, it'll be everything. But I decide. That's final."

Tallulah's face darkened with anger until it was hard to see where the fuchsia turban stopped and her skin began. "Well, I never!" She turned and marched down the stairs in a huff.

Carrie tried to imagine anything Tallulah had never!

She stood next to Nick, listening to the pounding footsteps. It sounded like the residents of the Dead Zone had come to life and were thundering down the steps, making their break after fifty years of captivity.

Oh, if only they would.

The back door slammed so hard that the attic windows rattled.

Carrie heard a loud grunt from outside. She whirled and ran to the window. Nick came up beside her, and they watched Tallulah lean over the edge of the Dumpster. Nick had phoned the city and had it delivered midmorning after his tenth trip up and down the stairs. He hadn't asked or Carrie would have told him she couldn't afford it. He said he paid for it out of Grandpa Leonard's thousand dollars because of all the building debris. It now sat below this open window so they could drop bags of garbage down into it and save the trips up and down the stairs.

"It's all just old clothes and empty packing boxes, Tallulah," Carrie yelled. "I promise I haven't thrown anything important away."

Tallulah looked up so far that her turban fell off.

Carrie flinched. Tallulah was mostly bald. Tallulah gasped, scrambling after her rolling turban. She retrieved it, shoved it back on, and scuttled away.

"That poor woman."

"You're sure she's a woman?" Nick asked. "That looked like male pattern baldness to me."

Carrie gasped. "Well, uh, yes. Why would you even think of such a thing?"

"Probably too much big city. You get so you've seen everything."

"No, I know she's got children. I know she had a husband."

Nick shrugged. "She sure yells like a woman."

Carrie smacked him.

Nick laughed. "Let's go wash up and eat something. I'm starving. Jansson's has tacos on Thursday nights."

"I hadn't heard that."

"Really?" Nick turned to her. "I thought everybody knew."

"Wow, clash with the smorgasbord." Carrie wondered if this counted as a date. She'd been wishing he'd ask her. She thought he'd come close a couple of times.

"Not really. They put lingonberries in the picante sauce. But it's drowned out by the jalapeno peppers, so it's okay."

Carrie shuddered. "Well, bless Olga Jansson for innovating. If this were Bjorn, she'd probably stick with strictly Swedish fare, but we can go a little nuts here in Melnik."

"I noticed." Nick picked up three-fourths of the stacks of papers they were keeping, and Carrie got the rest. They headed downstairs. "Where are we going to hide these so Tallulah or Hal or anybody else who might come snooping around doesn't find them?"

"There's really only one place I can think of that's completely safe."

"The Dead Zone again?" Nick stopped on the second floor.

Carrie kept going down. "Nope. Nowhere in there big enough, and the whole two lower stories are too clean. They'd be too easy to find."

Nick fell in behind. "Then where?"

Carrie felt the shuddering start in her belly and spread out to her limbs, her brain, her very soul. She moved quickly down the stairs, afraid she'd get clumsy with terror very soon. "The basement."

"Sounds good." Nick followed closely, sounding casual. He just didn't know.

"Sounds awful!"

"Why?"

"Because my great-grandma's basement is Mouse Ground Zero in the mouse capital of Nebraska."

18

He'd worked up the nerve to ask her out for dinner. It didn't really count because they were filthy and starving and no one had said the word *date* before or during their meal. It would have been hard to say a word of any kind since the good folks of Melnik all but stood in line to tell Carrie they were shocked, *shocked,* at her treatment of poor dead Wilkie.

By the end of the meal, when she never shirked from taking all the blame on herself, he was more impressed with Carrie's honor than ever.

Of course, word had gotten out — thanks to Nick's big mouth — that Gunderson had done it, but Carrie deflected all criticism of Gunderson, taking the whole load of blame on herself. Still, everyone knew the truth.

Once they were clear of Jansson's smorgasbord, Carrie quit being such a good sport. "I can't believe all those people yelled at me like that!"

Nick tried to lend moral support, but when he pictured himself hugging her, there was too much selfishness in it. "Give them a week. They'll get over it."

"Oh, they will not. They'll still be talking about this on Maxie's *Centennial* Festival, for heaven's sake. Are you kidding? They'll still be talking about Edith typing Stu Piperson's name as *Stupid Person*. No way will they forget a fiasco like my Wilkie story."

"Well, that's probably right." Okay, could he be any wimpier? "I mean, they'll move on. Yes, they'll remember, but it won't matter and . . ." So the hug was selfish. So what?

Just slip your arm over her shoulder. Classic junior-high move. She won't care a bit. She needs a white knight. Have-Mousetraps-Will-Travel. After all, I'm here, she's here . . .

He reached for her shoulder.

"I have to get out of here."

Nick dropped his arm to his side, hoping she hadn't noticed his clumsy move. He had no intention of ever leaving this charming village.

"That's why I'll never settle back in this lame little backwater."

His heart dropped as fast as his arm. He wanted roots. He wanted a small town where people knew him. Carrie was not a match for his dreams. But she was so cute and sweet and smart and funny and *cute*. Maybe if she knew he had enough money to travel a lot — thanks to the consulting he still did with his Chicago engineering firm — she'd be okay in Melnik. But trying to convince her to stay by quoting his bank balance was so bad, even a dope like Nick knew it was wrong. He felt sure God was ready with a lightning bolt if Nick had any second thoughts on the subject.

"It will pass. You're a good writer. You'll know to check up on the paper now, so it won't happen again. The *Bugle* could be a great choice for you. The writing would be personal. You could try everything: news, features, columns, advertising. It's what a newspaper is meant to be — someone's vision, someone's voice." Mr. Pep Talk. "You could make a great career at the *Bugle*." Nick's heart stirred. He could almost hear "Yankee Doodle Dandy" in the distance. He was almost eloquent, almost a poet. Why, running the *Bugle* was her patriotic duty.

"Running the *Bugle* is a waste of my life!"

Carrie apparently preferred to rant. When they got to her house, he scouted for mice — none — too bad — so no leaps into his arms. Nick paused in his fretting. What if the mice moved out? She wouldn't need him anymore.

He turned into a tongue-tied coward — or rather, he turned into himself. He left her without asking for another date or another kiss.

Dope!

For the rest of the week, Nick worked on Carrie's house, loving every minute of coaxing the grand old mansion back to life and hoping she'd come out and ask for protection. She rushed in and out, giving him updates on news stories and the search for Gunderson. He never saw her for more than "hi" and "good-bye."

Even Sunday morning at church he couldn't catch up with her. He picked a pew at church with plenty of room so that maybe Carrie would come in and sit next to him, but Dora got there ahead of her and plunked down beside him. Now, thanks to Dora, he had ten new personal hygiene–goals laid out in front of him. He also agreed to repair the cemetery fence, keep the sidewalks scooped this winter — he'd already done the lawn work all summer, so why not — and donate gravel for the parking lot.

When he caught up with Carrie after church, he said, "Wait'll you hear what they're going to let me do. I think I'm really starting to fit in here." Nick recited his list.

Carrie scowled. "They roped me into the funeral committee, the decorating committee, the cleaning committee, the choir, and teaching Sunday school."

"Wow, that's great. The town must be excited to have you home."

"They saw a sucker, just like with you. They're trying to dump every bit of work on the 'new guys.' "

"But you said yes, right?"

"Right. But it's no big deal for me. I'm not going to be here that long." Carrie patted him on the shoulder. "Bye." She joined her parents and grandparents. Nick overheard Carrie's grandma Helga invite everyone for lunch. Everyone in the family. Not him.

Dejected, Nick climbed into his pickup and went home alone to the little house he'd bought when he moved to town. It wasn't his dream house, not by a long shot. But it was old with pretty details. It needed him.

He did hang around Carrie's house later to make sure that Carrie got inside without incident, but no mice gave him an opening to sneak in another kiss. Which just made him the most pathetic human being who ever lived — that he needed a mouse to make that happen.

As he let himself out of her house Sunday night, he wondered if the day would ever come when he could kill off his inner overweight, nerdy bookworm.

And then it was Monday, and the *Bugle* monopolized every minute of her time. By Tuesday morning, desperate to have something Carrie needed him for, he decided to go apologize to Marian/Bonnie and find out if the museum wanted Carrie's old papers.

Nick gathered the papers into a file folder and drove to the Main Street building that now housed the Melnik Historical Society Museum. A very grand name for a fish tank containing a really large mouse. It shared an entrance with the City Hall. And right in the entrance stood the Maxie Mouse Monument. Someone had done some landscaping, and Nick saw that Maxie had some fake shrubs and a few bright colored rocks in his aquarium house.

The Melnik city hall boasted an entry area, about twenty by ten feet and had five doors: the city offices and two bathrooms on the left, the museum on the right, and straight ahead, a door to a large auditorium.

The Maxie Monument stood in all its verminy glory. Nick had done a considerable amount of business with the city office, applying for building permits and checking underground power and phone lines. But he'd never gone into the museum. Today, historic paperwork in hand, he tucked his folder under his arm and pushed on the chipped beige door labeled MELNIK HISTORICAL SOCIETY MUSEUM.

He fell in love.

It wasn't pretty or welcoming. It was just books. Oh, there were little displays, too. Old toys and rusty tools from a bygone era. Some slightly bent street signs, a few dozen replicas of Maxie on coffee mugs and stationery, and a few stuffed Maxies. There were also postcards of Maxie for sale. But mostly it was books. He took a deep breath and smelled books. The smell took him back to his childhood. Books and libraries, the refuge of the brainy dweeb.

The small Melnik museum was overwhelmed by ceiling-high shelves laden with books. The lights weren't bright enough to cut through the gloom. An aisle barely wide enough for Nick's shoulders led him to a little desk, with Bonnie "Marian the Librarian" Simpson, sitting quietly, reading a dogeared copy of *Les Misérables*.

She looked up, startled, as if no one had ever come in before. Nick wondered how close to true that was.

"Victor Hugo." He smiled at the memory of the sanctuary that books had been in his childhood. "My favorite. I read that book so many times when I was a kid, I could recite whole passages."

"I like *The Hunchback of Notre Dame* better."

"You identified with Esmeralda?" Nick couldn't see that. Bonnie was a quiet, sweet woman, not given to flashiness ala Esmeralda.

"Nope, I'm more the Quasimodo type."

Nick laughed. Even in the murky museum, Nick could see Bonnie blush, as if she'd never spoken so boldly in her life.

"For me it was more *The Count of Monte Cristo.*"

"Alexandre Dumas?" Bonnie nodded. "Revenge. One of my favorites."

"Yeah." Nick laughed. "Hey, I'm sorry I've been calling you Marian all this time. I thought . . ."

"Dora."

Nick nodded. "I apologize. It was the only thing I heard you called, and you answered to it."

Bonnie smiled, and Nick saw that behind the glasses and the plain dark blond hair scraped into a ponytail at her nape, she was a very pretty woman. Probably midforties.

"Well, who's going to fight with Dora over nicknames?"

"I haven't gotten one yet, but I'm new in town."

"So, you read the classics?" Bonnie lifted a bookmark off her desk and slid it in place. No folding over corners to mark her spot. No laying the book facedown on the desk. She didn't even stick her thumb in her place and hang onto it. She set the book down perfectly square with the desk. Besides the book, the desk held a small ceramic turkey wearing a pilgrim hat, its tail feathers spread and colored rich orange and red and yellow, a perfect Thanksgiving touch.

"I read everything."

"How come you haven't come in before?" Bonnie slid her glasses into a beige case and then looked around the dingy museum as if she were sitting in the very center of heaven.

"I knew it was the museum, but I never heard about the books. I'll be back."

Bonnie smiled. "Did you need something today, or did you just come in because Carrie told you my real name and you wanted to apologize?"

"I have some old papers here." Nick lifted the manila folder of documents and clippings. "Things that might be of historical interest to the town. They were among Carrie's great-grandmother's things, and she says that if you want them, she'd probably donate them. You could cross-check and see if you already have copies."

Bonnie's eyes lit up as if Nick had brought old Hugo back to life and brought him in for a book signing.

"I'd be glad to help." Bonnie rose from the desk.

"Really?"

"What, you think I look too busy?" She blushed again, as if surprised at her nerve. Nick couldn't help but like the painfully shy woman. He remembered too well countless hours spent in the library as a child, his three brothers and one sister joining him often as not. His scholarly parents sometimes, too. The O'Connor family of nerds. And he'd been the king of them all.

The engineering firm had been more of the same — long hours alone with his computer and calculations. His move to Melnik had been more of a prison break than a career change. Bonnie seemed forever trapped in this lonely wonderland.

Nick felt a deep connection with her. "I'd appreciate it. Thanks."

"Let me show you some of my favorite books that pertain to Melnik history. You might want to study them to see if the information in your papers is already in our collection." Bonnie slipped around the desk, turning sideways to fit between it and the nearest bookshelves. Nick had to back up to let her pass. She led him deep into the literary jungle past displays of Melnik mementoes.

"Look at all this stuff." Nick ran his hands reverently down the rows of books. "I like the old ones better than the new."

Bonnie glanced over her shoulder. A beige cardigan sweater draped over her shoulders set off her dark eyes in the dim light. Nick thought he saw mystery in those eyes, and loneliness, as if her thoughts were so private she hated to even think in the presence of others. He wondered how many hours a week she spent alone in here.

"These are all the yearbooks from Melnik High School," Bonnie pointed out as they went down the row. She tapped one book with a white spine. "My senior year."

Nick stopped. "Your year — hey, that's my year. We graduated the same time." Nick was stunned. He'd misjudged her age by over a decade. The poor woman was in her early thirties, not forties. He turned quickly to cover his expression.

"The books about Melnik history are in this section. They are more about the individual families and genealogy research, stuff like that, but put together they really do tell the story of the town." Bonnie led him to the furthest corner of the room and began pulling heavy tomes, their binding cracked with age, off the highest shelves. "There's one here that has a lot about the Evanses in it. That might be the best if your papers came out of Bea's house."

"Here, let me do that. I'm a foot taller than you."

Bonnie turned to face him. She couldn't get past him in the tight aisle. Nick turned sideways. "Just scoot past."

Bonnie stared at the floor as she approached him. Pressing her back to the shelves, she inched by.

She glanced up, and Nick wondered about her and worried. "I really am sorry about calling you the wrong name. I know that had to hurt."

Bonnie shrugged one shoulder. "It's okay."

"No, it's not." Nick rested a hand on Bonnie's shoulder. She quit pressing herself so solidly against the shelves. In fact, she might have leaned toward him just a bit. She blinked, her lips parted. Nick noticed it all. How pretty she was in an understated way, how lonely. She'd gotten stuck in her world of books while he'd escaped. He still loved reading, but not as a substitute for life. He could help her escape.

"Bonnie, I . . ."

"Having that stupid mouse outside the museum is like a repellant. No wonder you never have anyone in here. This is the first time I've ever come. . . ." Carrie came around the corner of the shelf, and Nick looked up, forgetting what he was going to say to Bonnie. Carrie's eyes widened. She looked from Nick to Bonnie to his hand on her shoulder.

"Oh, sorry, excuse me." She turned and disappeared.

Carrie thought she'd interrupted . . . something. Nick jerked his hand off Bonnie's shoulder as if he'd been burned and raced after Carrie.

He caught up with her on the sidewalk. It was easy enough.

"NoonestarveswhileClaralives."

Carrie stood in the icy, buffeting wind just outside the door of City Hall, forking over money for what looked like a cherry pie.

"Mouseishome."

"Wow, cherry. That looks great." Nick tugged his jacket collar up around his ears and reached for his wallet. Sure, it was probably poisonous. It made drinking antifreeze seem yummy. But still . . . "Cherry's

251

my favorite."

"Marbles," Carrie muttered under her breath.

Nick handed over a five, took the surprisingly heavy pie, and looked closer. Sure enough, red marbles.

Bonnie came out at a near run, as if she were chasing after Nick. He glanced at her flushed cheeks and saw her eyes bright with embarrassment and what might be the gloss of tears. Before Nick could apologize again, although he wasn't sure for what this time, Bonnie bought a meringue pie garnished with bright yellow cottonwood leaves.

"Areyouamanoramouse?"

Bonnie had a heavy book in her hand. "H-here's that book on the Evans ancestors if you'd like to take it and study it, Nick . . . uh . . . and Carrie." Bonnie looked up as if lifting her chin was too much effort.

"Thanks. Uh . . . do I need to sign something to take this out of the museum?" Nick tucked the file folder under his arm, balanced the pie with his right hand, and reached for the book with his left.

"No, but I can give you a brochure explaining how to join the Melnik Historical Society. It's not required."

"Melnik'sgotitsmouse. ButI'vegotmyownideas."

Nick saw the look Carrie slid between him and Bonnie. He couldn't read her expression now. But she hadn't liked finding Nick with Bonnie in that narrow aisle. It gave him hope. With a glance at Bonnie, who was not nearly as good at covering what she was feeling, Nick saw the same hope he was afraid gleamed in his eyes. Only Bonnie's hope was aimed straight at him.

He knew just how Bonnie felt. She'd found a kindred spirit. Another bookworm. Nick knew they could talk for hours. And Bonnie loved Melnik and had no plans to leave. Ever. She was perfect for him. Well, what relationship ever worked between two people who were perfect? He wanted the mouse-phobic woman who saw Melnik as a giant mousetrap.

"What are your ideas, Clara? Tell me." Carrie shifted the pie into her left hand and slid her arm around Clara's shoulder.

"Giantsizedmice." Clara's gray hair trembled as she flinched from Carrie's touch. "Runningwildkillingfolks."

"You mean Maxie." Carrie nodded her head toward the glass doors of City Hall. Maxie's case was clearly visible beyond it.

"Iknowafewthings."

"We need to talk, Clara. Let me go with you to sell your pies, and we'll talk all about how you take care of the people in this town."

"It'stheCommunists.They'rebehindallthetrou

Nick watched in fascination as Carrie walked away with Clara. Listening, cajoling. Being a reporter. But Nick wasn't sure what the story might be.

"So, Nick. Would you like . . ."

"Give me that book!"

Nick groaned.

Carrie abandoned Clara.

Bonnie clutched the volume.

Tallulah.

"I recognize that." The wind gusted and Tallulah's caftan billowed fit to keep a ship sailing. "I've got everything I need gathered and written — mostly — for the Maxie book. But I was just going into the museum to dig through some of the oldest material."

Carrie snatched the book out of Bonnie's arms. Nick couldn't control a sigh of relief when Carrie gained control of things. Bonnie was too sweet. Tallulah would crush her like a bug. He grinned at the fiery competitive gleam in Carrie's eyes.

"I was here first, Tallulah. I'll go through it and then get it to you. And I've gone through a lot of Great-Grandma Bea's things and found a few interesting documents and pictures. I'll start on the Maxie pamphlet as soon as I get the paper out this week."

Tallulah gasped. "But I thought we'd go with my vision for the book. I only need you to polish it and to give me any pertinent information lost in Bea's house."

"Do you have your book with you, Tallulah? Believe me, I'd prefer editing your work to creating the whole thing myself."

Tallulah nodded, her eyes flitting to the book. "It's in my car in front of Jansson's. I'll get it and bring it across to the *Bugle* office. We don't have a moment to spare. I've even settled on a title. *Maxie Mouse: The Glorious Rodent of Melnik.*"

Bonnie turned and headed straight back into the museum. Nick thought he heard a snicker before the glass doors of the possibly-soon-to-be-named Maxie Memorial Hall clicked shut.

To keep from laughing straight into Tallulah's vivid green turban, Nick began thinking through a particularly complex exercise he'd learned the semester he spent studying physics. He heard Carrie coughing as he examined the variety of conventions for describing vector.

She got control, and with a sincerity that impressed Nick greatly — considering it was completely fake, she said to Tallulah, "I'll look forward to getting the draft of your book. I honestly don't see myself making a lot of changes. I'll just double-check for grammar errors and misspelled words. I'm sure I won't find any."

Tallulah gave a jerk of her chins that set them wobbling and nearly capsized her turban. "We need that book within two weeks so it can be mailed to the media and federal, state, and local dignitaries."

Nick pictured the president waving from the back of a giant mouse and immediately began reciting, internally, the Declaration of Independence, something he'd memorized during his semester studying American History.

When in the course of rodent events . . .

"This is going to be a huge event. I fully expect the governor to attend."

"Maybe if it was an election year, Tallulah," Carrie said. "But I'd hate for you to get your hopes up."

. . . it becomes necessary for one people to use a great big mouse . . . Nick caught himself. That wasn't in there.

"I refuse to be denied this triumph. The governor *will* be here, or I'll know the reason why."

"Uh, Tallulah, the reason *why* might be because he's busy and every town around has some kind of Christmas festival."

"This isn't a Christmas festival, this is a *Maxie* festival."

"But it is *Christmas.* You may be losing your perspective a bit. I mean, it is our Savior's birth. Maybe we shouldn't focus *too* much on Maxie."

We hold these truths to be self-evident, that all mice are created equal . . . except for Maxie, who is gigantic.

Nick shook his head and decided to stay with the bizarre conversation. Reciting the Declaration wasn't helping anyway. Maybe if he paid more attention instead of daydreaming, he'd have figured out Bonnie's name faster.

Carrie headed across the street to the *Bugle,* and Tallulah lumbered toward her car. Nick traipsed along after Carrie for no good reason. Maybe he'd check to see if the *Bugle*'s front door needed more work.

19

Carrie finished with Tallulah, thanked Nick for her perfectly oiled door, and settled into her desk chair dreading the next part of her day.

She needed to find a Maxie photo. *Eeek!*

The door crashed open. Sven Gunderson stormed in.

Lifting her head to face him, she was actually grateful for the interruption. She'd been wondering when he was going to come in and fire her.

"I read that puff piece you did on Wilkie, retracting the first story." Gunderson jabbed an arthritic finger at her.

The man was her boss. She really ought to be polite. "You sneaking, lying coward!" Okay, forget polite. Maybe the paper in Bjorn or Gillespie was hiring. "It's bad enough that you wrote that garbage. But then you put *my* name on *your* story!"

Gunderson launched into a tirade, *none*

of which included the words, "You're fired."

Carrie gave as good as she got, and eventually Gunderson stormed out.

"It really is hard to get fired in this town," Carrie said to the empty paper office.

She finished her workday and went home to spend her evening writing something that she hoped marked her as the ultimate professional, unbiased journalist. A flattering story about that nasty, obese mouse.

Carrie looked at the time in the corner of her computer screen and was shocked to see that it was nine p.m. She sat alone in the mouse house, rope tied firmly around her jeans at the ankles so no mice could run up her legs. She was finished writing *Maxie Mouse: The Glorious Rodent of Melnik.*

"Is it any wonder I've got a phobia?" Carrie asked her living-room ceiling.

Grizzly came in howling like a demon-possessed Osterizer and leapt onto Carrie's lap.

She picked up the soft-bristled baby brush she'd unearthed in the bathroom. Grizzly liked having his hair combed.

Grizzly, who was turning out to be *not* the rampaging killer she'd hoped for at all, looked up. Carrie studied him. "Didn't it used to be the other eye that was closed?

Are you sandbagging your injuries to get sympathy?"

His unearthly yowl eased into a rugged purr. He twitched his strange, L-shaped tail, and Carrie hugged him.

"Okay, even if you're faking the eye thing, you've had it hard. I'll keep babying you. I hope a diet of mice will give you all the vitamins you need, because I'm not feeding you while I hear scratching in the walls. You" — she tapped him on the nose — "hunt your own supper."

She'd have rather had Nick nearby protecting her, but after a very promising start, he'd pulled back. She kept hearing herself yell, "Let me go!"

"I believe those were my very words, Grizz. You don't think he took them wrong, do you?"

How could he take them any way but wrong, idiot?

"Did I tell you I'm a genius writer, Mouse Breath?" Carrie smoothed the brush over the cat again, finding fewer knots. "A dope about men, but I can really write."

Grizzly rubbed his head on Carrie's knee. "I told the Maxie Mouse story as it's meant to be told. It's a story of freedom and courage and creativity. This book isn't about Maxie; it's about America. It's about a small

260

town's struggle to hold onto their heritage while building for the future, all to preserve a way of life they love." Satisfied with Grizzly's now-smooth back, Carrie set the brush aside. She didn't want the old boy to get irritated with her. Besides, they needed to talk.

"It's really good. The governor really might come. And in writing it . . ." She whispered in his good ear, almost afraid to speak out loud. "I'm going to give the good people of Melnik something to really be thankful for." Carrie hugged Grizzly again, loving the softness of him. Even his coarse growl seemed like an offer of friendship.

"I've convinced myself that Melnik is where I belong, too." And if she belonged and Nick belonged, then maybe, just maybe, she and Nick belonged together.

It was way too late at night, but she reached for the phone.

"Nick, can you come over for a while?"

Nick's eyes fell shut. This was it. Carrie was going to tell him she'd found a job and was leaving forever. He swallowed and tried to speak. Nothing came out. He swallowed again.

"Did I wake you?"

"No, just . . . uh . . ." Nick couldn't even

think of an easy excuse. "What did you need?"

"I have to go up to the attic again and I'm . . ."

He breathed a sigh of relief. This wasn't good-bye. This was mice.

"I'll be right over." He jogged out the door into the frigid wind, tugging on his down-filled jacket. November wound down aiming toward Thanksgiving. The trees were as bare as his future would be if she left him.

Pulling to a stop in front of Carrie's house, sitting alone in his cold, empty truck, he thought of his cold, empty life. "I don't want you jumping into my arms tonight," he said to the cold, empty air. "It hurts too much to let you go."

"This time when I see a mouse and jump into his arms, I'll hang on," Carrie said to the ceiling of her cold, empty house.

Quit being such a dope and just tell him you care about him and you've decided to stay in Melnik. You don't need a mouse. Still, a mouse would make things easier. When Carrie realized she was actually *wishing* for a mouse to appear, she knew that either she'd completely lost her mind . . . or that this was love.

Nick walked up her back steps, and Carrie swung open the door. The bite of the November weather chilled her, even in her red Cornhusker sweatshirt and blue jeans.

"You called?" Nick smiled at her.

Her heart turned a twisty somersault. Nick's smile was going to give her internal injuries. She stepped back to let him in.

"I've been writing the book Tallulah wanted, and I've come up with some questions. I need to search the attic to answer them. Do you mind keeping me company?"

"It's my pleasure." Nick followed her into the kitchen just as Grizzly jumped up on the table and then leapt at him. Nick caught him by reflex.

Carrie stopped. "Before we go up, I-I'd like you to see something I wrote."

"The Maxie book?"

"I've been working on that, too. But I wrote a story for next week's paper about Maxie, and I really feel like it came out well." Her cheeks heated. "I wouldn't mind a second opinion."

Nick's expression lightened.

Carrie lifted the laptop off the couch and handed it to him. He sat and began reading. The room was still. Carrie's nerves crackled until she was sure Nick could hear them. The moments stretched. She considered making coffee or unsnarling more of

263

her snarling cat or maybe checking the kitchen pantry for new dead guys.

Instead she sank down on the couch beside Nick and read over his shoulder. About the time she started, he was done.

He lifted his head. "This is beautiful. How did you do this — make a story about a big dead mouse seem important?"

Carrie shrugged. "You like it, then?"

Nick set the laptop on the coffee table. A week ago the table had been buried in refuse.

"I love it. You made the words . . . sing."

Carrie's throat closed. Nick seemed closer than he had before . . . bigger, nicer — which wasn't possible. He'd been the nicest man Carrie had ever met right from the start.

She managed a hoarse "Thank you."

Nick studied the computer screen. "I'm sure the minute you contact them at the *World-Herald,* they'll take you back. It seems like you've been regretting making this move back to Melnik. When you want your job back, they'll jump at the chance."

Guilt and the weight of all she'd left unsaid made it hard to talk. "Sure, maybe."

His blue eyes, lit by the computer screen, shone with the honesty and decency she'd come to expect. "Can you answer a question for me?"

Carrie wouldn't have denied him much right now. "Sure."

"Why are you here? Why did you give up the *World-Herald* for Melnik?"

Carrie's heart pounded. "I got fired." Her face heated until she had to resemble a matchstick, with her hair the white tip on the end.

"Fired? Why? You're brilliant."

Carrie's humiliation morphed into pathetic gratitude. "I accused a man of a crime. A man who, it turns out, was a good friend of my editor. When I took my suspicions to him, I got my head taken off. The worst part is, I was wrong. I looked a whole lot closer and found out I'd jumped to the wrong conclusions. Of course, I didn't know that until I'd faced down my editor and given him a rousing speech about Rich Man's Justice. I burned my bridges at the paper. I can't go back."

She dropped her chin and looked at her hands twisted together in her lap. She couldn't meet his eyes. "I was out of work. I couldn't make the rent, and Great-Grandma's house came along. Instead of admitting I'd messed up, I took the house. I'm not a big success, Nick. I may just qualify for the Guinness Book of World's

Records as the World's Youngest, Fastest, and Most Complete Failure. Maybe they'll stuff me and give me my own case at City Hall."

Nick lifted her chin with one finger, startling her. She forced herself to meet his gaze, braced for his disappointment and his contempt. She deserved it.

"You're not a failure, Carrie. You're a genius."

All she saw in his eyes was kindness. "What?"

"I just read the proof of it on your computer. Anyone who can write like this can never be called a failure."

Carrie felt her eyes burn with threatening tears. "You're the nicest man I've ever met."

His hand relaxed on her chin and eased around to the back of her neck.

Carrie waited for a mouse to jump out or a robber to break in or a neighbor to drop by.

He kissed her.

She made a point of *not* yelling "Let me go."

He tilted his head and deepened the kiss.

A loud thump came from underfoot. The cellar. Mouse Ground Zero.

Nick eased back. His lips twisted in a wry smile. "Another home invasion, I suppose.

But remember where we were, huh?"

Carrie nodded, not particularly interested in whoever might be robbing her blind.

"Let's go. Maybe we can add a new member to the rogue's gallery in the Melnik jail." Nick stood up and rounded the couch. He wrenched the basement door open with a nasty squeak, and when his feet hit the hollow-sounding boards to the cellar, another crash echoed up the steps.

Carrie came out of her kiss-induced stupor, jumped up, and chased after Nick.

Her feet reached the cement floor of Ground Zero just as Nick clicked on the pull string of the bare bulb and reached down to pull Tallulah to her feet, where she'd stumbled over one of Great-Grandma's ten rusty water heaters.

Carrie hoped the woman hadn't broken a hip.

When Nick pulled Tallulah to her feet — pretty gently, Carrie thought, all things considered — Tallulah's *turban du jour* dropped off her head and rolled across the floor like an electric blue tumbleweed.

Tallulah, hairless except for a ring of bright red perfect male pattern baldness fluff, made a dive for the hat. Nick held on. A gun shook loose from somewhere in Tallulah's voluminous color-splatter caftan, clattered across the basement floor, went off, and shot a dusty canning jar to death.

Carrie jumped and squeaked, but it wasn't as bad as if she'd seen a mouse.

Nick pulled Carrie close to his side, shielding her with his own body.

"A gun?" Nick turned to Tallulah, his brow arched.

Carrie let herself be held for a few seconds and then stepped away to focus on Tallulah, who was struggling against Nick's hold, reaching for her turban. "Leave the gun and the turban. You're not going to be able to keep them in jail anyway."

"Jail!" Tallulah covered her head with her one free hand, as if she had no bigger problem than her hair. Carrie decided Tallulah might be right. It was bad hair.

"Unless they make turbans to match the orange jumpsuits, you're going hatless for a long, long time. This time no one's going to talk me out of pressing charges. I'm sick of you breaking into my house."

"No, not without my turban!" Tallulah waved her hand and an object flew straight at Carrie. With a soft thud, something hit her chest.

Carrie looked down, as the little ball of . . .

"EEEEKK!!!"

She landed in Nick's arms, shrieking, slapping at her shirt as if it were on fire. Carrie had just been hit by Maxie Mouse.

Tallulah, free, raced for her turban, ignoring the gun.

Nick stepped well away from the bedraggled, rolling mouse. "Don't cry. Run up and change your shirt, quick. Take a shower if you need to."

Carrie hadn't noticed she was crying. She'd have wiped her face, but her hands had touched her mousy shirt. She buried her face in Nick's chest. She was going to have to boil her shirt, her hands, maybe her whole body. She was pressed against Nick — she was going to have to boil him, too.

Nick carried her to the bottom of the stairway, set her on the first step, and picked up the gun.

"Oh, what's the use?" Tallulah took a second to pick up Maxie and slip him in her caftan pocket and then buried her face in her mousy hands to cry with sufficient drama. "I'm ruined anyway. I might as well admit everything."

Carrie knew what was coming before the woman even opened her mouth. She almost held her ears, but she'd touched her shirt and her shirt had touched Maxie. Still, she didn't want to hear it.

"I did it." Tallulah's sobbing deepened

until it didn't even seem like she was acting. "I shot him. I killed Wilkie Melnik."

20

The cell door rolled shut with a metallic *bang.* "I'm not like the other trash you keep in this jail." Once her turban was restored, Tallulah's inner diva fully reemerged.

Shayla rolled off her cot and stood, looking like a lifer in a no-death-penalty state. The type of person with no fear of punishment. So why not mop the floor with the lady who'd just called her trash?

Tallulah was too busy emoting to notice that she was insulting a young woman with antifreeze flowing where her paternal love should be.

Hal strolled over to the cell wall that separated him from Shayla and Tallulah and looked through the bars. The women's and men's correctional facilities weren't exactly across town from each other.

"What's Hal still doing here?" Carrie whispered to Junior.

"I think his apartment's being painted.

He refused to pay his bail, and then when I told him to just go home anyway, he wouldn't leave. I quit feeding him unless he chips in for meals."

"This isn't a bed and breakfast, Junior. Send him and Shayla home."

Junior shrugged. "They're not hurtin' nothin'."

A man lay snoring to humble a sawmill, with his back to the action. Ned Gaskell, the town drunk, sleeping off a brawl he'd had in the local bar. Someone had questioned the skill of the Cornhusker's starting quarterback, and Ned had defended the honor of one of Nebraska's finest.

Nick knew Junior would have let the man go home. Badmouthing the Huskers amounted to someone begging to be punched. But Ned's wife was too mad to let him in the house, so he'd sleep here a night . . . or two. However long it took Mrs. Gaskell to cool down and Ned to sober up.

Nick glanced at Carrie, still pale even for a Swede. Her hair was wet and slicked back, her face raging pink from the blazing-hot water and scrubbing during her shower. Her clothes were fresh out of her drawer. Nick had her whole outfit from the Maxie incident stashed in the back end of his truck, destined for the burn barrel. Nick didn't tell her he'd seen a mouse dash into her clothes drawer while he was tearing up the kitchen flooring. Amazing that somebody had covered a perfectly good solid oak floor with Congoleum.

"I want a lawyer. I demand a phone call."

"Tallulah, give it a rest." Junior shook his head and rubbed his bare scalp with his beefy hand.

It occurred to Nick that Junior had more hair than Tallulah.

"It's after ten p.m.," Junior went on. "You've confessed to murder, and the only lawyer in town already took his nighttime meds and is out cold until breakfast."

"I know my rights!" Tallulah's fists punched the air. The woman couldn't act her way out of a paper bag, let alone a jail cell.

Ned jerked in his sleep and grumbled something about women and bowling a three hundred. He yelled, *"Giant mice . . . crawling!"*

Hal looked at the man and shuddered. Nick noticed goose bumps on Carrie's arms.

"Actually, I get to hold you for twenty-four hours before I press charges. And it's not that I don't know what charges to file. I've got a list as long as my arm. But it's late, and my wife told me that if I don't get back and help with the slumber party she's having for our son and his twelve best friends, she'd throw away my share of the leftover lasagna instead of letting me have it for lunch tomorrow. But before I go . . ." Junior grabbed a folding chair and plunked himself down in the narrow hallway in front of the two cells.

"You let me out of this cell, Junior Hammerstad." Tallulah wagged the scolding finger of death under Junior's nose. "Or I'm calling your mother!"

"I've quit letting Mom tell me who to arrest ever since she got lost driving the three blocks from her house to mine and ended up in Kansas City. So don't bother her. You're staying."

"I'm leaving!"

"Knock it off."

"I ought to be above suspicion. I'm an upstanding member of this community!"

"Tallulah." Junior scrubbed his face with both hands. "You confessed."

"You said he was already dead."

"You didn't know that when you started spraying him with bullets."

"One bullet!"

"Oh, like that makes it okay."

"You're going to regret this."

"I wouldn't be surprised." Sounding

exhausted, Junior scowled at his three prisoners. "Now, I want all three of you to listen up. I love my wife's lasagna." Junior glanced sideways at Nick and Carrie loitering in the jailhouse door. "Get some chairs in here."

He turned back to the criminal element. "I'd let you out of the cell to talk — just so Ned gets a good night's sleep, but my office is too small for all six of us."

Nick ducked out to grab the chairs. He was the new guy in town. Rule of thumb: The new guy did it. He was glad to be outside the cell.

Junior pulled his notebook out of his pocket. "Now you say you shot Wilkie — is that right, Tallulah?"

Nick was losing track of the confessed murderers, the motives, and the weapons of choice. That struck him as a bad, bad sign.

Tallulah jammed her fists on her rotund hips. "But you said he was already dead." Tallulah had gotten over her confession real fast when Junior gave her that bit of news.

The turban to cover her hair problems. The caftan to cover her weight problems. Nick wondered if there was anything she could get to cover her mouth.

"I said *most likely* he was already dead. The coroner's report tells me something and then one of you confesses. I ask the coroner, 'Could it have been antifreeze poisoning?' and she says, 'Wow, gunshot wound, blunt force trauma wound . . . I never thought to check for poison.' She's got a limited budget, you know."

"What did kill him, Junior?" Carrie asked, crossing her legs as if they were at a tea party instead of Murderer's Row.

"The results are sketchy. The coroner said all these things contributed. The gunshot seems to be postmortem, but with him unconscious, weakened by the poison, and showing obvious signs of suffocation, there's some question of which came first."

"You said the gunshot *was* postmortem, not *seemed* to be," Tallulah screeched.

Nick wondered if she subconsciously dressed to look like a parrot to match her voice.

"Even if you didn't kill him, Tallulah, you're still under arrest for breaking into Carrie's house *with* a gun. Plus, you've admitted to doing the same thing the night Bea died. That's *four* felonies, so *settle down!*"

"There's a concealed-carry law in Nebraska. I've got a license. I can carry a gun in my pocket."

The top of Junior's head turned red. "*Not*

if you're breaking into a house. That's committing a felony with a weapon."

Tallulah sniffed. "A technicality."

"*A felony is not a technicality!* Not even close."

Nick wondered if he should get some duct tape to wrap around Junior's head so it wouldn't explode.

"You want me to walk all the way home just to put my gun down before I break in? That's very inconvenient."

"Well, sitting here talking while my wife rides herd on a dozen junior-high-aged boys is inconvenient, too."

"I brought the gun for protection. I wasn't going to use it on anyone."

"It went off twice. Once into *maybe* already-dead Wilkie and once into Carrie's canning jar. *You stop carrying that gun around until you learn how to use it!*"

Nick thought that maybe Tallulah ought to quit carrying the gun under any and all circumstances.

"Well, fine then." Tallulah crossed her arms, a gesture of defiance somewhat weakened by the bars on the jail.

Junior clutched his hands together in front of his paunchy belly as if he were wrapping them around Tallulah's neck. "And we haven't even talked about you breaking into

City Hall and stealing Maxie yet. The break-in is a felony. Stealing Maxie, well, I don't know about that. He isn't worth much; probably can mark that down as a misdemeanor."

"Maxie is extremely valuable."

"You *want* another felony count?" Junior's voice rose until it might hurt a dog's ears.

"But I didn't *steal* him. I have a key to Maxie Memorial Hall . . ."

"It hasn't had its name changed yet, Tallulah. Don't call it that." Carrie clutched her hands together as if she were begging.

"I sometimes get Maxie out and take him home overnight, just so he's not so lonely."

Carrie dropped her face onto her clasped fingers. Hal grabbed the cell bars with a faint nauseous-sounding groan.

Nick asked, "Does anyone else do that? Carry Maxie around? That could explain the mouse fur on Wilkie."

Carrie whimpered. Hal backed away from the bars.

"They'd better not." Tallulah looked affronted that anyone would take Maxie for a sleepover except her. "As for Wilkie, I went in the pantry to hide. . . ."

"With the gun drawn . . . ," Nick said.

"I'd just seen Bea dead and heard a noise. I pulled the gun out of fear. Then I opened

278

the pantry door and Wilkie was in there and . . ."

"Why'd you wanna kill Dad?" Shayla interrupted.

Nick braced himself. If seventy-year-old Tallulah announced she was forty-something Wilkie's child, he was just going to believe it and add another seat on the Maxie float.

"I told you it was an accident. I went to Bea's house to talk to her."

"That late at night, Tallulah?" Carrie shook her head. "You've been prowling around that house too much. What's so important that you think is in there?"

Tallulah had a mulish expression on her face.

Carrie said, "I'm pressing charges on the break-in, Junior. Give her four felony counts right now."

"Okay!" Tallulah cracked. "It's just that — that there have been rumors about Maxie maybe not belonging to the city. There might be a will lost somewhere that puts his ownership into question. I'd heard that maybe the will is in Bea's house. I just need to make sure. We need to clear up even the slightest shadow on Maxie's ownership."

"What you mean is, you hoped to find proof that it existed and destroy it."

"No, that's not what I mean. And it's not *four* counts. I didn't break in the night Bea died. I saw she'd fallen. I *went* in. To help. Then I heard someone upstairs and it scared me. I decided to hide and accidentally shot Wilkie in the pantry. That's why I didn't call an ambulance for your great-grandma. I promise you, I'd have called if there'd been any hope of saving her." Tallulah gave Carrie a beseeching look.

Carrie nodded, and Nick could tell Carrie believed the woman. Actually, he did, too.

"After the gun went off, I slammed the door. I ran out and didn't look back. I didn't mean to shoot Wilkie. I didn't want him dead. I wanted him to be the grand marshal of this year's Maxie Festival. I had no motive to kill that poor man."

Junior's face had returned to a color compatible with life while Tallulah talked. He exchanged a look with Carrie and Nick then turned to his trusty notebook. "Here's how I see it. Shayla" — Junior jabbed his pencil eraser at her — "served up the antifreeze cocktail, and Wilkie drank it and went out about six p.m. He spent the evening in the bar. By ten o'clock, he ended up at Bea's. Hal" — Junior looked up and glared at his deputy — "for no good reason I can figure out, was in Bea's house. Care

280

to explain that, Hal?"

The deputy went sullen. "Look, I heard rumors, okay? I was paying real close attention to Dad because I wanted to know everything about him. I knew he was spending more money than he should have, and I heard there might be a lot more. I knew it had something to do with an old will and the will might be hidden in Bea's house. I figured if I got it first, I might be able to keep Dad from getting it. I didn't want the money, but I didn't want him to have it just to gamble away. So I tailed Dad when I had the night off that Tuesday. I was cruising around town, and I saw Dad through a window in Bea's house. He was standing over Bea. I assumed he'd hurt her."

Junior shook his head in disgust. "Hal clobbers Wilkie and leaves him for dead on the floor next to Bea."

Tallulah sniffed. "That was tacky, Hal."

"Well, bad manners are all over murder near about every time it happens." Junior wet his finger and turned a page, then settled his notebook on his stomach as if it were a handy TV tray. "Somehow, between ten and eleven thirty when you say you went there, Tallulah, Wilkie gets in the closet. I'm guessing someone found him unconscious and smothered him to death with Maxie or some other mouse."

Carrie scooted her chair two feet farther from Junior. Nick patted her on the knee and prepared to catch her. Hal backed up. Nick was going to let Hal handle his fears alone.

Tallulah looked appalled. "They could have ruined Maxie. He needs to be treated with care."

Junior rolled his eyes. "Then the murderer set Wilkie in the pantry like a can of cream of potato soup."

"You know, Junior . . ." Carrie sounded the next thing to crazy, in Nick's humble opinion. Which might be why she was glaring at the man who seemed destined to arrest half the population of Melnik. "I've been meaning to tell you, you never should have told Gunderson all those details about Shayla and the crime scene. That's unethical."

Nick decided not to remind Carrie of all the stuff Junior had told them.

Junior sat up, obviously surprised. "What are you talking about? You're the one who wrote that story with all that information in it about the crime. You wrote about Shayla's confession and the autopsy report in that stupid pack of lies about Wilkie."

"I didn't write that article."

"Who did?" Junior lifted his notebook, pen ready.

Nick couldn't believe Junior hadn't heard. Everybody knew who'd written that story. Of course, Junior had been busy arresting confessed murderers. "Gunderson."

Junior and Carrie stared at each other. Nick was adding things up, too. That noise in the newspaper office. Behind the door that opened into a building owned by Gunderson. He'd gotten the information on that hatchet piece on Wilkie by eavesdropping on Shayla's hysterical confession. Why would Gunderson be eavesdropping on Carrie at the paper?

"I'm adding his name to the suspect list. Someone strong had to pick up Wilkie and stuff him in that closet." Junior jotted away.

"Don't forget Mom," Shayla said. "She might've killed Dad because of Donette."

"Or Donette might've killed Wilkie because he wouldn't leave your mom." Junior did some more writing. Then, satisfied with his notes, he gave a tiny jerk of his head toward the three prisoners and went back to his notebook. "My gut tells me the mouse smotherer found Wilkie unconscious from the skillet and the poison, but alive. Finished him off and stuffed him in the closet. Neither your mom nor Donette could've

283

moved his body, Shayla."

Shayla looked mutinous, like she'd fight to prove her mother was a killer. Dysfunctional-family poster child at your service.

"I've got one other detail from the state police detective who's in charge of this investigation."

"I thought you were in charge," Nick said. Although, when he thought about it, that seemed unlikely. Junior was nobody's image of a competent police detective.

"Nope, but while they're waiting around for the autopsy results, I'm looking into it myself. They did check financial records, though. Hal's right about Wilkie coming into money. He was gambling more than usual and spreading cash around for the last couple of months. He had two payments of five hundred dollars. Wilkie kept records."

Carrie said, "You think maybe he was blackmailing someone?"

"Maybe." Junior glared at Tallulah. "But even if someone else smothered him, your reckless gunplay could have finished him off. I'm not about to let you off the hook for murder until we've got a final autopsy report. Right now Dr. Notchke, the coroner, is so fed up with me for phoning her with new confessions that she'll barely take my calls, so that slows everything down."

Junior sighed. "I don't think any of you did it." He pulled the keys off his belt. "You can all go home, but I'll need to ask you more questions, so don't leave town."

Shayla shook her head. "I don't have anywhere to go."

Hal settled into the cot next to snoring Ned. "My apartment won't be ready until the day after tomorrow."

"Everyone in town will have heard about it, and they'll be gossiping." Tallulah crossed her arms stubbornly. "I'm not leaving until you admit you were out of line to arrest me in the first place."

"I want you all out of here. I'm tempted to kick Ned out, too. It's aggravating, hauling in food for the bunch of you."

All three glared at him but didn't budge, not even when Junior threw both doors open. "Fine, stay if you want, but no free meals."

"What it really comes down to is . . ." Carrie leaned forward, her elbows on her knees. Nick saw her eyes lose focus as the investigative reporter added everything up. "There's still a mouse-wielding murderer running loose in Melnik."

Nick sighed. He was never going to get a date with Carrie. "Well, isn't this just going to be a happy Thanksgiving, compliments of Maxie?"

Carrie nodded. "And a very merry Christmouse."

21

Four days until Thanksgiving. Maybe more to be thankful for than I'd thought when I moved home to Melnik. Carrie jingled her keys as joyfully as sleigh bells as she opened the *Bugle* on Monday morning.

Her Maxie-Makes-America-Great story had set the town to buzzing with joy last week. This week, Thanksgiving week, she was going to cause trouble. She still needed to transcribe the city charter and Rudolph Melnik's last will and testment.

Tallulah, Hal, and Shayla remained in jail, even though Junior now left the door wide-open night and day. Shayla was homeless; Hal's landlord had decided to remodel his bathroom. Tallulah was sneaking home to sleep in her own bed, but she always beat Junior back before he could lock her out of jail.

At least Ned had gone home, bless his heart.

Olga Jansson had taken to dropping off meals, which annoyed her because everybody knew she didn't do takeout. But Tallulah was an old friend who paid for all three meals — and she tipped well — so Olga made an exception.

Junior refused to apologize for arresting Tallulah, citing her confession. He threatened at least five times daily to physically heave all three of them out onto the street, but Tallulah said that if he so much as touched her, she'd whack him with her purse so hard he'd have to arrest her for assault, so what was the point?

Carrie was pretty sure none of those three had killed Wilkie. She was convinced that the killer was the person who had stuffed Wilkie into the closet.

During a quiet moment at the *Bugle* while Donette and Viola were out chasing hot-breaking news — or possibly having coffee at Jansson's — Carrie pulled a couple of documents out of her desk drawer. One of them was the Melnik City Charter, the other Rudolph Melnik's will. If she was reading them right, both contained a motive for murder. One about wealth; the other about the ownership of an oversized mouse. Anywhere else on the planet there would be no doubt what the motive was. But this was

288

Melnik. As Carrie read, her hands began to tremble. Finally, she thought, they had the answers they needed.

She reached for the phone to call Nick, knowing he wouldn't be home, but glad for an excuse to try anyway. She didn't bother with his cell. Cell phones didn't work well in Melnik. She needed one of those books from Bonnie's museum, and Nick had it. Knowing he'd drop everything to bring it over warmed her heart.

Not enough to make her blood stop running cold from getting whacked by Maxie, but it was a start.

Nick didn't answer. She remembered that he had planned to hunt for more historical information at the museum. Shuddering at the very thought of walking past the Glorious Rodent of Melnik, she shoved back her chair and marched out the door. Nick's truck was parked in front of the Melnik Historical Society Museum and the City Auditorium, soon to be renamed Maxie Memorial Hall if Tallulah had her way.

She entered the dingy hallway dividing the museum on the right from the city offices on the left. She tiptoed past Maxie's aquarium, keeping far to the left.

Maxie was in the aquarium looking none the worse for hitting her — Carrie swatted at her chest. She couldn't quit wiping away the Essence of Rodent that now clung to her like a death shroud despite taking ten boiling-hot showers — the theory being she could change into a whole new layer of skin more quickly if she burned the old one away. Forget that Maxie had never actually *touched* her skin.

She made the mistake of a true phobic. She glanced at Maxie, his teeth bared as if he wanted to go for her throat. He stood frozen in all his rattish splendor, in his case, as if trying to terrify children away from learning about Melnik's past.

She dashed past the wretched vermin, remembering Bonnie and Nick in a very close situation when she went in last time. A flash of jealousy made her swing the door open quietly. She heard the murmur of voices — back in the corner where she had found them before.

Carrie was absolutely sure Nick liked her — maybe. But there was no denying that Bonnie was his perfect match. Bonnie loved Melnik. Nick loved Melnik. Bonnie loved books. Nick loved books. Bonnie was an obsessive-compulsive neat freak. Nick was an obsessive-compulsive neat freak.

Instead of being jealous, Carrie knew she should push Nick and Bonnie together. A little light matchmaking. Instead, she decided she'd invite Nick to her family Thanksgiving right in front of the little poaching OCD bookworm.

She rounded the corner and saw Nick reaching for books off the top shelf while Bonnie stared at him with abject misery, as if all her dreams were just out of her reach on a high shelf.

Jealousy and pity created a toxic-waste dump where Carrie's Christian charity should be. Shamed by her unkindness, Carrie knew Nick really did deserve someone good enough for him.

Too bad.

She stepped forward to stake a claim. Then Bonnie opened her mouth.

"Would you like to have Thanksgiving dinner with me, Nick?"

Carrie clamped her jaw shut. Bonnie had beaten Carrie to the invitation. He answered her without stopping his search, a search that stretched out his long, lean body and reminded Carrie of what good shape he was in and how tall and broad and strong he was. And how he'd been a hero from the first moment she'd jumped into his arms.

"That would be nice. Thank you." Nick pulled a book down, studied the title for a minute, then looked back at Bonnie. "My parents are in Florida, and I dreaded spending the day alone."

His eyes went past Bonnie to Carrie. "Hi. We've found some more interesting information."

Nick the Clueless had just broken her heart, and he was too stupid to even notice.

Bonnie turned, her cheeks faintly flushed. Her eyes met Carrie's, and behind her embarrassment was just the tiniest bit of triumph. Carrie wanted to crush her like a bug.

"I've found something, too. I may have figured out who killed Wilkie. But I need some books and the papers we brought in."

"Let's set these up on Bonnie's desk. Bonnie knows Melnik history forward and backward, don't you?" Nick smiled at the shy woman.

She nodded and stepped closer to Nick, as if she were a moth and he a light in the darkest night.

Boyfriend stealer!

"She'll be a lot of help." Nick turned to leave the narrow book aisle, and Carrie had to go first and then Bonnie. They shifted to let Bonnie take her seat behind her antique desk.

Nick went to the side of the desk and laid his books down. Carrie stood so she faced

Bonnie. She outlined her suspicions to both of them and explained what she needed. The pair of Melnik-loving, perfectionist brainiacs went to work.

After much discussion, they had a plan of action.

"First," Nick said, "we have to spring Tallulah from jail."

Carrie shook her head. "She won't go home. She's so determined to punish Junior, I don't think she'll ever leave."

"She'll leave," Bonnie said with confidence.

"She will?" Carrie looked up from her notes. With Tallulah locked up, they'd never spring this giant mousetrap.

"Sure. Right now I'm subbing as the organizer of the Maxie Festival. She trusts me."

"So how does that get Tallulah out?" Nick asked, closing the books and stacking them neatly.

"Simple. I quit. I nominate Carrie to be the chairperson."

"Me? I hate Maxie. I despise that mouse and think we need to emphasize Jesus' birth. I'll even change the name back to *Christmas Festival*. I think the parade is a stupid idea, too. It's freezing cold in Nebraska in December! Everybody knows that."

Nick grinned. "Of course everybody knows. Tallulah will be out of the county lockup before the sun sets."

That pinched. But Carrie had to admit the truth. "Bonnie, you're a genius."

The shy woman grinned, and Carrie had a hard time hating her. "For the rest of the day, I'm in charge. But I'm not touching that raggedy, nasty, flea-bitten, overactive-thyroid *mouse*."

"How do we get the word to Tallulah without making it seem obvious?" Nick asked, as out of touch with Melnik as Crazy Clara would be at a Mensa quiz bowl.

Bonnie stood and brushed nonexistent wrinkles out of her drab, cream-colored blouse and her tidy, khaki skirt. "Easy. I'll go have coffee at Jansson's."

"Perfect." Carrie smiled. "Dora was just pulling in when I left the *Bugle*."

22

Forget nightfall. Tallulah resumed control of the Maxie Festival by noon.

In a fit of pique, she took Hal and Shayla with her to her house as if she'd opened a foster home just for children of Wilkie Melnik. Hal's apartment had no functioning plumbing, and Rosie, still furious about the antifreeze, didn't want any part of her daughter.

Nick expected to hear that Shayla's little brother had moved in with Tallulah, too. Not because Rosie was mad at him. Just because the Melnik family was gathering like migrating geese.

A flock of Melniks.

Nick had volunteered to help with the parade. He stood now in Tallulah's garage, coating the gigantic replica of Maxie with the gray felt "mouse hair." Maxie would be the crowning touch to a float Tallulah had special-ordered from Mexico for the big parade set during the Maxie Festival, in the second weekend in December. Carrie was right about the float; it was completely realistic. It looked like a real mouse. Hal wouldn't touch it and privately told Nick he wasn't riding on it . . . although he held out a bit of hope to Tallulah. Maybe to get a free place to live. He did agree to ride a hayrack pulled along behind Maxie.

Carrie's sentimental Maxie story came out in the paper. Nick, after some research on the Internet, carefully cut out several copies of the story and, with regret, mailed them away to newspaper contests and some national publications who used syndicated material. If Carrie wanted the big city and a big paper, then she should have it. Even if it meant leaving Melnik . . . and him . . . behind.

Rosie Melnik had been persuaded to ride on the hayrack if Shayla rode on the mouse and didn't speak to her. Shayla wasn't speaking to her mother anyway, so that was easy. Then Shayla found out that Donette and the soon-to-be-born baby were riding mouse-back and threw a fit. Donette and baby had been moved to the hayrack. Rosie balked, although she was okay with Hal riding beside her and Kevin.

Tallulah rigged a sidecar somewhere

around Maxie's small intestine for Donette, and the whole feuding family planned to be aboard for the parade.

Tallulah had a special turban made out of faux mouse fur and had a Maxie aquarium created for the parade with the sides made of magnifying glass because, World's Largest or not, Maxie was still pretty small.

As he worked, Nick thought of Bonnie's Thanksgiving dinner invitation. How lonely must she be to ask a near stranger to Thanksgiving? Nick knew she had three brothers — one a lawyer in Omaha, two others still in college. Bonnie had dropped out of college to raise them after their parents died. None of the ingrates were coming home for the holidays. He felt sorry for her, but he'd been praying for Carrie to ask.

Nick inserted teeth fit for a horror movie into Maxie's felt mouth and muttered, "Jurassic Park IV — The Verminator."

Carrie stepped into Tallulah's garage. "Eeek!"

Nick rushed to her, hoping she'd jump.

Instead, she backed away. "You've got mouse fur on your hands — stay back!"

"It's gray felt." Nick couldn't hold back a grin. "C'mon, let me save you." He remembered that kiss right before they'd caught

Tallulah. It had been a long time since that happened.

Carrie smiled, a little pale but coping. "I can't believe you can stand to build that disgusting mouse."

"Boy, Tallulah was sure right to fire you from the festival."

"Absolutely. When I handed in my crown . . ."

"The one with the foot-tall picture of Maxie's face?"

Carrie shuddered. "That's the one. Guess what? I never put it on."

"There's a shocker."

Carrie managed a smile, and most of the color returned to her pretty, fair skin, pinking up her cheeks. He couldn't even see the whites all around her eyes anymore.

"When I handed in the vermin crown — apparently Tallulah wears it at all the historical society meetings — I told her I thought we ought to at least let the baby Jesus go first. You'd have thought I asked her to toss Maxie into a wood chipper."

"The Catholic church made a really nice nativity scene float, too." Nick wiped his hands on his pants and realized he was actually thinking that if he got all the mouse-colored felt off his hands, he might try to sneak in a kiss. "Father Calvecci asked

Donette to let them use her baby in their manger and it was a total no go."

"I heard that. They're using a Cabbage Patch doll instead."

Nick nodded. "Might be for the best. Tallulah said that the doll they used last year rolled out of the manger and off the float, and the hayrack rolled over its head."

Carrie winced.

Nick stepped closer.

The door banged open, and Tallulah stormed in. She saw Carrie and stopped in her tracks. She came over to them, now friendly again, with her power and turban fully restored.

"That was a beautiful story, Carrie. Thank you so much for writing it."

"Did you like the final copy of the book?"

"Yes, but I don't think we need all those pictures. One of Maxie on the cover is enough. Ink costs a fortune." Some of the pictures included a photocopy of the Melnik Town Charter they'd found in Carrie's great-grandma's house and the slightly altered version that hung in City Hall. They'd also put Rudolph's will in. The same things that would show up in this week's *Bugle.*

"Whatever you say," Carrie agreed, exchanging a furtive glance with Nick.

Nick tried to remember one single instance of this festival where Tallulah had worried about the cost. Just maybe Tallulah was taking the bait.

"I'm just double-checking that the float really resembles Maxie." She pulled her hand out of the pocket of her exploding-parrot-of-the-day caftan and, lifting her hand up to her nose, opened her lightly closed fist to reveal Maxie.

Carrie landed with a shriek in Nick's arms.

Tallulah rolled her eyes. With a huff of contempt, which struck Nick as a little arrogant for a woman who'd shot a corpse recently, the woman went into the room she insisted on calling the Artistic Vision Studio.

Carrie opened her eyes. Nick held her close.

A long, drawn-out moment passed as their eyes met.

"If you kiss me, it's just like you're begging someone to break into my house." Carrie grinned.

Nick said, "I'll risk it." Their lips met. He pulled away after far too short a time. "I didn't want to have dinner with Bonnie. I wanted to be with you."

A mouselike squeak grabbed their attention. Carrie grabbed Nick more tightly around his neck. They turned to see Bonnie standing in the doorway — her cheeks flaming red, her eyes brimming with tears. "The in . . ." Bonnie's voice broke. "The invitation is withdrawn." She whirled and stormed out, slamming the door.

"Oh, no." Nick set Carrie down.

Her feet swung to the floor while she clung to his neck. "I thought you liked her."

"I do like her."

"No, I mean . . . I thought you *liked* her."

Nick quit looking after Bonnie. "Not like I like you."

Nick's heart leapt at the longing in Carrie's eyes, and he pulled her close again.

"Nothing like you." No one came in until he was good and done showing her just how much he liked her.

"Have dinner with me?" He'd done it. He couldn't believe he'd said it, and it hadn't even been that hard.

Carrie nodded, as agreeable as he'd ever seen her.

"But I've got to apologize to Bonnie. And if she'll have me, I'm going to her place for Thanksgiving dinner. Not for a date, but she's alone. Accepting her invitation was always about sharing a lonely meal."

"And that, Nick O'Connor, might be why I lo-like you."

Nick smiled. "Friday night. We'll drive out

301

of town, go to the big city, and find something great to eat."

"Omaha?"

"I was thinking of Bjorn, but Omaha
works for me."

Carrie laughed. "Bjorn, population one
thousand and seventy-two."

"Big compared to Melnik. We could go to
the Dairy King." He pulled Carrie back for
a long hug.

"It closes for the winter."

Nick came to his senses, or as close as he
ever got since he met Carrie. "We've got the
community Thanksgiving dinner Friday.
How about Saturday? We could leave early
and make a day of it. Dinner and a movie?"

Carrie shook her head. "Pastor Bremmen
wants us at the young adult potluck. He
thinks he needs us to help the group get off
to a good start."

"He's right; he does need us. We're the
only people coming except for him and his
wife."

Carrie's smile spread. "Sunday, then?"

Nick shook his head. It didn't matter
about dinner; they were spending every
evening together, even if it wasn't at a nice
restaurant in Omaha. "You know we can't
do it on Sunday."

It took a minute, but the dreamy look

faded from Carrie's eyes. Nick thought it was a really good sign that he'd driven most of the thoughts from her head.

"That's right. We can't leave town."

Nick rubbed his hands together in anticipation. "Because sometime this weekend, one of our suspects is going to walk right into our trap."

23

After consulting Junior to make sure she didn't end up in jail, Carrie made a pea-and-spam casserole and spent Monday in the late afternoon with Rosie Melnik, spreading Christian compassion and dropping a few hints about what would be in the newspaper that would scare her good if she was a killer. Except, instead of acting guilty, Rosie bemoaned the death of Wilkie the Wonder Jerk.

Nick's job was to make sure Gunderson would read the *Bugle* articles when they came out Wednesday. Gunderson either wasn't home or didn't answer the knock. Nick slid a note under the door of his decrepit old house.

Carrie met Nick back at her place. He kissed her hello just as if he had the right to. Carrie kissed him back and led him inside.

Nick hooked up his computer printer to

Carrie's laptop so she could do all the work at home on the story they were planning to use to expose a killer. Carrie would later sneak it into the paper without anyone, especially Donette, knowing.

Carrie flexed her fingers and reached for the keyboard. "Let's get started."

The back door slammed open. Nick stood. Carrie loved a man of action.

Donette charged into the room, her face soaked with tears. Her hair was scraped back in a ponytail. She wore blue jeans and a stained white maternity T-shirt, with the words "There's a Pea in my Pod" across the front in green sequins. Carrie had just barely finished reading the shirt when Donette threw herself into Carrie's arms. A child having a child. Carrie wanted to cry, too.

"He dumped me." Donette flattened Carrie against the back of the couch.

"Who, the guy from the funeral?" Carrie held on and closed her eyes to pray that she could somehow undo the damage from the story about Wilkie.

Donette nodded. "I — I told him I'd had enough of guys treating me like dirt. I told him I wanted some respect and . . . and that God loved me."

Carrie's eyes flew open, and she stared

over Donette's shoulders at Nick.

Nick gave Carrie an encouraging nod.

Tightening her arms around Donette, Carrie tried to apologize. "I'm sorry about that awful Wilkie story. I did *not* put that in the paper. I took responsibility for it because I'm the boss. But it was sneaked in when I thought the paper was done. I've been heartbroken to think you would give up on God because of me."

"I forgive you."

Donette jerked upright with a little scream.

Carrie looked frantically for mice. "What is it?"

"I-I'm not sure. But I think my water just broke."

Nick jumped up from the couch and fell over the coffee table.

Carrie stood up and pulled Donette to her feet. "Are you going to the Bjorn hospital?"

"Nope, Gillispie."

"Nick!" Carrie tried to break through the panic she saw in his eyes. She expected him to say *"Eeek!"* and leap into her arms. She regretted that her hands were full of Donette.

Nick's eyes focused — some.

"Get Donette to your truck. I'm calling

the hospital and telling them we're on our way. She could go fast."

"I'm not letting her drive."

Carrie sighed. "I mean, go fast as in having the baby, not go fast driving your truck."

Donette groaned and clutched at her stomach.

"Is she having a labor pain?" Nick's eyes went wide. Carrie could see white all the way around his pupils, like a scared horse.

"They're called contractions now, not pains. I think it's so an expectant mother won't know that having a baby might hurt — like they want it to be a surprise or something."

"It hurts to have a baby?" Donette grabbed Carrie's arms.

Wrenching loose, Carrie dashed to the phone and called the hospital quickly, thanks to Great-Grandma Bea having one thousand numbers posted by her phone.

Nick supported the apparently now-made-of-china Donette out the door. Carrie was beside them before Donette scaled the truck with Nick boosting for all he was worth.

When Donette had two contractions before they'd gotten out onto the highway, Nick set out to break the land speed record getting to Gillespie. Another Guinness entry for Melnik.

As the nurse hustled Donette away in a wheelchair, it occurred to Carrie just who ought to attend this birth. She phoned and then waited with Nick until . . .

"This baby is a gift from a providential God!" Tallulah flew into the ER like a flapping, squawking parrot descending from the treetops. "I demand to be the birthing coach!"

Carrie waved her hand toward the maternity ward, and Tallulah fluttered off.

Donette and her doctor must have agreed, because Tallulah never came back.

"So much for baiting our trap, right?" Nick sighed and settled into a utilitarian brown chair in the waiting room.

"A large percentage of our prime suspects are busy doing Lamaze breathing." Carrie shook her head. "We'll just have to push back the timetable a bit. We don't really turn up the pressure until the *Bugle* comes out, anyway."

"We still haven't managed to have a dinner date." Nick seemed really glum.

Carrie's heart warmed irrationally. "Let's leave this baby to the pros and go have pizza."

"Are you sure we should?" Nick sat up straight and smiled.

"He's destined for greatness!" Tallulah

shouted from the depths of the extremely shallow Gillispie Hospital. "And I will be his mentor!"

Carrie shrugged. "We can't compete with that."

Nick smiled, and they ran.

On Wednesday afternoon, Carrie lugged the newspapers over to the post office then took twenty-five copies each to the Mini-Mart, the grocery store, and Jansson's café. Deliveries took ten minutes; everybody would know the news in fifteen. Mission accomplished. Article written. A niggling fear had grown in her stomach until she felt like she'd swallowed a bucket of mice.

She swiped compulsively at her dirty black T-shirt. She always came away from Wednesdays coated in printer ink.

She hopped into the Cavalier and tore away from the post office like a kid who'd batted a ball through a picture window. She'd sure tried to break things wide open.

Donette's baby boy only made it better — or worse — if you happened to be a murderer.

Nick waited at her back door. "How was your day?"

Carrie almost heard him add "dear." Like they were a real couple. Her heart beat harder. "I did it, Nick. I wrote the story just the way we planned."

"Good. Come on in and see what I did to the kitchen linoleum."

Carrie wanted to talk crime and punishment.

Nick wanted to talk vinyl.

Her heart slowed to normal.

Then she saw Great-Grandma's kitchen. No, *her* kitchen. He'd been working on it for days, making a terrible mess, but Carrie could see the finished project at last. "It's beautiful." The linoleum was no more. Instead, bare wood was in its place.

Carrie crouched down and slid her hand over the sleek, honey oak floor. Then her conscience stood up and she followed it. "Nick, I love what you did —"

"It still needs wax and polish. Wait'll you see it after it's finished."

"— but you have to have worked off all Grandpa Leonard's money. I can't afford you."

Nick smiled. "I am completely in love with this house. I'd be glad to work here for free in my spare time."

Carrie's hands left black smudges on the oak. What had she come to? She was dirtier than Great-Grandma's kitchen. She pulled her hand back and went to wash up at the kitchen sink. Confession time. "As for that, you seem to have a lot of spare time. I can't ask you to give up whole days to work for me. You need the money, and I can't . . ."

"Have I ever mentioned that I'm rich?"

"No." She looked up from the flowing tap water. "I'd have remembered."

"I made really good money in Chicago, and I lived in my parents' house because they travel constantly. So I didn't spend much. Plus, I still do consulting work for the firm. They pay really well, so I haven't had to touch my investments, which were extensive."

"How could you quit such a well-paying job?"

"I have enough money to live on for the rest of my life. Now I'm doing what I love. Sanding and waxing this floor is what I love. Restoring beautiful old things feeds my soul." Nick shrugged as if he were embarrassed.

It sounded like poetry.

"I find time to pray and meditate. I'm closer to God using my hands and the gifts God gave me. Please don't make me stop."

"I can't even afford the wax." While she was admitting things, she added, "I'm living on what the *Bugle* pays, which is next to nothing. I'm already worrying about property taxes. I might agree to let you invest your time, but I can't ask you to spend your own money."

"Okay, then don't ask. Just let me do it. Please."

Carrie stared at him. The man was preparing to beg — beg to do something she seriously needed done. She still felt like a leech. "Okay, for now. If I ever get ahead, I'll pay you what I can."

Nick's shoulders rose as if she'd lifted a weight. "Great, because I need to strip the rest of the floors and paint the walls and varnish the woodwork. I want to strip the paint off the kitchen cupboards. They're solid oak. Who painted them? What were they *thinking?* Then next, I'll . . ."

"Wait!" Carrie raised her hand like a school-crossing guard. "That all sounds wonderful. But first, we've got a murderer to catch."

"And I know where we have to start. Maxie Memorial Hall."

Carrie shuddered. "Stop calling it that!"

"I promise. You'll never have to touch him. By the way, welcome home." As if it was their home, not just hers. Then Nick pulled her close and kissed the living daylights out of her.

■ ■ ■ ■

They finished deep cleaning the living room together and put up a Christmas tree. The freshly cut tree almost made the room — not stink. It would be better than that when Nick was done. He saw the majesty in the old house and he wasn't going to settle for less than complete restoration.

They moved out Bea's ugly furniture and hauled away the cheap area rug that had to be fifty years old. Next they centered the white Douglas fir Nick had chopped down in front of the living room picture window. They'd brought down the Christmas ornaments from the attic that Carrie told him she'd never seen before. Cleaned and polished, the delicate glass figures of Santas and angels and nativity scenes and shining balls were truly beautiful. They probably didn't have any great antique value, but from the shine in Carrie's eyes, Nick decided Bea had saved something precious after all.

Nick knew they didn't need to do any of this tonight. But they did need to wait for darkness to fall.

When even Dora had probably . . . hopefully . . . gone to sleep, so she didn't notice them slinking around under cover of night. Nick knew better than to underestimate Dora.

They slipped out the back door and scurried like mice down alleys and between buildings until they got to the back door of the city hall. Nick produced a key.

"It's no wonder we can't pin down who had Maxie. Everyone in this town has a key to this building. Why don't they just leave it standing open, for Pete's sake?"

Nick grinned at her. "You think anybody saw us?"

"I don't think so, but this is Melnik."

"If we get away with it, it'll be the caper of the decade." Nick moved quickly through the high-ceilinged city hall to Maxie's case. He pulled out another key.

"You're sure this is okay with Junior?" Nick asked before he inserted the key.

"I talked to him. He said that since you're on maintenance, he could call it cleaning Maxie's cage."

"Good, because it'd really be embarrassing to have to tell my mom and dad and younger brothers and sister that I'm doing hard time for Grand Theft Mouse." Nick unlocked Maxie's cage.

Carrie stayed back about fifty feet.

Nick had rubber gloves and a Ziploc bag

for Maxie. Dropping the mouse in, he zipped the yellow and blue into green to close the bag, Carrie gritted her teeth, and in the dim light of city hall at midnight, Nick saw her bite back an *eeek*.

Nick put the first bag into a second one, tucking his gloves into the second bag before he zipped it and put it in his jacket pocket. "Are my hands mouse-free enough?" Nick extended his fingers in front of her.

"As long as you don't touch me."

Nick chuckled. "We'll see about that."

They left the hall the way they'd come and were back home in minutes.

Nick stuffed Maxie into the battered bear in the Dead Zone. There was a nice opening in his stomach cavity, thanks to Hal's collision. Grizzly — the cat, not the bear — had followed Nick into the Dead Zone, licking his lips at the huge mouse in the sandwich bag. Who could blame him for thinking dinner was served?

Worried about the cat's mouse-eating binge that had turned him from a lean alley cat into a fat pig, Nick stuffed a wad of newspaper — somehow overlooked by the Compulsive Cleaning Housewives League — into the bear's belly to keep Grizzly out.

Grizzly turned his back with a flick of his

bent tail and pouted his way out the door. Nick firmly closed the door on the Dead Zone and followed the cat downstairs.

Carrie had insisted on being in on the Maxie Heist but refused to escort the mouse a step further once the "cage cleaning" was over.

Nick washed his hands eight times while Carrie looked on. He said, "They've already read the paper, which should tip off a murderer that the truth is out there. Tomorrow the town will discover Maxie gone."

"Or Friday. The city hall is closed tomorrow. The crime might go unnoticed."

"And soon after —" Nick dried his hands and turned to her.

"I still can't decide who," Carrie interjected.

"But we've got a really short list. Hal, Tallulah, and Shayla are out."

"Probably," Carrie said with some skepticism.

"Rosie had a motive, but she couldn't have moved Wilkie's body." Nick was envious of Junior's notebook.

"Unless he was semiconscious and she somehow coaxed him to get in the closet before she smothered him. Or she had help."

"Let's don't start with conspiracy theories.

I can barely keep the suspects straight now. And don't forget Gunderson." Five suspects? That was four too many. "He had to want Wilkie's name blackened for some reason, or he'd have never given you that story."

"He's an awful man, but that doesn't give him a motive for murder. Maybe he enjoys printing hateful things."

"Gunderson is strong enough to hide a body. And if that will was forged, Gunderson stands to lose a fortune. He's the only one except Tallulah in this mess who could afford to pay blackmail." Nick shrugged. "Anyway, someone is going to make a move, and that's when we'll catch him . . . or her." Nick gave her a long look. "Uh . . . are you going to be okay in here with Maxie?"

"Look, I'm never going to like that glandularly challenged rodent, okay? But I'm phobic, not stupid. I can handle it."

A mouse dashed out from under the couch and raced on its teensy, clattering claws straight toward them.

"Eeek!"

She found herself in Nick's strong arms as the mouse ran toward them. Carrie, looking frantically to keep her eye on the danger, saw the evil little beast run up inside Nick's pant leg.

Her next scream almost peeled the ancient cabbage-rose wallpaper off Great-Grandma's living room walls.

Nick stomped his foot several times, acting as unconcerned as if his leg had just gone to sleep. The mouse ran back out and vanished into the kitchen with Grizzly hot on his disgusting, long, dragging, pointy tail.

Carrie quit screaming and looked at Nick. In horror, she said, "You're going to have to live with that for the rest of your life!"

"You mean live with knowing a mouse ran up my leg?" Nick tilted his head, considering. "Okay, no problem."

"And so am I!"

"Honey, you're strangling me."

Carrie loosened her hold. "Uh, is that what mice always do when they run up your pant leg?"

Nick shrugged. "I suppose. What else?"

"I figured they ran all the way up and crawled inside my underwear and got stuck in the elastic and started biting and squeaking and . . ." Carrie buried her face in his chest.

"And yet none of that happened."

Carrie thought Nick sounded a speck impatient. Couldn't blame him. "It's my lifelong dream to live on the fifth floor of an all-glass building."

"I'm an architect. There aren't any of those. I know that for a fact. What if someone threw a rock? Five stories of dangerous broken glass raining down on everybody? Nope, bad idea." Nick pressed a quick kiss onto the top of her head.

Carrie looked up.

"Before I leave, how about I make sure you've forgotten all about mice?" Nick smiled and leaned down.

24

Kissing hadn't worked, but not for lack of trying. And to give Nick full credit, it *had* worked during the actual kissing, but he'd had to quit eventually.

After Nick left, Carrie lay awake for hours shuddering over the stupid, disease-bearing vermin crawling inside her walls, under her furniture, and even in her bed, for all she knew. She fell asleep and dreamed of mice running up her leg, squirming in her unmentionables.

She woke up screaming twice.

She had Thanksgiving dinner with her family and heard talk of how boring the special section of the paper was, the one containing the fine print of the town's charter and Rudolph Melnik's last will and testament. The one who wasn't bored was guilty of murder, so impatient though Carrie was to solve the crime, she was glad her family was bored.

Carrie had printed the exact words of the charter that hung on the wall in the museum and then printed the words from the one in Bea's house, knowing that only someone who really cared would notice. Someone who'd figured out that Wilkie had a legal claim on all the Gunderson property. One of his heirs could end up rich. Or Sven Gunderson could end up broke. Excellent motives for murder.

She had a great family time with one thousand cousins and two big feasts, one with each grandma. Being with all of them almost controlled the jealousy she had over Nick spending Thanksgiving with Bonnie. Almost.

On Friday Nick showed up at Carrie's house neat as always, in a knit, two-button, hunter green shirt that didn't have his company logo on it.

He'd gone casual.

"How was Thankgiving?"

"Fine. I had to do some fast-talking to convince her to still let me come. But it was okay. Bonnie knows. . . . I mean, I told her I wanted to be friends. That . . . I'm . . . uh . . . well . . . seeing you." Nick shrugged. "Bonnie's a good cook."

"You really told her that?"

"Well sure, we . . . uh . . . are . . . aren't

we? Seeing each other?"

"Oh yeah." Carrie wasn't jealous. That was an unworthy emotion. She just wanted to know every detail. Every word. Every look Bonnie and Nick exchanged.

He didn't tell her a thing, but he did kiss her until she was convinced that Nick and Bonnie had shared nothing more important than turkey and pumpkin pie. Which didn't take long. After all, she trusted him.

He refinished the living-room floor while Carrie gingerly pulled junk out of kitchen cupboards. They got a lot done despite Carrie being a spaghetti-spined coward.

But it was Friday night and time to face the music. On Wednesday, the paper had come out with the articles that few people would notice contained a motive for murder. On Thursday, Thanksgiving Day, the city hall was closed, and word of Maxie being missing never hit the street. On Friday morning, however, the atrocity had come to light.

Time to attend the community Thanksgiving potluck at City Hall. The place had been in an uproar all day over Maxie.

Tallulah took over the microphone and raged.

Pastor Bremmen tried to calm her and talk about giving thanks to God and preparing their hearts for the holy season.

It almost turned into a fistfight.

Carrie got scolded for the first Wilkie article, fawned over for last week's Maxie Festival article, was informed of a few typos in this week's *Bugle,* and heard the word "boring" a lot.

Donette was there with her baby, accompanied by Hal, of all people. Dora whispered that if they got married, Hal would be his brother's father, his wife's son, his stepsister's stepfather, and his own uncle. Or something like that.

Nick was coerced into washing dishes. Carrie wiped tables.

Rosie Melnik, the most injured Melnikite of all, approached her. Carrie braced herself to be told off yet again.

Whispering a prayer for the right words, Carrie turned to face the music.

"Can I talk to you, Carrie?"

Interested in the frightened voice as opposed to anger, Carrie said, "Sure, but before you say anything, please let me apologize again for the article about Wilkie. That never should have gone in the paper. I'm so sorry."

Tears welled in Rosie's wounded eyes.

Yell at me. Please, don't cry.

Carrie patted Rosie's slumped shoulder.

"Is there anything I can do to help?"

"I — I want to put a few personal touches on the Maxie float. I just — I know you hate mice, but I don't want to go in there alone. If I go when there's a crowd, I'll have to face them. If I go alone, it's spooky. Would you please come with me?"

Carrie's arm got a gentle tug. "You mean, go now?"

In the night? To that garage containing a giant mouse?

She pumped up her courage.

I did ask if there was anything I could do to help.

I am a stupid, loudmouthed idiot.

"It won't take long. I've already told Nick I was going to ask you, and he gave me his key to Tallulah's garage." Her open hand displayed a brass key. "I told him we'd only be gone a few minutes."

Carrie knew this was a perfect opportunity to talk about faith and repentance. Rosie couldn't move a body. With a prayer to God for opening this door, Carrie nodded, snagged her leather jacket, and walked out of the hall.

Controlling a shudder she glanced over her shoulder, looking for Nick to wave good-bye. He had his back to the room, hard at work scrubbing casserole dishes.

It was two blocks to the garage. Shivering in the November cold, Carrie hurried along, praying for the right words.

"God loves you, Rosie."

"There's no God. How can you believe that stuff?"

Carrie jumped a bit at the harsh response. Where had Rosie's tears gone?

Lots of people in small towns didn't go to church. A small town was no guarantee of faith. But most of them acknowledged that God existed. And even if they didn't, they were a little too afraid of God's wrath — should they turn out to be wrong — to say so out loud.

"Sure there's a God. His Son, Jesus, died for all our sins, and if we believe in Him we can be saved." It sounded a little rushed, not the sincere testimony Carrie had wanted to give. But this might be her only chance. She'd better get the basics in.

"I don't want to hear about what a sinner I am." All the quiet fear from earlier had vanished.

"We're all sinners. Me, Nick, you, Pastor Bremmen, everyone. We all fall short of perfection. That's just part of being human. And since we're all going to die someday, we need to live this life in preparation for the next."

"I'm not going to die for a long time. Then, when I do, they'll stick me in the cheapest coffin they can find and throw dirt over me."

They reached the garage at the rear of Tallulah's huge, tree-lined lot. Carrie unlocked the door and pushed it open. Carrie waited, but apparently she was supposed to go in first. Fumbling around the wall, Carrie found the light switch, and the garage lit up from one small bulb. The small room being used for the float was partitioned off. Carrie had avoided it up to now, coming in no farther than this. She gritted her teeth and marched across the chilly building filled with storage boxes, with barely room for a car. Right now, the car must be at the Thanksgiving party.

Rosie twisted the doorknob. Something about her demeanor made Carrie's stomach jump.

"After you."

Taking a deep breath and calling on all her courage, Carrie stepped in this tiny room full of giant Maxie. Just as she crossed the threshold, she stopped and looked back. Her stomach sank as she realized something she should have noticed right away. Rosie was empty-handed. "Weren't you going to include some mementos in this float? Where are they?"

The smile had turned to gritted teeth. A hard shove sent Carrie stumbling forward, and the door slammed shut. Carrie heard a lock click before she could open it.

Carrie fought with the doorknob then pounded on the door. She yelled, "What is going on?"

"Just shut up." The voice rose unnaturally high. "I'm not letting you ruin everything we've planned."

"What do you mean? What plan? Who's we?"

The outer garage door closed, leaving Carrie's question to echo in the silence.

And then the echoing was replaced by something else. Something rustling and skittering. Like a thousand frantic mice.

25

"Where'd Carrie go?" Nick hung up his apron and tossed his dishcloth onto the pile of towels and rags he'd offered to take home, launder, and return.

Dora handed an empty pie pan to Crazy Clara. "Excellent pie, Clara."

"Pecanpieismyfavorite."

Nick moved casually to the trash and dropped a stack of used paper plates over the upended pies. Clara had brought five of them, bless her heart. Near as he could figure out, instead of pecans she had chiseled bark off a tree and broken it into pecan-sized pieces.

"I haven't seen her, Nick." Dora handed out another container and another as the ladies finished up their cleaning. Nick looked through the big window into the social hall.

Carrie's chair sat empty, and her coat was gone. He glanced around the kitchen.

Everything was in order. He picked up the bundle of linens, and, with a quick good-bye to Dora and the other few ladies still chatting in the kitchen, he headed out. Carrie wouldn't have walked home without him. Not with that most recent mouse-up-the-pant-leg experience so fresh in her mind.

She wasn't out in the hallway. A quick look at Maxie's cage reminded him of what Carrie had written in the *Bugle* and how it ought to trap a murderer into revealing him- or herself.

He hurried outside. They'd set a trap. Carrie wouldn't have gone anywhere with their main suspects. If someone dragged her out, there would have been a scene.

"Micerunningloose. Nobearbigenough."

Nick turned to look at Clara. How had she known about the bear? Maybe God whispered in his ear, using the mouth of a crazy woman.

"Clara, tell me about this big mouse."

Clara looked past Nick to the cage. "BetterthanSvenrulingthistown."

"Sven Gunderson rules this town?"

"Ownsit,doesn'the? Lock,stock,andbarrel. Deathof Melnik."

"Gunderson owns the town, but why would that kill Melnik?"

"Thinksheownsthetown. Melnikthought-different."

Clara headed for the door, pulling her cart, which was empty because she'd donated all her pies to the Thanksgiving dinner. A woman fixated on feeding a dying town. Or was it a dying town? Maybe she meant it was a dying Melnik. Wilkie Melnik.

"Clara." Nick caught Clara's arm before she meandered off. "Did Sven Gunderson kill Wilkie?"

"Everybodykilledhim."

Nick knew that was the absolute truth. Everybody had killed poor, worthless Wilkie. But right now Nick couldn't focus on that. He had to find Carrie. He prayed a quick prayer for help and then looked at Maxie's empty cage. He guessed that solving the crime would lead him straight to Carrie.

Then another thought struck Nick like one of Clara's pies in the face. Whoever had killed Wilkie had used Maxie as a murder weapon. Nick died a little inside as he imagined someone coming after Carrie with a mouse. Carrie in danger was bad enough. But her phobia was well-known. If whoever did this enjoyed cruelty . . .

Clara tugged at Nick's hold, and Nick realized he'd been hanging on tight enough that he might have bruised the addled old woman.

"I'm sorry. Did I hurt you?" He massaged her wrist carefully as he released her. She went out the door, and he followed, trying to catch every word she muttered.

"You *saw* everybody who killed Wilkie? Can you tell me who?"

Clara listed three people he expected and one he'd pretty much eliminated. Rosie Melnik.

Carrie turned to face the pitch-black room, fumbling for the doorknob behind her. It held as if it were made of iron. The tiny, clawing footsteps came closer. Had the slamming door scared them into their holes, but now, in the silence, they felt bold?

Something raced over her toe.

"Eeek!" Of course, she had shoes on, but she felt it. She was sure she felt it.

A weary voice sounded from the farthest corner.

"Carrie, is that you?"

Carrie screamed and staggered backward into the wall. It wasn't her mouse scream. It was one she'd never heard before, one that she'd been saving for if she wanted to curdle someone's blood.

Unless the Maxie float had learned to talk,

there was someone else in the room.

Please, dear Lord Jesus, let it be someone else.

"Yes, it's me. Who are you?" She braced herself to hear, "It's Maxie, and I'm your worst nightmare."

True, all true.

"It's Tallulah, honey. Someone hit me."

Carrie realized that it was just barely possible that the horrid, teensy, clawing, zipping footsteps had been Tallulah moving around. No one could fault Carrie's ability to imagine mice in every situation.

Carrie edged toward the voice, trying to avoid colliding with Giant Maxie while dodging countless electric lawn beautifiers. "Talk to me, Tallulah, so I can find you. Who hit you?"

Carrie realized that she knew very well who. The same person who'd lured her here.

"I don't know. All I know is that I heard footsteps and turned just in time to see a rolling pin crashing toward me. I woke up with a throbbing head when I heard the door slam."

Carrie slowly slid her feet forward, the cement floor scratching under her tennis shoes as she closed in on Tallulah. A soft object on the floor rolled as her toe connected with it. It felt turban-like. She was getting close.

"I'll help you. I'm locked in, too, but we'll find a way out."

A moan of pain almost directly under her feet stopped Carrie in her tracks. The black in the windowless room was absolute. She crouched and reached forward, hoping for Tallulah's silky caftan instead of the felt of a Maxie suit.

Her fingertips touched a slippery bulk that could only be the elderly fanatic. "I'm here." Carrie fumbled for Tallulah's hand.

Tallulah reached out, her breath broken and ragged. Their hands met and they clung to each other for a few seconds. Carrie was desperately glad there was someone else in there. Even Tallulah.

"Thank God you came. I've been praying and praying for help. It's so dark." Tallulah's voice broke, and weak sobs set the caftan wiggling like Jell-O.

"I'm glad you're here, too, except I'm really sorry that either of us is here." Carrie toughened her voice to brace Tallulah's backbone. "Now, how do we get out?"

"We can't. This room has one door, with a good lock, and no windows. I designed it specifically to house the Maxie float. I wanted maximum security."

Since Carrie couldn't quite picture anyone stealing a six-foot-tall mouse float, she changed the subject. "What about these tools I bumped into along this wall? Is there an ax? We could chop a hole in the door or the wall. Or a crowbar — maybe we can pry the door open."

"There's a weed whacker."

Okay, not useful for beating down a door. "Why did Rosie bring me here? Why would she lock me in here with you? It's awfully cold, but not cold enough to kill us. We'll get out and get away and tell everything."

Tallulah interrupted. "What's that smell?"

Carrie inhaled once, and that's all it took. "Smoke."

26

Nick pounded on Gunderson's door. The house was dark. There was no sign of life. Nick knew the old goat was in there. Maybe.

"Burntpies! Burntpies!"

Nick quit pounding and stared at the mad baker sitting in his truck. He turned to pound some more. "I know you're in there, Gunderson! I want some answers!"

An orange light caught his eye from the far side of Gunderson's privet hedge. *Burnt pies? Fire?* It looked as if Tallulah's garage, where the Maxie float was being assembled, was on fire.

Nick had a frantic second to wonder if the fire was the result of Tallulah — in some mad experiment involving lightning and spare parts she'd stolen from the Melnik Cemetery — trying to bring Maxie back to life.

That'd make the Christmas parade special.

Nick knew as well as a man can know anything that he doesn't really know, that this fire had something to do with Carrie's disappearance.

"Carrie!" He ran for his truck, jumped in, and roared out of Gunderson's driveway.

"Tallulah, stay down. I'm going to find a way out of here, and I don't want you be hurt if I knock something over." Carrie flailed her hands along the wall of the garage, searching for anything heavy enough to knock the door down. Even a weed whacker might be enough. Tools clattered down around her feet, barking her arms and shins and toes. Finally she caught hold of some wooden handle that seemed to have enough heft to be useful. She rushed her hands down the circular wood and found a hoe at the end. She made her way as she dared the few feet to the door.

Orange light gleamed through the door frame. The dim light lifted the gloom in the float room, but now Carrie glanced over her shoulder to see the huge, skulking mouse and wished for the dark.

A crackle of fire sounded on the other side of the garage. Something whined as if it were under pressure. Who knew what? Aerosol cans, gas — garages were notoriously full of flammable liquids.

Something exploded and slammed against the door, sending Carrie staggering backward into the float. The mouse seemed to reach for her as if he needed a snack.

Carrie's *eeek* barely registered, even with her. She approached the door again and gingerly touched the knob. Jerking her hand back from the burning-hot metal, she knew that knocking down the door would just let the flames in.

"Start praying again, Tallulah. We need a miracle."

"I'm way ahead of you." Tallulah's voice sounded as if she'd stood.

"Stay back. I'm going to swing this hoe."

"No, I can see the fire from here. We can't get out that way."

"There's no other way!"

"I know! I know!"

Carrie turned back to the door, scared to death, and swept the hoe back to take a swing.

Nick lay on his horn the whole three blocks to Tallulah's house. He saw a light flicker on in Dora's house as he roared past. He skidded into Tallulah's driveway and saw the flames.

"Clara, can you stay in here and keep

honking?"

Nick noticed Tallulah's car parked behind the garage and knew a way to get inside that building. He should make sure Clara was safe, but there wasn't time. The flames had circled the structure and were eating their way up the walls. Nick knew the fire wasn't accidental. A jagged line of flames danced across the lawn like an arrow pointing straight to Tallulah's outbuilding. Nick caught the whiff of gas among the smothering smoke.

The side containing the Maxie float wasn't nearly as engulfed as the other. If Carrie was in there, he prayed she was in the small room. Alone with Maxie. Terrified. Nick prayed. He threw open the truck door and poked his head out. "If you're by the garage door, get back! Get back from the door!"

The sound of a fire siren streaked through the night. Help was on the way, but Nick didn't have time to wait for the experts.

He reached over and clicked Clara's seat belt then turned back to the raging fire. Something exploded with a deafening roar. One corner of the garage door blew open. Nick grabbed the steering wheel with both hands. He jammed his foot on the accelerator. His truck spun out, and the back end slewed. Nick aimed for the garage. And the fire. And Carrie, burning alive.

His front bumper smashed into the garage door. Wood snapped. His windshield shattered. An iron brace jammed with a sickening thud into the seat between Nick and Clara. Sparks erupted. Ash filled the cab of his truck. Fire crackled down from the ceiling. Suffocating smoke choked him. Clara screamed. Nick coughed, his eyes stinging, his lungs roasting. He had to get the elderly woman out.

He shifted into REVERSE, shoved the accelerator to the floor, and barreled backward. Wood and metal clattered off the roaring truck. He slammed on the brakes as soon as they were far enough for Clara's safety. Nick's safety wasn't high on his agenda.

Nick leapt from the truck and raced toward the billowing smoke.

He ducked under the fire, his arm covering his mouth and nose. Flames reached like greedy fingers toward the sky, out of the destroyed garage door. The inside walls were consumed by the ravenous inferno. Lungs burning, Nick nearly fell to his knees.

Shrill sirens grew closer. He could barely hear them over the snapping, snarling inferno.

"Carrie! Carrie, are you in here?" There

was no sign of her in this side of the garage. He heard something bang into the door to the Maxie float room.

"Carrie?" Dashing for it, he shouted, "Carrie, is that you?"

"Nick!" The fear in her scream cut his heart.

"Get back! I'm coming in!" Nick noticed the heavy padlock on the door, snapped shut. Fury blazed as high and as hot as the fire.

Carrie shouted, "Okay! We're away from the door."

We? Nick had a split second to catch that. He drew in a short breath full of gritty, hot ash. He lashed out a foot. The blackened door smashed open. The padlock ripped from the burning door frame. Carrie stumbled forward into his arms.

"Tallulah's in there."

"Go! I'll get her."

Carrie shook her head. "She's close to unconscious from the fire. It'll take both of us."

There wasn't time to argue. They charged back into the room that was clogged with the overpowering fumes and smoke. The fire was now so loud they couldn't talk. Carrie kept a hand on Nick's arm and led him straight to the corner where Tallulah crouched behind Maxie. They lifted her.

"We've got to save Maxie. We can't let him burn!"

Nick and Carrie exchanged an incredulous look. They towed the woman out the door, cinders raining down on their heads.

"No, save him. Save Maxie!" Tallulah fought them.

They dragged her outside while she was screaming for Maxie.

A blast of cold water hit them in the face.

It served to calm Tallulah down.

The valiant men and women of the Melnik Volunteer Fire Department raced toward the building with their hoses cannoning water ahead of them.

"We've got everyone." Nick shouted at Marc Swenson, who led the charge. Deputy Steve was right behind Marc, his yellow fireproof suit and hat askew. Hal came next. Just because he was a confessed murderer didn't mean he couldn't fight a fire.

The two men took over supporting Tallulah as the Melnik ambulance shrieked into the yard. Tallulah screamed for Maxie as they dragged her away.

Two other paramedics grabbed Nick and Carrie.

Carrie waved them off then began coughing until Nick had to hold her up.

"Let them help you. Just to give you some oxygen."

"I'm fine. I'll go with them in a minute, but first I need to talk to Junior."

Junior huffed up to them, his pajamas sticking out of his unbuttoned uniform shirt. "Is everyone all right?"

"They're seeing to Tallulah. She took a blow to the head." Nick patted Carrie on the back and held her. He'd come so close to losing her.

Carrie broke in.

"Rosie Melnik tried to kill Tallulah and me."

27

The governor came to the Maxie Festival. So did both Nebraska senators and a congressman, two state senators, ten area newspapers, news crews from six television stations, and a reporter and photographer from the *Omaha World-Herald.*

The festival came off in grand style. It was a fairly balmy twenty-degree day. Everyone dressed for the cold, there was no wind, and they were Nebraskans. It was lovely.

The Country Christian Church float, the St. Barnard Catholic Church float, the Swedish Covenant Church float, and the Lutheran church float led the way. Each had a nativity scene, and each had a different piece of the Christmas story immortalized with chicken wire and spray-painted facial tissues. Jesus had made it into the starting line-up of the Melnik Christmas Parade after all.

Of course Maxie wasn't to be forgotten.

Carrie understood that. She just wanted some perspective.

Nick glanced at Maxie's aquarium, centered on the quaint gazebo from Melnik Park. Today it had been rigged with wheels so it could carry Maxie in style.

After the parade, Carrie went into City Hall, and members of the press started shouting questions at her. She climbed up on the stage in the front of the auditorium so she could see who was yelling and give them answers.

Before Nick followed Carrie in, he offered to help Tallulah carry in Maxie's display case from the gazebo.

"No." Tallulah flinched as if he'd attacked her, her turban pulled on more tightly than ever. "I've put new locks on Maxie's home, and no one has a copy of the keys but me."

Nick thought that was for the best. The mouse needed to stay put.

He left the woman to it and quietly slipped into the press conference, staying well back. He got there just as Carrie got the news that her Melnik and Maxie article had been named as a finalist for six Nebraska Press Association Awards. The crowd broke into applause.

She stood on the stage in front of the social hall, by a microphone. Nick watched her furrow her brow.

"That's not possible. I never entered anything. I've only been in my job a few weeks."

The *World-Herald* reporter shrugged. "It must have made the deadline."

She looked up and her eyes met Nick's, and that's when she knew what had happened. She mouthed "Thank you," and Nick touched his forehead in a two-fingered salute.

"So what exactly was Rosie Melnik's motive?" A reporter shouted out the question.

Nick saw Carrie's shoulders raise and lower in a deep sigh. "Wilkie was blackmailing Sven Gunderson. Wilkie found out that Gunderson had forged an old will and stolen the Melnik fortune. The truth was in the real city charter, now posted in the Melnik Historical Society Museum. The one formerly posted there was switched by one of Sven Gunderson's ancestors."

"But why is that a reason to kill her husband?" someone shouted. "Why not help him claim his rightful inheritance?"

"She didn't know about it until the very end." Carrie shook her head. "If Wilkie died and Rosie married Sven, he could keep everything. He began manipulating her. She decided to work with Gunderson when

Wilkie asked for a divorce to marry Donette."

"When Chief Hammerstad arranged for Maxie to go missing and for the original charter to appear in the paper" — she glanced at Junior, who gave her an encouraging nod — "he knew it would provoke someone to go to great lengths to protect their secret. He knew someone would fall into his trap."

Nick saw Carrie glance at Tallulah. They'd thought Tallulah was a strong suspect, but she hadn't been their first choice. They'd stolen the mouse to force Tallulah's hand, if she was the culprit. The charter was to goad Shayla, Hal, Rosie, and Donette, all possible heirs to the fortune, if owning Melnik Main Street could ever add up to a fortune. And since Gunderson stood to lose his inheritance, it would have brought him out to destroy the new charter, too, before someone got a good look at it.

Donette had been a long shot to get caught, what with a new baby to care for. But Nick hadn't been all that suspicious of her anyway.

They'd all had their eyes on Gunderson.

None of them had suspected poor, distraught Rosie.

"Rosie's pretty mad about Gunderson

tricking her into killing Wilkie, so she's talking. That's filling in a few blanks. It looks like Wilkie found the original city charter a few months ago while sneaking around in my great-grandma Bea's house, before he started blackmailing Gunderson. He went back the night of his death to snoop around some more. Rosie followed him, thinking he'd drink himself into a stupor, which he did most nights, and she could strike. She saw it all. Wilkie frightened Great-Grandma into falling. Hal knocked Wilkie cold with the skillet. Rosie sneaked in, urged Wilkie, groggy from the blow and the poison, into the closet, where she wedged him in and smothered him."

"With Maxie the Mouse?" the reporter from Channel Six asked.

"Not really." Carrie voice faltered. "Rosie always liked the mouse . . ."

Nick bit back a smile. All this horror, and the only thing that fazed her was that stupid mouse.

"Rosie had a key to City Hall."

"Maxie Memorial Hall," Tallulah interjected, as she approached the front carrying the heavy aquarium. Nick again offered to help and was rejected. Tallulah made her way forward, obviously determined to take center stage.

"And she liked to visit Maxie and take him home for the night. She'd been petting him . . ." Carrie's eyes filled with dread, and someone snapped a picture.

Nick definitely wanted a copy.

"So there was mouse fur on her hands, and she left some behind on Wilkie's mouth." Nick edged nearer Carrie. He'd try and catch her if she jumped and went flying off the stage.

"Miss Evans?" the *World-Herald* reporter called out. "My boss mentioned your name when that award was announced. I have it on good authority that he's ready to offer you a job in the *World-Herald* feature section."

The crowd gasped aloud, but with dismay rather than joy. Nick wanted to join in. But she'd never be his if she didn't have a real choice. Nick didn't want her to make a commitment to him because she needed money or her life was boring or she'd given up on her dreams.

He prayed quietly because he knew that, if necessary, he'd give up his own dream of small-town life. If she'd have him, he'd follow her anywhere.

"Gunderson is now in jail as a coconspirator in Wilkie's death, and the will has been broken." Carrie kept talking, but her eyes were fixed on the approaching Maxie. "The Main Street businesses revert to the city, and are all for sale or rent at a more reasonable price. Six of the empty buildings are already under new ownership."

Nick had bought one himself.

"Plus, a good-sized chunk of the Gunderson estate will be divided up between Wilkie's heirs," Carrie concluded.

Tallulah unsteadily made her way up the three steps to the stage. Carrie had her eyes locked on Maxie, so Nick suspected the interview was over. Just as Tallulah got to the top step, she wobbled, her fingers slipped, and she shrieked. The aquarium tumbled to the stage, shattering into a thousand pieces. Maxie bounced out of the shards of glass, rolling straight for Carrie. Nick jumped onto the stage to save her.

Out of nowhere, Grizzly leapt onto the stage and swallowed Maxie in one gulp.

Tallulah shoved her askew turban out of her eyes and screamed loud enough to shatter crystal. Good thing the aquarium was already destroyed.

The whole crowd yelled. Carrie relaxed immediately and Nick put her down.

The cat hunched, opened its mouth wide, gave Tallulah a look of absolute contempt, and regurgitated Maxie onto the floor.

Carrie's ear-splitting shriek was like a warning that screamed, "Incoming!"

Nick caught her, marveling at her perfect weight and size. She looked at him and smiled.

"Are you taking the *World-Herald* job? Let me know so I can start packing."

She smiled and held him tighter.

"I've already got a job I love, in a town I love, near a man I love."

Tallulah's screams faded away as Nick got lost in Carrie's beautiful blue eyes. Or maybe, now that Maxie had reappeared, Tallulah just quit screeching.

"I love you, too, Carrie Evans. I want you to marry me."

"Can we live in my house? Will you take care of the mice in there for the rest of your life?"

Nick frowned. "You're not marrying me just to protect you from mice, are you?"

Carrie giggled. "Not just."

Nick looked at Maxie, who was lying in an unmentionable condition with Tallulah kneeling beside him, her hands clenched. Grizzly stood nearby. Maxie was in the center. No crying he made.

Nick shook his head. "We're one star, a heavenly host of angels, and a herd of sheep away from an extremely twisted nativity scene." Nick looked past the little scene and saw the real nativity set in front of the twinkling Christmas trees.

Pastor Bremmen hustled up on the stage and pulled Tallulah to her feet. "Really, Tallulah, there are limits." He gently but firmly urged her toward the manger and helped her back onto her knees. "I think a few moments of prayer would do you good." He left the stage.

"Much nicer." Carrie patted Nick's chest. "You know, I think Maxie actually looks a little better. He's got a nice sheen to his coat."

Nick conceded the point with a one-shoulder shrug.

Carrie turned to look out at the reporters, her family, and almost everybody in Melnik. "I'm not taking the *World-Herald* job," she announced, loud enough for them all to hear. "I'm staying right here. I'm going to keep living in Great-Grandma's house. Nick's going to turn it into a showplace, and I'm going to make the *Bugle* the best small-town newspaper in America. Oh, and Nick and I are getting married."

Dora snorted, emphasizing an unfortunate resemblance to a member of the hog family. "Everybody knows that."

The crowd broke into cheers. Carrie saw

her mother and two grandmothers mopping their eyes and smiling.

Carrie exchanged a look with Nick while Tallulah finished what looked like a sincere prayer; only God knew for what. Then she tore a sleeve off her caftan and lovingly returned to Maxie to dry him off.

"Feel free to keep jumping in my arms," Nick whispered, stealing a quick kiss.

"I want to be there." Carrie kissed him back. "But I much prefer it to be for some reason other than mice."

Nick nodded. "Or murder."

ABOUT THE AUTHOR

Mary Connealy is an author, a journalist, a teacher, and a true musophobe (Look it up!). She has written books for three different divisions of Barbour Publishing. She teaches GED by day and writes her novels by night, a transformation worthy of Superman!

Mary's dream is to tell love stories that make people laugh while drawing them closer to God. She lives on a farm in Nebraska with her husband, Ivan, and their mostly grown daughters, Joslyn — married to Matt, Wendy, Shelly — married to Aaron, and Katy. Writing is great, but her family is her true lifework.

You may correspond with this author by writing:

Mary Connealy
Author Relations
PO Box 721
Uhrichsville, OH 44683